Coming Out on the Sidelines

Dev Hahn

Fox Arrow Publishing

Also By Dev Hahn

<u>Standalones</u>
Beyond Broken Colors

<u>Bellwood Lady Baller Series</u>
Coming Out on the Sidelines
Catching Feelings in the End Zone
Tackling Temptations on the Line
Opposing Hearts on the Field, *Coming Fall 2025*

Dedicated to...

Every person who ever had to hide who they really are from the people they love out of fear of rejection and hatred. Never feel ashamed to be your authentic self. Those who truly love you, will love ALL of you, no matter what.

Contents

Chapter 1

Payson's POV

"How is the unpacking going?" Colton asks as he tosses the football to me.

"We're getting there. Mom and dad got a good bit done this week. I got almost everything in my room unpacked and put away. The twins' room however looks like a twister went through it." I laugh but it's no joking matter. Judson and Grayson just dumped all their stuff in the middle of their new room and didn't bother putting any of it away. At least, that is how it looked when I passed their room on my way out. Mom has been begging them to get their room together but she's not having any luck. Lucky for me though, I'm going to be gone before dad gets back. I do not want to be around when the retired four-star general goes all boot camp sergeant on them.

I had decided to drive over to my aunt and uncle's house to hang out with my cousin, Colton. We just moved to Bellwood, South Carolina from Fort Morrison Army Base. My dad finally decided to retire and moved us across the country to his old hometown. I can't complain, though. It's nice that we get to be close to family again, even if I have to start my senior year in a completely new high school away from the friends I had made in Cali but that's the life of an Army Brat. You tend to get used to relocating, new schools and having to make new friends all over again without a say-so. At least here, I already have someone I know and am close to.

I throw a beautiful spiral back to Colton. We're hanging out in his backyard, tossing the football around trying to enjoy this Sunday before football conditioning starts tomorrow. Colton and I will both be on the varsity team. I'm looking forward to playing on the same team as him. It brings back memories of when we were younger and did this all the time in his backyard. Mom, the twins and I would take vacations in the summers when dad was deployed to stay with Aunt Charlotte and Uncle Richard. Being surrounded by our loved ones when dad was away helped to keep our minds occupied.

I overestimated my throw and the football looks like it's about to go over the fence into his neighbor's yard. Colton runs, jumps up in the air and clutches the football one handed before it does.

"Damn, Colt. That was incredible!" I don't think I've ever seen him jump so high or run as fast as he just did. "Have you been working with a trainer or something?"

"Some of the guys on the team and I hit up the gym and I wake up early every day to go on runs. I want to be in my best shape and level up my skills. Got to be the best wide receiver on the team." He swipes the sweat from his forehead before he flexes his arms to show off the hard work he's put in.

"You are going to kick ass. Especially when I'm throwing these tight spirals on the field at you. Going to have those college scouts looking our way for sure." I grin. We are both hoping to get scouted to lock in some college scholarships. I have my eyes set on USC. They have produced the most NFL players, with over 400 being drafted so far. It's a dream to be on an NFL team one day, possibly as the first female quarterback.

"You know you are going to have to try out against Brady. He's been the starting quarterback the past two years. He's pretty good, but man, he is an arrogant asshole. If the game isn't going well, he blames everyone but himself and I can't stand it. I'm hoping when Coach sees your arm, he's going to give you the starting spot."

Colton told me about Thomas, the star quarterback. Typical popular jock with a cocky attitude who thinks he's God's gift to the ladies. *Gag me.*

"I'm going to have Brady shaking in his cleats. That starting position is going to be mine."

"Okay, Champ," Colton laughs. "Don't get cocky on me now just because you took your old high school to the California state championship two years in a row."

"That's right. TWO state championships. How many times has Brady taken the team, huh?"

"Zero."

I cup a hand to my ear. "I'm sorry. What was that?"

"Zero."

"I still didn't hear you."

"ZERO!" He says a little bit louder. He knows I'm just pulling his leg though.

"That's right. Zero, zip, nada to my two." I'm a competitive person. It's a part of who I am, and Colton knows it.

He shakes his head before he glances back at me and throws me the ball.

"Are you nervous?"

"About trying out?"

"Yeah."

"Nah. I am going to do what I always do. Show up and show out. I want that starting QB position and I'm claiming it."

"Well, you know I'm rooting for you Pace."

"Thanks Colt." I pause, holding the football in my hands. "Can I tell you something that I never told anyone?"

"Of course."

"You know, I wasn't too happy about my dad retiring and moving us back before senior year." I glance at Colt and see a bit of sadness in his blue eyes. "It wasn't because I didn't want to be close to you and Thea. I love you guys, more than anything. And I love Aunt Charlotte and Uncle Rich." It's true. I love being back around my family. They are everything to me, not to mention loving, nurturing and very supportive.

"I didn't get a chance to tell you, or anyone really but my old football coach has a friend who works at USC, and he mentioned to me they were going to send a scout out to see me play during my senior year. Maybe even when conditioning started. He said my record put me on their radar. I was so excited. I couldn't wait to get home and tell mom and dad because I wanted them to be the first to hear about it. Then when I got home, dad dropped the bomb about moving back to Bellwood. I was devastated. And if I'm honest? I was so mad until dad explained it was about Gramps and his health going downhill. Then I felt guilty for being upset so I kept that from them."

"Damn, cuz. I know how badly you want to get into USC. Can't your old coach contact his friend and inform them of your situation?"

"I don't know. Maybe? The move happened so fast, and I never got to see my coach before we left."

"Don't lose hope yet, Pace. You can kick Brady's ass for the starting QB position and take our team to the state championship. I mean, think about it. The first female quarterback to win the championship game in the state of South Carolina!? That's breaking history! You will be all over social media for it and then USC is going to know where to find you."

I always loved Colt's positive enthusiasm.

"You make a valid point there."

"This is why I'm your favorite cousin," he smirks.

"Second favorite. Thea is number one."

His jaw drops and the look of shock on his face has me laughing.

"Take that back. Take that back right now!"

"Okay. Okay. I kid. Sheesh. Don't get your panties in a twist."

"Thank you. And my boxer briefs are not twisted." He crosses his arms over his chest and pouts.

"Okay first, ew. Don't need the underwear info. And second, you know I'm just messing with you. The truth is you are both equally my favorite. You can't make me pick one."

He sighs dramatically. "Fine. I guess I can share the title with Thea."

At that moment, Colton's cell phone rings. He pulls his phone from his shorts pocket and glances at the caller I.D. before answering.

"Yo Z. What's up? No shit. Of course, I'm down." He glances in my direction. "Hang on a sec. Pace, you want to go to a pool party?"

"I don't have my swim stuff with me."

"We can go by your place for you to change. Your house is actually on the way."

"Sure. I don't mind."

"Hey Z, yeah man. I'm bringing my cousin with me. I want to introduce you guys. We should be at the party in like 20 minutes. Yeah, see ya there." He ends the call. "That was Zealand. Said the cheerleaders are hosting a pool party and invited the football team."

"Oooh! Any hot cheerleaders?" I waggle my eyebrows.

"Pace, they're cheerleaders. Any and everything about them is hot."

"Partially true. Their character plays a huge factor in how hot they truly can be."

"Yeah. I guess you're not wrong. I'm not sure any of them are into girls so you may be out of luck."

"It's cool. Honestly, I'm not really looking for a girlfriend. I'm solely focusing all my energy and time on football, graduating, and getting a college scholarship."

"Damn. Mir—"

I hold my hand in front of his face, cutting him off quickly. "Please don't say her name."

"Sorry Payson. What I meant to say was *she who must not be named* really did a number on you."

"Yeah, she did, and I rather just forget her altogether. She's history and I never want to talk about or hear her name again."

There's a moment of silence between us before Colton speaks again.

"Oh, I may need you to be my wingman at this party."

"Wingman, huh?"

"Yeah…" He lowers his head, but I don't miss the way his cheeks turn a slight pink.

"Awww. Does little Colty have a crush?" I cooed at him. I love teasing him and getting him riled up.

"Shut up," he gives me a light shove, "and maybe I do."

"What's her name?"

" Keplinger."

"Let me guess. Stacey is a cheerleader?"

"A smoking hot cheerleader. I'm talking about long tan legs, killer body, hair that looks like caramel and amber eyes with these little flecks of gold in them." He stares off like he's daydreaming. From the looks of it, it's more than just a little crush. She sounds gorgeous and if Colton needs a little assistance in locking down a girl, I'm always down. I know he would do the same for me.

"I guess as your favorite cousin, I can help you out."

"Who said you were my favorite cousin? Judson's my favorite."

"What!? How the hell is that pipsqueak your favorite and not me?"

"That kid is crazy funny, and I know he would be down to do some crazy shit with me." He laughs for a moment until he notices I'm glaring daggers at him. "Calm down. I'm kidding. Just a little payback for saying Thea was your favorite."

I roll my eyes at him. "Fair enough I guess."

"Alright, let me go grab my stuff so we can head out."

We fist bump before he goes. I walk around the side to the driveway towards my yellow Jeep Rubicon. I am in love with this vehicle. So much so that I even gave her a name. Connie. Mom and dad gave her to me for my 18th birthday last month. On days like today, where the sun is bright and it's hot as hell outside, I love having the top off and feeling the sun kiss my skin and the wind in my hair as I drive around.

I hook up my playlist while I wait for Colton to get what he needs for the party. After a few minutes, I honk my horn annoyingly until he comes jogging out of the house, throwing his stuff in the back and hopping in the passenger seat.

"Hey, I was coming. And out with the horn or Mrs. Garrett is going to have a bitch fit. The last thing my parents need is drama from that woman."

"Who the hell is Mrs. Garrett?" I ask.

He points to the blue colonial on the right side of his house. "The old lady next door. She's such a grump and she's nosey as hell. Likes to gripe about anything and everything. Thea always thought she was a witch or something."

I look over to the house he pointed at and see an elderly woman peeking through her front window curtains.

"Maybe Thea meant bitch but knowing Aunt Charlotte, she said witch to avoid getting soap in her mouth."

"Yeah. Mom's always saying..." he clears his throat then makes an impression of a woman talking, trying to impersonate his mom. "Young ladies should never cuss. It's not very ladylike." Colton bats his lashes before he breaks out into a laugh.

"Aunt Charlotte sounds nothing like that. What would she say if she saw your impersonation of her?"

"Please don't tell my mom!" he begs. "She will find some way to embarrass me on a level that the whole town would know and that could ruin my chances with Stacey!"

"Speaking of Stacey, we better get us to that party so I can help you get the girl."

I back out of his driveway and head towards my house. I only live a few streets over, so we get to my house in about five minutes. When I turn onto my street, I spot our Craftsman cottage house at the end. It's a nice dark army green color with black window shutters and a big white porch. I think dad solely wanted this house for the color.

I don't see dad's vehicle which means he must still be out, and mom is stuck with my brothers. Judson and Grayson are wild when they are together but when you separate them, they can be tolerable. I pull into the driveway behind mom's car just in case dad comes home while I'm here and doesn't block me in.

"You should probably come in with me. Dad isn't home yet which means the twins are probably driving my mother insane. Plus they would be happy to see you. Maybe you could help tame them while I get my stuff? My mom is probably going to ask you for some deets about the party." My parents allow me to attend parties based on the important information I can give them. It's how we have trust and I rather just be straight up with them. I don't like lying and never saw the point in it.

"Yeah, no problem. And maybe I can convince the twins to unpack their room."

"Five bucks says you can't."

"Are you betting on my ability to get your brothers to do a task?" One of his eyebrows goes up.

"Oh, I definitely am," I quipped back.

"Alright. How about I double your five dollars I can get them to unpack their bedroom and put everything away."

"Okay, okay. I can do ten. Shake on it?"

He grabs my hand and gives me a firm shake. If he only knew how bad their room is right now. This is going to be an easy ten dollars for me.

We hop out of my Jeep and walk up the walkway, up the steps and into my new home. I'm impressed with how much mom and dad have managed to unpack, even with dad's constant visits to see Gramps at the nursing home. After grandma passed earlier this year, Gramps's health had taken a bit of a decline to the point a nursing home was needed to look after him. That was the reason why dad closed the chapter of his military career and moved us back. He wanted to get as much time with the only parent he still has while he can. It was the reason why I couldn't tell dad about the USC scout opportunity. I couldn't be upset when I would have made the same choice.

"Mom?" I shout into the house. Colton steps in after me and I shut the door.

"In the kitchen sweetie," she responds. I nod to Colton to follow me to the kitchen.

As we pass the staircase, I hear my twin brothers yelling, and the sounds of gunfire and explosions. It sounds like they are playing their video games and I wonder if they finally took care of their bedroom.

We walk into the kitchen and spot my mom standing at the white marble top island, unpacking a box of dishes. I don't miss the glass of red wine next to her, nearly empty. It's only 1:30 in the afternoon which can only mean the twins must have driven her to the end of her nerves. Mom stops what she is doing when she hears us enter.

"Hey you two!" She hugs Colton. "My goodness. Look how handsome and tall you are, Colt. I bet you have all the girls vying for your attention."

"The ladies just love me, Aunt Lee," he responds as he hugs her back.

"Oh yeah? Does Stacey know about all these ladies? And how come you need me to be a wingman to get her to notice you?"

My mom looks between Colt and I with a sly smile on her face. "Stacey? Who's Stacey?"

"Some cheerleader Colt's got a major crush on and needs my help to get."

"Gee, thanks Pace. Tell your mom everything, why don't you? You know she's going to blab to my mom, and I'll never hear the end of it." He sits down on one of the island stools and covers his head. He can be dramatic sometimes.

"Oh, sweetheart. You have nothing to worry about. I promise my lips are sealed." My mom does that little locking key motion in front of her lips and throws away the invisible key.

"Speaking of Stacey. Colt got a phone call regarding a pool party that she and the cheerleaders are hosting. They invited the football team, which is why we are here. I wanted to ask if it was cool that I could go with Colt?"

"But you're not on the team—" Mom starts to say until she sees my face, "—yet. You are not on the football team *yet* Pace. Calm down. You didn't let me finish. I know how talented you are."

Colt lifts his head to speak. "Auntie Lee, we all know Pace is going to make the team with her killer arm. I figured I could take her with me to the party and introduce her to the team so she can get acquainted with them." And then he does the puppy eyes. "Please, Auntie."

My mom falls for it. She has tried to deny she doesn't fall for Colt's puppy eyes but I'm seeing before my own how quickly she's giving in to his begging.

"Well, I guess it wouldn't hurt to meet the team before tomorrow. Where is this party going to be? Are the parents going to be there? Is there any alcohol or drugs involved?" The typical mom rundown. Her and dad's checklist of questions to determine if they will let me attend a party.

I point to my cousin. "Colt, take it away." He's the one who can give her the answers she's looking for. He's busy texting someone before he responds.

"Give me a sec. I'm waiting on Rhett to text me since he is there now." The swoosh of an incoming text is heard. "Okay, the party is at Lydia Johnson's house. The Johnson's live over on Brimview Lane, which is just a few streets over from here. Lydia's father is away on a business trip, but her mother is around. No drugs and no alcohol." He looks up at my mom and gives her a big ass grin.

"What happens if someone sneaks in drugs or alcohol?"

"I will say 'no thanks.' And if they keep pressuring, I'll leave." I can see my mom thinking this through, but she really has nothing to worry about. "Mom, I'm an athlete and I care about what goes into my body. If I'm going to be my best, I have to feel my best. Trust me, no drug or alcohol is worth risking me not getting to where I want to be in life."

"Then it sounds perfectly okay for you to go. I do, however, would like for you to be back by 6:30 p.m. for family dinner."

"Not a problem, mom. I wasn't going to miss family dinner. Plus, I want to get to bed a little early. Conditioning starts at 9:00 a.m. and I want to be well rested for it."

Mom lifts her glass of wine to finish it and I don't hide the expression on my face. She usually has a glass with dinner on Sundays.

"Isn't it a little early for wine, mom?"

She gives me her signature mom glare for a second. "I'll have you know your brothers are not listening to me at all and your father isn't home yet. They haven't taken care of their room and have been bombarding me with random questions. I needed twenty minutes of quiet, so I gave them their video games to leave me alone for a bit. The wine is just helping me to relax."

"How about this," Colt says. "I will deal with the twins while Pace gets ready. I can get them to take care of their room for you."

"I appreciate that Colt, and no offense sweetie but I just don't think anyone can get those two to do anything except for Hank."

"Would you care to make a bet, Aunt Lee?"

"Eh, no. Do not take that bet mom. Colt and I already have one going about this. I don't think he can do it either."

"Alright, alright. We'll see, won't we? You got a party to get ready for and I got a bet to win." He really thinks highly of himself that he can pull this off. Guess we will find out.

Chapter 2

Sadie's POV

"This is exactly what I needed," Stacey says as she lays down on the lounge chair beside me. She's wearing a cute, emerald green two piece string bikini that accentuates her figure and makes her tan skin look impeccable.

We are laying out by the pool at Lydia's house. She's hosting this year's varsity cheer get-together. It's our Bellwood High cheerleading tradition that goes back for however long. At the end of the previous school year, the junior cheerleaders, who are about to be seniors, place their names in a bowl and the graduating cheer captain will draw a name. Whoever's name is drawn has to host the get together the Sunday before cheer camp. It's a wonderful tradition to help us relax before we spend the next week helping the incoming freshman learn our cheers and routines. Then it's full squad practice the following week to gear up for the first game of the season.

"You are not kidding. I'm so stressed out," I tell her. I'm the captain this year and I can already feel the pressure of that title weighing me down.

"What? Why?" Stacey asks.

"For starters, it's senior year. I still have no clue where to apply for colleges or what I even want to do with my life. I have got to keep my grades up. My mom is constantly on me to maintain my 4.0 GPA. Says it will impress all the colleges when I finally start applying." I hate that I have not applied yet but I'm pretty sure I still got the time to get my applications in. I guess mom just worries that by the time I decide on a career and college, it will be too late to get accepted.

"And let's not forget, I'm the cheer captain. It comes with a lot of responsibilities and being a role model, not just to varsity, but also the JV squad. Especially the incoming freshmen. You remember how impressionable we were at that age."

"Relax, Sadie. You got this cheer captain thing in the bag. There's a reason why you were voted cheer captain," Stacey states, "I'm just grateful it wasn't Lydia who got it. I don't trust that wench as far as I could throw her."

Stacey and I have been friends since fifth grade, when her family moved down the street from mine. I always liked her positive personality, but I love her honesty even more.

"Hey all you sexy bitches!" Lydia shouts as she comes out of the back sliding doors of her home and turns the volume down on the music playing through the outdoor speakers. "Listen up!" Everyone quiets down so they can hear her. "Who's ready for some delicious eye candy?"

"Oh my god, did you get male strippers?" A girl with fair skin and auburn hair asks. She's sitting on the edge of the pool, letting her feet soak. I spoke to her shortly after I arrived and introduced myself. Since I'm the Captain, I want to ensure I get to know everyone on a more personal level to help build trust and strengthen our squad. I remember she said her name is Morgan and she's an incoming junior.

"Oh, honey. No. That would be too pedophilia being that some of you are under 18," she says arrogantly. "Any who, I just got off the phone with Brady and he's letting the varsity football players know about our party. They should be here soon so, perk those breasts up, girls, fix your makeup and look hot!" She winks before she turns the music back up and heads inside the house.

I look over at Stacey. "Did she just say she got off the phone with Brady?"

"Yeah, I'm pretty sure I heard her say Brady. Why?"

"Brady is at some family function today and he told me he wouldn't be able to talk much, if at all," I tell Stacey. "He wasn't sure if he would have a signal. Plus his dad is very anal about quality family time. No way she could have spoken with him. Right?"

"She may have. We all know Lydia tends to get her way so I wouldn't put it past her. If it makes you feel better, you could text him and find out but try not to make it sound like you're questioning him. It will make him feel like you don't trust him," Stacey says. Stacey is one of the few people who knows about the real dynamic of my relationship with Brady. Things between us have felt rocky lately. Sometimes I think he is with me because my father is the of Bellwood. He runs the town and since I'm his daughter, I've been known as Bellwood's town "princess." My family is well liked by everyone so we get a lot of attention and Brady loves it. Me? Not so much.

I pull my cell phone out of my beach bag. There's a few texts from Jenna and one from my mom, making sure I let her know when I'm coming home. I ignore their messages for now and pull up Brady's number to send him a text.

I hit send and wait to see if the bubbles pop up. After about a minute, he reads my text and responds.

> It's going ok. Rather be with you tho ;) Can't chat. G2G before Dad catches me on my phone and chews my ass out for it.

I show Stacey his response and she looks like she's trying to solve a riddle. I'm about to ask her what's with her face when there's shouting coming from the side of the house. Sounds like the football team has just arrived. Lydia rushes out her back doors to the side gate and unlatches the hook to allow them entry.

"Hey boys," she sing-songs, her hazel gray eyes roaming over every guy coming in. The majority of the guys are shirtless, wearing their swim trunks and showing off their muscular physiques. Some are carrying coolers while others are carrying bags of snacks and chairs. Lydia takes some of the bags and walks them towards the pool house to the kitchen inside where the snacks are lined along the counters and table like a buffet.

"Hey, I'll be right back," I tell Stacey.

I walk past groups of players and cheerleaders chatting, heading towards the pool house. I spot Chad and Nathan standing near the pool house bar, talking to Christina and a few of the guys from the team. They're Brady's best friends and usually if one is around, all three of them are around, which makes me wonder if Brady could be on his way here. Chad spots me before the rest of the group and I don't miss the way his eyes roam over my body as I approach. I wonder if he's always checked me out when Brady's not around and I just haven't noticed before.

"Yo, if it isn't Bellwood High's newest cheer captain, Sadie Adams!" he yells. This makes some of the football players hoot and holler. I can feel my cheeks warm from the attention. Being the mayor's daughter, you would think I am used to it.

"All hail, the Queen!" Nathan hollers and he bows before me. Chad does the same before Christina smacks Chad in his shoulder.

"Knock it off!" She says through gritted teeth.

Chad stands and pulls Christina into his side. "Aw. What's the matter, babe? Are you jealous?"

Christina shoves his arm off her and storms away.

"What was with that, Chad?" I nod in Christina's direction. "Is there something going on between the two of you?" I give him a sly smile.

"Who? Me and Christina?" he asks. "Psh. Hell no! I mean I heard she got some crush on me but I'm not the dating type. I'm enjoying the single life and getting my dick wet with as many hot chicks as possible. But if she's up for some midnight twister under the sheets, I'd happily oblige." He gives me a wink before he lets his eyes roam over my body again, but this time Nathan catches it and hits him on the back of his head.

"Ow, what the fuck was that for?"

"What the hell is wrong with you? You were totally checking out Sadie!"

"Dude, bro code. You know she's Brady's girl," one of their teammate's states. He's a big guy who looks like he could squash a watermelon easily with his bare hands.

"Speaking of Brady, is he coming a little later, by any chance?" I figured I would ask. If anyone would know for certain, it would be them. Nathan is the one to answer. "I spoke to him earlier this morning. Said he had that family reunion thing today. Said it was going to be an all-day event."

"Oh. Yeah, he mentioned going to a family thing to me and that he wouldn't be able to talk much. Just thought I would ask since the three of you always seem to hang out together. Kind of hoped he was going to show up." I tried to disguise the hint of disappointment in my voice, but I think Nathan picked up on it.

"Sorry, Sadie. You know he would rather be here with you than at that reunion."

I nod my head in agreement. "Thanks. Well, I'm going to go and let you guys get back to talking about whatever it is you were talking about."

I turn to walk inside the pool house to use the restroom. As I walk away, I overhear the guys talking about some new guy Coach said will be joining the team which makes me wonder if Brady knows too. He used to tell me everything going on with the team but this I haven't heard of.

I open the door to the Johnson's pool house. I guess it is more of a guest house, though. There's a decent sized living room area with a 55-inch TV hung on the wall above an electric fireplace. There are two heather gray couches for sitting and a white ottoman with a square wood tray sitting on top to double as a coffee table. It's got an open floor plan to the dining and kitchen area, which is crowded with football players and cheerleaders grabbing snacks, drinks and chatting amongst themselves.

I make my way down the small hallway. There's a master bedroom suite on the left and a second, smaller bedroom across from it on the right. Each room has its own bathroom. The door to the master suite is shut and from the sounds coming from the room, it's currently occupied. I notice the door to the other bedroom is open and make my way inside to ensure I use the bathroom before anyone else decides to occupy this bedroom.

After I wash my hands, I check my reflection in the mirror and notice my curls are starting to frizz from the humidity. This is one of the cons of having naturally curly hair. I decide to pull my hair up into a messy bun before I make my way back outside. I head to the lounge chairs by the pool where I was sitting with Stacey. As I approach, I notice that there's two people sitting on the chair I was laying out on. A guy who looks to be pretty tall with shaggy blonde hair and bright blue eyes. He appears to be enamored with Stacey. She's laughing at something he says, and I can't help to think they would look cute together.

My eyes fall onto the person next to blondie and I think my heart skips a few beats. She's got long, straight chocolate brown hair pulled into a ponytail. She has a baseball cap on with the ponytail pulled through the back. She's got what looks like a black sports bra paired with black cargo shorts and crisp, clean white chucks on her feet. She must be athletic because her body is nicely toned. You can make out the slightest hint of her abdominal muscles when she leans back to stretch out her legs. I have never been so drawn to another girl like I am right now.

Wait, I have never been this attracted to a girl before.

"Oh, hey Sadie. Here, have a seat next to me!" Stacey pats the spot next to her on the lounge chair.

The brunette beauty looks my way and I think I stop breathing for a second. Her eyes are a beautiful jade green and when she smiles, two little dimples appear in her cheeks. I don't think anyone's ever taken my breath away.

I take a seat next to Stacey, across from blondie and the girl who has captured my attention. She's staring at me, eyes never leaving mine. It makes butterflies go off in my belly with how she's looking at me.

The golden-haired guy next to her breaks the stare down. "Hey, Sadie. I'm Colton."

"Nice to meet you, Colton. Last name is Reynolds, right?"

"Yeah, that would be me. Heard you made cheer captain. Congrats! You will get to meet Thea, my sister, this week at camp. She's a freshman and made the JV squad."

"I look forward to meeting her. I'm assuming you're here because you play football. What position do you play?"

"Wide receiver. Planning to make the first-string offense." He plasters a big cheesy grin on his face.

"What do you mean planning? You *are* making the first-string offense!" The brunette tells him. Gosh, she has a nice voice. "What have I told you? When you want something, believe it's already yours and claim it!"

Stacey chimes in the conversation. "You know, I like that. The whole making something your bitch and claiming it? I'm going to start applying that to my life, starting with this school year."

"Yes! This girl knows what's up!" The brunette stretches between the chairs to high five Stacey before sitting back, her eyes falling back to mine.

"Sorry, my cousin has seemed to have lost his manners being in the presence of your friend here. I'm Payson."

She reaches her hand out to shake mine and I return the gesture. There's a small tingling sensation when our hands touch, like electricity is zapping through us. We both pull away quickly, making me wonder if she felt what I just felt.

"Ni-nice to meet you, Payson." I smile warmly at her. *Why am I nervous? I don't normally get nervous.* "Are you new around here? I don't think I have seen you around before."

"My family and I just moved recently. Dad was a four-star general in the Army and recently retired before uprooting us from a base in Cali to here. He's actually from this area. Both my parents are. They were high school sweethearts who married shortly after graduation and dad enlisted in the Army."

"Oh my God, that's so sweet!" Stacey exclaims. "Well, the high school sweethearts and marriage part. I'm sure the military life was challenging."

"Um, yeah. There were definitely some hard times. Especially when my dad got deployed into dangerous situations. I'm just grateful he always made it back to us. He was one of the lucky ones." There's a bit of sadness in her tone and I have to wonder if she lost someone close to her.

"Well—" Stacey stands up, adjusting her bikini. Colton glances at her, swallowing the drool that's probably pooling in his mouth. She looks down at Colton and smiles. "—I'm getting kind of hungry. There are snacks inside the pool house. You want anything?"

"Yeah, sure. I could eat." Colton stands up and judging by the look on his face, I don't think it's the food he wants to eat.

"You want anything Sadie?"

"No, thank you Stacey. I'm good for now."

"Payson?"

"No, thank you. I'm good."

"Okay. We'll be right back." She heads towards the pool house while Colton lingers back. He's staring at Stacey's backside for a moment before he looks down at Payson.

"Oh, uh, hey Pace?"

"Yeah, Colt?"

"Pay up. You owe me $10."

"Damn it! I was hoping good looking Stacey made you forget, especially with the way you just eye fucked the hell out of her." She lets out a small laugh, reaching into her pocket to pull out a $10 bill from her wallet and hands it to Colton. He rushes off to catch up with Stacey who was a few feet ahead.

Wait. Did they make a bet? Were they betting on if Colton would get Stacey's attention? I don't think I like that, and I *know* Stacey wouldn't appreciate being the object of a bet. I mean, what girl would?

"Did you and your friend make a bet on Stacey?" I ask, a hint of anger in my voice that Payson picks up on.

"What? No! No, no, no. It's not like that. You totally got it wrong."

I cross my arms over my chest. "Then why don't you explain it to me? Because the way I just saw it, it looked like you two had a bet over my friend." I really hope I'm wrong. There's something about this girl and I don't want to view her in a negative way.

"Okay. Yes, there was a bet made but not about them. I promise you. Yeah, Colt's mad crushing on Stacey, which is why he brought me along. He wanted my help, and I said I would. He would do the same for me if I needed him." She stares at me as if she is thinking of something, biting on her bottom lip and pulling it in her mouth. There's a hint of a smile, her white teeth glistening against her sun kissed skin. Not sure what she's thinking but damn if it didn't do something for me. When she sees me staring at her mouth, she sits up straight, adjusts her hat and clears her throat.

"Before we came here, we had to stop by my house so I could change. I have two younger brothers, and they can be pains in the asses. My mom was struggling with getting them to unpack their room. They don't listen to anyone but dad and he wasn't home so Colton had it in his mind that he could get the twins to take care of their room. That was when we made the bet. If he couldn't get them to unpack their room, I won $10 and if he could, well, clearly you see who won that."

"I'm sorry I took it the wrong way." I avoid looking at her, feeling ashamed of myself for judging her and not showing her grace.

"Hey." She reaches across the space, gently grabs my chin and forces me to look into her eyes.

Whoa, why is that gesture so hot?

Her eyes are soft as she looks at me. "No worries. I would have gotten defensive too if I was in your shoes. It just goes to show your loyalty to those you care about, and I respect that."

She's staring me down, taking in my face. She glances down at my lips a few times and damn if I didn't wish she would kiss me. I almost think she's about to when I hear someone yell cannonball before cold water drenches my skin.

"Oh my gosh, that's so cold!" I jump up from the chair and try to shake off the water.

"Do you have a towel?" Payson asks.

"Yeah, um, you're sitting on it actually." I point to my leopard print towel laying on the chair.

Payson stands up, grabs the towel and wraps it around me, ensuring it's securely around my shoulders.

"I'm sorry, I hadn't realized you had been sitting there. Is that better?" She's standing super close to me and when I breathe in, I get a hint of her scent. She smells like coconut and vanilla with a note of salty sea, reminding me of the tropical beaches we vacationed at in summers past.

"Yeah, I'm feeling a bit warmer already." The way she is looking at me, the longing and maybe a hint of want, makes me feel a way no one has ever made me feel. I can feel the blush creeping in, and I hope it's not noticeable. How can this one person make me feel so desired, like I'm the sun in the center of their universe?

Payson reaches out and places a strand of hair that fell in my face behind my ear. She moves even closer to me and some part of me starts to move closer to her.

"Ahem." The sound of a throat clearing startles me from the little trance-like bubble I was just in, and I take a few steps back. Payson and I turn to see Lydia standing next to us, a smug look on her face.

"Am I interrupting something?" She crosses her arms over her chest and juts her hip out.

Payson looks her up and down, and damn if the notion didn't bother me a little.

"Actually, I think you were." She cocks her head to the side, glaring at Lydia. The last thing I want is for Payson to end up on Lydia's bad side. Lydia is like the devil in smooth, tan skin and she is the last person you want to cross.

"Sadie and I—"

"We were just talking," I interrupt. I give Payson a look I hope she can read, pleading with her to be cool. "Payson, this is Lydia. She is the hostess for the party. Lydia, this is Payson. She is new in town, and we were just getting to know each other." Payson smiles lightly at me and oh heavens, the dimples!

"Yeah, I can clearly see that," Lydia replies. She quirks an eyebrow. "I came over to introduce myself. Thank you, Captain, for doing that for me. As the hostess, I have to ask why are you here? This is strictly an invitation only for football players and cheerleaders."

Payson stands up straighter, crossing her arms. "For your information, I was invited."

"Oh, really. And pray tell, who invited you?" Lydia questions her.

At that moment, Colton and Stacey returned with plates loaded with a variety of snacks and bottled waters.

"That would have been me," Colton says. "We were hanging out when Zealand called about the party. Figured I would bring Payson to meet everybody before tomorrow." He grins widely, like he's so proud of himself.

Lydia's demeanor changes. "Oh, hey Colton." She flutters her fake eyelashes at him. If you were to look up the definition of a jersey chaser, Lydia would be pictured next to the word. She has no shame in it. "How are you?"

Colton seems to ignore the way Lydia is trying to flirt with him. "I'm good," he says before popping a chip into his mouth. "I would be better if you apologized to my cousin. Where is your southern hospitality, Lyd?"

"Oh, I had no idea she was related to you!" Lydia turns to face Payson. "I'm sorry Peyton. I hope you can forgive me."

"It's Payson. And that was a weak ass apology." I can't help the smug smile I feel on my face. Most people don't ever give it back to Lydia. They fear the retaliation she would dish out, so no one really wants to put her in her place. Something tells me Payson isn't like that and I admire her for it.

Payson gives a sly smirk. "You might want to watch how you flutter those falsies there, baby doll. They may fly away."

Stacey spits out some of the water she was drinking, and I can't help the laugh that slips out before Lydia gives us both the death glare.

"And uh, you can stop trying to get Colt's attention. He ain't interested in you and you are nowhere near his type."

"First off, don't call me baby doll. I'm not some carpet muncher, you dyke!"

"Okay, whoa Lydia that's so fucking not cool—"

Payson puts her hand up, halting whatever Colton was going to say.

"Whoa, whoa. Now hold on Colt. You don't have to defend me. I got this. Lydia thinks she can hurt me but really, she is clearly telling me everything I need to know about the type of person she is." Payson takes her hand and moves it across her chin. "You see Lydia, yeah, I am a carpet muncher. I love pussy! I will shout it in front of everyone here at this very party if you want me to. You got a mic? I will make sure everyone hears me say it. I'm not afraid of what people think of me, and I don't care either. I'm happy with the person I am. Can you say the same about yourself?"

There's a small crowd near us, people who moved in closer when Lydia started to go into bitch mode. Everyone is quietly waiting to see what will happen next, waiting for Lydia's reaction.

Lydia's jaw clenches tightly, I think you can hear her teeth grinding each other.

"Why don't you take your little rainbow happy ass and get the fuck out of my party!"

Payson gives a smug smile. "I'd be delighted to. This party sucks balls anyway." Lydia shoves through the crowd and storms off.

"Colt, are you coming or staying here for a bit?"

Colton looks like he's trying to figure out what to do, eyes bouncing between his cousin and Stacey.

"Um, well uh..."

"You know what? Stay. It's cool. I'm sure someone can take you home, right?"

"I can take him home!" Stacey speaks up. "If that's okay with you guys?"

"Yeah, it's not a problem," Payson smiles. "See you tomorrow, Colt! Text me if you need me to pick you up." Payson pulls her keys out of her pocket and heads toward the gate to leave.

I don't miss the small, hurtful look on Payson's face as she goes.

I grab my bag, pull on my cut off denim shorts and cherry tank top over my swimsuit, slide on my flip flops and grab my things.

"Hey, Stace. I'm going to head out too. I will see you tomorrow for the cheer camp."

"Okay, are you sure? I mean we can eat our food really quick and then I can take you home."

"It's okay. I can walk home from here." I give her a reassuring smile.

"At least text me when you make it home?"

"Absolutely! See you guys later!"

I wave them off and nonchalantly hurry my way to the gate, hoping I can catch Payson before she leaves. As I turn the corner of the house, I look through the rows of cars lined up along the street, searching for the long brown ponytail in a black baseball hat. I spot her as she is getting into a bright, yellow Jeep.

"Hey!" I shout, hopefully loud enough to catch her attention. I see her head pop up, looking around until her eyes fall on me. She releases a slow smile and it sends the butterflies fluttering in my belly again. I hurry across the front lawn to where she is parked, carefully trying not to trip and make a fool of myself.

"Mind if I catch a ride?" I ask. I'm hoping she will say yes.

"Are you sure you want to leave your party? Being that you are the cheer captain, isn't it some cheer law you have to stay?"

I let out a small laugh and swear I hear Payson mutter, "That's beautiful," under her breath. "Uh, no. There are no such things as cheer laws and Lydia was voted to host this so I can leave if I want to. I'm not needed for this."

"Okay. Well, Captain, hop on in. Just tell me where I got to take you and I will see to it you get home safely."

"Thanks."

I get in the passenger seat and buckle up before we head to my house. I tell Payson which streets to take and before we know it, she's pulling into the long driveway of my parents' home.

Payson and I sit in her Jeep, a moment of silence passing between us.

"Look, Payson. I want to apologize for the awful things Lydia said to you back at the party."

"Apologize? You want to apologize for something another person said to me?"

"I mean, yeah. What Lydia said was uncalled for. It was disgusting hearing her say those things to you.""You don't have to apologize for her. You don't owe me that. She does and, this is just a guess, but I don't think I will ever get one from her. She showed me the type of person she truly is, and it's clearly someone I don't plan to be around."

"I wish I had the chance to warn you about her before she approached us. Lydia can be awful, and no one has ever stood up against her, especially after what she did to a girl in freshman year. Everyone's afraid of her wrath."

Payson just shakes her head and grins. "Nah, she doesn't scare me that easily. I've got some thick skin. There is nothing she can say or do to me that probably hasn't been done before."

She kind of zones out for a moment and I want to ask what's happened to her. But I don't think it's my place. I mean, we just met, and I hardly know much about her. I don't realize I'm staring at her until she speaks up.

"What? Do I have a pimple or something on my face?" She pulls down her visor to check her reflection.

"No, your face is perfect." I thought I whispered it quietly enough so she wouldn't hear me but the look on her face says she did.

Shoot. Why did I say that out loud!?

"I mean, um, can I see your phone?" I ask, feeling the heat of a blush on my cheeks.

"Sure. What for?" She hands me her cell phone after she unlocks it. I go into her contacts, put in my name and number then send a text to my phone.

I hand her phone back. "I thought you should have my number since you're new to town. Figured you may need some assistance finding your way around school. And after the verbal showdown at the party, you may need an extra friend..."

"You think I need backup or something?" She says jokingly.

"Well, no. Definitely not. But you can always use a friend, right?"

"I guess I don't see the harm in an extra friend. Especially when they are as gorgeous as you." I feel my heart skip a few beats. *Did she call me gorgeous?*

Payson leans across the center console and into my space. Her face is a hair breadth away from mine. She reaches up, cups the side of my face and her thumb gently swipes under my eye. She pulls back, just a smidge, eyes still locked on mine.

"You had an eyelash under your eye."

"Oh. Thanks for getting it for me," I whisper back.

We are both lost in the moment. Thoughts are swirling in my head, wondering what is going through her mind and if she is drawn to me like I am to her.

The moment ends quickly when the sound of my cell phone starts ringing and reality sinks in. I realize the ringtone that is playing and know exactly who is calling me. It's the one I have set for Brady, my boyfriend.

What am I doing?

I fumble, trying to quickly grab my things and get out of the vehicle.

"Sorry. That's my mom calling. I got to get inside and help prepare for dinner. It was nice to meet you, Payson. Thank you for the ride!"

"Yeah, no problem. I guess I'll see you around?"

"Yeah. I'll be around." I give her a quick smile before getting out and rushing up the walkway to the front door. I pause for a moment, turning to look back at Payson. She's still sitting there, and I'm not sure why but I give her a little wave before I enter the house. Once I'm inside, I peek out of the little side windows that frame the doorway and watch Payson drive off. I lean my forehead into the door with so many conflicting emotions swarming in my mind. What am I doing having these feelings over this girl when I have a boyfriend?

Chapter 3

Payson's POV

B *eep. Beep. Beep. Beep.*

Is there a more annoying noise than the sound of your alarm going off and waking you up too damn early?

I quickly turn off my alarm and lay in my bed for a few minutes. I'm not a fan of early mornings but today is the first day of football conditioning. I have to get up and ready so I can make it to the field a little early. I want to make a good impression on the coaches, especially the Head Coach. He's going to determine who gets the starting quarterback position and damn, I want to be the starter more than anything.

I throw the covers off and make my way into my bathroom. The upside of moving to this house is I don't have to fight my brothers for the bathroom anymore. Thank God for no more pee on the toilet seats.

I make work of cleansing my face, brushing my teeth and putting my hair into Dutch braids. It's my go to style when I'm on the field. It keeps the hair out of my face and makes my helmet fit comfortably on my head.

I throw on some clothes and do a once over in the mirror hanging on the back of my door. I grab my cell phone off my side table and head downstairs to the kitchen.

"Mmm," rumbles out of my mouth as the smell of French toast, eggs and bacon greets me when I enter the kitchen. Mom knows it's my favorite breakfast.

Mom is busying herself at the stove, plating breakfast for everyone. Dad is sitting at the head of the table, looking over the newspaper while he drinks his coffee. He looks up from whatever he is reading and smiles.

"Morning, Champ. Are you ready for today?"

"As ready as I'll ever be," I reply.

"You're not nervous, are you?" he asks.

"Me? Nervous? Dad, please. Are you forgetting what I did back in Cali?"

"Of course not, Champ. But it's also okay to feel a little nervous. It's a new school, with new coaches and teammates who are going to judge your skills all because you're a female."

"I swear, I'm not nervous at all. It's an adrenaline rush knowing they have no idea what I'm capable of and I get to show them that." I give him my biggest grin. I love nothing more than showing guys that just because there isn't a dick between my legs, and I have boobs, granted they're very small, I can play the game just as well as they do, possibly even better.

I take a seat next to my dad when mom sets my plate in front of me.

"That's my girl," she says before planting a kiss on top of my head. "Did I ever tell you you're my shero?"

Mom has always loved my spirit that nothing should be garnered to gender. Women can do anything men can and it's time people stopped seeing the world through gender roles. This isn't the 1950's anymore.

"All the time, mom," I beam. "Where are the boys? I'm surprised they aren't down here at the first smell of bacon."

Dad looks at his watch on his wrist. "Give it about three...two...one..."

As if on cue, the sounds of a stampede come charging down the stairs followed by my brothers yelling.

"I'm going to beat you to the table first!"

"No, I'm going to beat you to the table first."

What can I say? The Moore kids are just naturally competitive.

Judson and Grayson come running into the kitchen. Judson shoves Grayson into the island before he slides on his socks across the gray laminate floor to the dining table.

"Ow, Judson! You totally cheated!"

"Boo-hoo!" Judson mocks Grayson with the crybaby gesture. "You're such a baby, Gray."

"Am not!" Grayson yells.

"Yes, you are. I barely shoved you."

"Boys—" mom starts but they keep going back and forth.

"Tell that to my bruised ribs!"

"They're not bruised. Suck it up, you big baby."

"Boys, you need to stop." Mom tries again to no avail.

Judson continues to antagonize Grayson. "How can you be a football player if you cry like a baby getting hit?"

"We wear pads in football, you idiot!" Grayson retorts.

"BOYS, ATTENTION!" Dad yells, bringing out that commanding general tone. My brothers shut their mouths and face our father.

"Come here."

The boys walk over in front of father, who stands up from his spot at the table. They stand side by side, like dad's former soldiers used to do.

"That is completely unacceptable behavior. Judson, this is not football practice. We do not tackle or shove our siblings in this house. And we most certainly do not mock or call our siblings names. You need to apologize to your brother, right now. Then I want you to drop and give me ten. If your apology isn't good enough, I will double it."

Judson lets out a sigh before he turns to face Grayson. "I'm sorry for shoving you into the island that may have caused you pain. It was wrong, as was me calling you a baby. You are not a baby. You are actually a pretty kickass football player."

"Judson Cole Moore!" Mom is glaring at Judson for his use of a cuss word. "You do not have permission to use adult language until you are eighteen years old!"

"You have just earned yourself an extra ten," dad says.

"Yes, sir." Judson hangs his head.

"You apologize to your mother for cussing."

Judson turns to look at mom. "I'm sorry, mom. I shouldn't use adult words before I'm an adult. No matter how cool they may be to say."

"Oh, Judson. What am I going to do with you?" mom asks, shaking her head. "You are forgiven. Now, do your twenty push ups before your breakfast gets cold."

"Yes, Ma'am."

Judson drops down and pumps out twenty push ups before he retreats to the table and digs in.

"You good, Gray?" I ask Grayson.

"Yeah Pace. I'm good."

"You know, I think Judson should give you half of his bacon for what he did. Don't you think so, Grayson?"

Grayson smirks in agreement. "Yeah, I think so too. You know, for pain and suffering."

"What!? No way! I just did twenty push ups, an apology and even gave you a compliment."

"Pain. And. Suffering."

"Mom!" Judson exclaims.

"It wouldn't kill you to give your brother a few extra pieces. Consider it a peace offering and move on."

Judson drops a few pieces of bacon onto Grayson's plate before he slumps in his own chair and folds his arms over his chest.

"Thanks, Payson," he snarls at me.

"Anytime little bro," I smile back. My phone chimes with a text from Colton. "Alright fam. I got to go. Colt needs me to pick him up for conditioning and I want to be early. I will see you guys later!"

I give dad a quick side hug before dropping my dishes off into the sink and give mom a kiss on the cheek.

"Good luck, sweetie. Go kick some asses."

"C'mon mom. You know I plan to." I smile at her before I grab my gym bag and keys from the foyer and head out. It feels humid out already and I can tell it's going to make conditioning even more unbearable.

I send a text to Colt letting him know I'm headed his way before I hook up my playlist to Connie and drive off. A few moments later, I pull into my aunt and uncle's driveway and honk the horn.

Colton emerges from his house with his duffel bag on his shoulder and water bottle in hand.

"Who's ready for some football?" Colt asks as he hops into my Jeep, his megawatt smile in full shine.

"Aren't you a little chipper this morning? I take it that things went well with Stacey yesterday?"

We never got to talk about what happened after I left the party. I was so caught up in Sadie and our little moment when I dropped her off at her house. I know I told Colt that I'm not looking to date anyone, but there is something about Sadie that draws me to her. For starters, she is absolutely gorgeous with her honey blonde curly hair, steel blue eyes, and a killer toned body. It was a challenge when we were talking not to let my eyes roam over her in that pink bikini she was wearing. I didn't want to come off as a creep or scare her off if she caught me ogling her. But beyond the exterior beauty, she seems like a genuine girl who cares about others more than herself. She's loyal to the ones she loves, and I admire and respect it.

I was so tempted to kiss her. I was about to pull her into me before her phone rang and ruined the moment. After I made sure she got in her house okay, I went home to change into some gym clothes and went for a run. Lydia's words were still buzzing in my head, and I needed to run off the anger that was simmering beneath my skin. I know it looks like I'm not fazed by people's ignorance and hateful comments, but I'm still a human being with feelings.

"Well, after you and Sadie left, Stacey and I finished our snacks then dipped out. There was no point in staying. Lydia ruined the whole vibe. So, we went to the outlet mall and just walked around. You know, talking and stuff."

"Stuff, huh? Would that happen to involve possibly kissing?" I quirk an eyebrow in his direction.

"No. No kissing."

"Really?"

"Yes, really. Look, I'm not like Chad or the other sleazeballs who want to jump right into the physical stuff. Unlike them, I do happen to want to know the girl on a more personal level."

I lightly punch him in the shoulder. "Chill dude. I'm just giving you a hard time. It's cool that you are taking things slowly. You're giving her time to see what she feels about you and I admire it."

"Did you also forget who raised me? Because you know they would bury me six feet down if I ever did anything that was not consensual."

"Yeah. I think I remember your mom's exact words were, 'If you ever do anything to make a girl uncomfortable, I will cut off your manhood and blend it to mush!'"

Colton shivers slightly at the memory. "Yes, and I have had those fearful words embedded in my brain since she made that statement."

"Good to know Aunt Charlotte's words still resonate with you. Now, let's get our asses to this football field, shall we? I got a quarterback position to claim."

We make it to the high school across town in great timing. Conditioning doesn't start for another ten minutes, which I'm hoping will leave a great first impression on the coaches. I want them to see just how much I take football seriously. Being a young woman in a male dominant sport is already a challenge, one most of the misogynistic society mocks and looks down on. They tend to view women as weak or too soft to handle a sport where bodies slam into each other, and can leave you with sprains, broken bones, torn ligaments and even concussions. It's no different than any other sport girls and young women play. Soccer, volleyball, and cheerleading have just as many risks of serious injury as football.

Colton and I grab our duffel bags from the back seat and head towards the football field.

"Yo, Colt! Wait for us!" someone shouts from behind.

We turn to see three guys jogging towards us from across the student parking lot. When they catch up to us, Colt shares a fist bump with the guys.

"Surprised to see you guys here early," Colton says.

The tallest one smiles wide. "Yeah, well, it's varsity. Got to take it more seriously." He notices me standing next to Colton and does a quick look over. "Who's this?"

"This is my cousin, Payson. Payson, this is Zealand, Rhett and Jeremiah." He points to each guy as he says their name. "Zealand plays safety. Rhett is a tight end and Jeremiah is a linebacker."

"Wait, *this* is Payson? The newbie coming in to go against Thomas?" Zealand asks.

"Yeah. I thought I told you guys. Why is this news to you?" Colton asks.

"Because Brady and his ass kissing friends have been assuming it was a new *guy*. Not a chick."

I roll my eyes. Of course, no one expects to see me. They automatically assume I'm a dude and it doesn't help that my name comes off masculine.

Rhett smirks. "Oh, this is great. Brady's about to get the shock of his life."

"Well, I can't wait to see what you do out there," Jeremiah speaks up. "I really hope you swipe that quarterback position from under him." He gives me a fist bump, one I reciprocate.

"It was great meeting you guys, but I'd like to get in there." I point towards the entrance to the stadium behind me. "Trying to make a good impression on the coaches. Since I don't have a penis, I have to make them see I'm serious about playing."

"Shall we then?" Jeremiah makes a gesture, showing me to lead the way.

"Hey, for what it's worth, I think it's badass that you are gunning for QB," Zealand states. "And just know, we all got your back. Anyone who gives you any trouble, you let us know."

"Thanks, man. I appreciate it."

We make our way through the entrance of the stadium where families and students pay to enter. We bypass the restrooms and come out to where a black gate surrounds a black track. The track surrounds the football field, bright green turf with freshly painted white lines. Bellwood and Eagles have been painted on the end zones in Carolina blue and gold.

I spot a few men chatting amongst themselves with hats on their heads, silver whistles hanging around their necks and clipboards attached in their hands. I can assume that's the coaching staff. They are standing by the home team bench where tables are set up with drinking stations to keep everyone hydrated with the heat beating down on us.

I tap Colton's chest to get his attention for a second. "Hey, are those all the coaches over by the bench?" I point in the direction I'm referring.

"Yeah, that's them. The big, burly guy is Coach Watson. He's the head coach. The one standing beside him on your left is the offensive coordinator, Coach Freeman. And the one who looks like he could be Dwayne Johnson's stunt double, he's defensive coordinator, Coach Wells."

"The silver fox looking one is Coach Harbaugh. He's the assistant head coach. You'll like him because he isn't kissing Brady's ass," Rhett chimes in.

I look at Rhett. "Silver fox, huh? Is there something I should know?"

"Nah, Rhett's straight as a pole," Jeremiah chimes in. "Coach Harbaugh is the talk of the school with the ladies, and gays. They all call him a silver fox."

"Good to know." I pull my bag up onto my shoulder and let out a deep breath. "Alright fellas. I'm going to go introduce myself. Wish me luck!"

I walk across the field to the circle of coaches. As I approach, the one who looks like he could pass for the Rock's twin notices me first.

"Good morning, young lady. How can we help you?" he asks. The other coaches stopped their conversations to stare at me.

"Sorry, I don't mean to interrupt. I just wanted to come over and introduce myself. I'm Payson Moore, the new player from California." I reach out to shake their hands.

"Payson Moore?" The one everybody calls the silver fox asks.

"Uh, yes sir. That would be me," I answer.

The big, burly guy who Colton mentioned is the head coach is staring at me. "You're Payson Moore?" He checks his clipboard to scan it, looking for something. "The incoming...quarterback?" He chuckles and shakes his head. This grinds my nerves. I have a feeling why he's in disbelief and am not surprised by what he says next.

"My second string quarterback is a girl? Is this a joke?" He chuckles.

Did he just say second string? And is he seriously laughing about me playing because I'm a girl? I can feel the anger boiling under my skin, until I feel a light touch of a hand on my arm that's clenching down on my duffle bag strap.

"Excuse me, Coach?" Colton asks.

"Ah, Reynolds. How are you, son?" Coach Watson asks, his tone a bit more chipper than a second ago.

"Good, sir. But I couldn't help overhearing you claim Payson already as our second string quarterback. Excuse me for saying this but how can you say that when she hasn't had the opportunity to prove her worth? Are you really going to assume her second best because she's a girl?"

Coach Watson is quiet. His face is hardened and he's staring at Colton, an expression I'm certain that says Colton's walking on thin ice for that comment.

Good job, Colt. I think you just screwed your chances of being a starting wide receiver by defending me.

"Reynolds makes a valid point, Watson." The coach with russet brown skin speaks out. "You got to give Ms. Moore here the opportunity to showcase her skills. And frankly, I'm excited to see what she's got." He gives me a big smile, one flaunting his perfect white teeth. "I'm Coach Freeman. Being that I am the offensive coordinator, I would like to see some competition for Brady. Let the best QB win." He gives me a wink. I think he and I are going to get along just fine.

"Fine," Coach Watson sighs. "Ms. Moore, place your bag somewhere and find a spot with the boys. We will begin momentarily."

"Thanks, Coach." I replied.

Colton and I head over to the gate by the track to set our bags down before I smack Colton upside the head.

"Ow! What the hell was that for?"

"What in the hell were you doing back there? I was handling that conversation before you put your two cents in!""Well, uh, excuse me for wanting to have your back and make sure Coach treats you fairly. Is that so wrong?"

"Yeah when it jeopardizes your chances of making it as a starter, Colt!" I whisper shout. "I appreciate you having my back, I really do. It means the world to me, and I love you for it. But I can handle coaches like Watson. This isn't the first time I've dealt with this. I just have to prove myself to him and he will see my skills over my gender."

"Look, I'm not that worried about making it as a starter this year. I'm just a junior. I have time to hone my skills and give the coaches something to look forward to next season. As long as I'm starting next year, I'm fine.

But what I'm not okay with is you getting passed over on an opportunity simply because of your gender. It's not right."

"It matters to me. This is our only year of playing together. I want us to make big plays and win games before I head off to college."

"Who's to say we won't end up at the same college together?" Colton shrugs.

"True, but are you even smart enough to get into college?" I tease him.

"Hey, I'm plenty smart. Okay?"

"Whatever you got to tell yourself to sleep at night," I smirk.

The sound of a few whistles blowing gets everyone's attention. Looks like the rest of the football team has arrived.

"Alright everybody. Listen up!" yells Coach Wells. I'm not surprised the biggest coach has the loudest voice. "Welcome to the 2022 football season. I'm Coach Wells, for anyone who doesn't know me. I'm the defensive coordinator. We are going to take attendance then run through some warmups before we begin with conditioning. Therefore, I need five rows of players on a line, starting on the 30-yard line."

Everybody scrambles to go stand on a line. I make my way over to the 50-yard line. Call it quarterback paranoia but I like to be able to see all around me.

Colton stands to my left on the 40-yard line. Jeremiah is behind me. Rhett is to my right and Zealand is behind him. I guess they weren't kidding when they said they have my back. It makes a small piece of my heart smile.

Once everyone is lined up, the coaches motion for us all to sit down. Coach Freeman begins to run through attendance when some of the guys start whistling and hollering. That's when I notice the cheerleaders entering the track, walking over to the opposite side of the field. I think back to the pool party and Sadie, the beautiful girl who wanted to make sure I was okay. I haven't been able to forget her..

My eyes search through the crowd of people entering the track until I spot her curly blonde hair pulled up in a high ponytail. She looks gorgeous with her long tan legs in black little shorts and a white Bellwood Eagles t-shirt tied in the front showing off her toned abs.

"Alright, alright. Let's reel it in fellas," Coach Freeman says, chuckling. "We got a lot to cover this week before we can move to pads and work on play calls. So, I need all your attention." Everyone settles down a bit before Coach Freeman resumes going through the list. "Alright. We are going to do some stretches and warm up exercises. Then I want you to run two laps around the football field. After that, you can get a water break before we break off into drills. Got it?"

Everyone shouts, "Yes, Coach!"

By the time I made it to my water bottle after my laps, I'm covered in sweat and my lungs are on fire. I glance over to where Sadie is with the cheerleaders, and I catch her watching me. For the hell of it, I decide to spray some water on my face, letting it drizzle down my neck, into my sports bra and down my body. I look back at her, taking note of the way she bites her bottom lip and damn if I didn't want to just pull it out and bite it myself to see how she tastes.

"Why...is it...so damn...HOT!" Colton pants through gasps of catching his breath.

"It's South Carolina. What do you expect the summer weather to be like in a state so close to Florida?"

"We need an indoor facility...with air conditioning...for all of this..."

"Colton, you're such a wuss. Just dump some water on your head and you'll be good."

He gives me the middle finger, so I return the gesture back to him when the coaches blow their whistles.

"Everyone who is finished with their water break, come back to the field so we can divide you up for drills," yells Coach Freeman.

I place my water bottle back inside my bag and head back to the coaches when I accidentally bump into a wall, or what felt like a wall. I look up to see a guy, about six feet tall. He has long, tousled brown hair on top with the sides faded and chocolate brown eyes that slowly rake over my body. He gives me a sly smirk and I have no doubt he just checked me out.

"Sorry. I didn't see you." I try to walk past him, but he blocks my way.

"Kind of hard to miss, don't you think?" he says slyly.

I cross my arms across my chest. "Okay. I see what you are doing and to save you the trouble, I'm not interested. You're not even my type."

"Pretty sure I'm every girl's type."

"Mmm, yeah. Not this girl. Now if you could move the hell out of my way, that'd be great."

"Whoa, calm down there, Shortstack. I'm just trying to make conversation."

"How about you don't block my path so I can get back to the coaches, will you?" I sneer.

"You mean the cheer coaches over there?" He points his thumb behind him, directing it to where the cheerleaders are.

I let out a small, fake laugh. "How cute of you to assume that because I have a pussy and boobs, that's where I belong. If anything, my place would be with one of those cheerleaders riding my face while I make her scream. Particularly, the cute cheer captain with the curly blonde hair. She looks like she would be down for a good time."

His smirk disappears before he lets out a low growl. He's about to say something before Coach Watson yells, "Brady Thomas! You're late!"

Ah, so this asshole is my competition for starting quarterback. I'm going to have so much fun when I take it away from him.

"I'd watch what you say," he says with clenched teeth, lowering himself to look me in my eyes.

"Or what?" I retorted.

"Brady, now!"

"Better go. Wouldn't want to keep Coach waiting."

Colton comes to my side as Brady storms off towards Coach Watson.

"So, I see you finally met Brady and by the looks of it, it didn't go so well," Colton says.

"Yeah, and you were right. He is a complete ass wipe. Getting that starting QB position is going to be even better. Especially seeing how it will wipe that smug ass look off his face."

"Well, you know I'm rooting for you, Cuz." Colton and I fist bump then head back on the field to run through all the conditioning drills.

After an hour's worth of participating in each station, we are split off into offense and defense. Defensive players went to one half of the field with Coach Wells and offensive players are with Coach Freeman on the other half.

Coach Freeman blows his whistle to get our attention. "Alright everybody, listen up!" We gather around him, waiting for instruction.

"I'm going to split you up into two groups. I want all my offensive linemen to be over on the 50-yard line. You are actually going to work with the defensive linemen and practice blocking each other. I want my centers, quarterbacks, wide receivers, running backs and tight ends in the end zone. We are going to be working on some passes, running plays, and I want to see how well our quarterbacks throw."

When we get to the end zone, Coach calls for Brady and me. "Alright, give me my quarterbacks, Moore and Thomas."

Brady is looking around, confusion all over his face. "I'm sorry, Coach. I think I didn't hear you clearly. Did you say quarterbacks as in more than one?"

"You heard correctly, Thomas."

I walk up to the coach and stand next to him. Coach Freeman points at me. "Fellas, let me introduce you to our other quarterback, Payson Moore. She's the new teammate from California."

Brady and some of the guys start to laugh. "Is this some sort of joke?"

Coach glares at Brady with a firm expression. "Does this face look like I'm joking, Thomas?"

The laughing halts and Brady's face is one of disbelief. "Uh, no sir. The guys and I assumed the new kid was a guy. I'm just having a hard time seeing how a girl can be on a football team, especially as a quarterback. Do you know how embarrassing that would be——"

"Hey Colt!" I interrupt Brady's little tantrum tirade. "Go long!" I snatch the football from Coach's hands and throw a perfect spiral. Colton's running down the field, eyes on the ball. He leaps up around the 45-yard line and snatches it before coming down to the ground. There are gasps and shocked expressions being whispered from the rest of the guys but Brady who is awfully quiet.

I smile at Brady. "What were you going to say about a girl being a quarterback and how it embarrasses the team?"

"Alright, alright. Calm down. Moore, I have to admit, that was impressive. But next time, ask to take the football instead of snatching it out of my hands. Okay?"

"Sorry, Coach. I have a tendency of needing to prove myself to others who think I'm not good enough solely based on what I have between my legs."

"Noted." Coach Freeman shakes his head. "Alright, why don't we work on some passing throws first. Pitman, you will be the center for Thomas. Lambert, you have Moore. I want Mason, Olsen and Calloway with Thomas. I want Reynolds, Turner and Sanchez with Moore. We are going to start with the quick out route. Ms. Moore, I'm sure you are familiar with the different routes?"

"Yes, sir. Colton and I have been running routes since I've moved here. Just throw them out, Coach. I've got this." I give him a smile.

"Very well. Alright I want to see a quick out route. On my whistle. Three...two...one..." The sound of the whistle blows. Turner runs out and cuts left. I throw the ball, but not too hard as this is for quick passes when I feel the pocket collapsing on me in the game. Turner reels in the ball and I fist pump the air.

"Yes!" It's always a great feeling when you make a successful pass.

"Chill there, Shortstack. That was so simple a toddler could have done it." Brady rolls his eyes, as if he's annoyed.

"Oh, I'm sorry. I didn't realize I'm not allowed to celebrate my small victories. How about you stop focusing on me and worry about that wobbly pass you just threw." I give him a smug smirk before waiting for the coach to give out the next route play.

Colton stands next to me at the ready.

"Hey, just ignore Brady. I think he's intimidated by you and it's not sitting right with him."

"Damn straight, he better be." I smile back at Colt.

"Since defense is taking their water break, let's try a deep go route. Receivers, when I blow my whistle, you're going to run down the field. I want my quarterbacks to give a three second count then throw it as far down the field as you can go. Receivers, on my whistle. Three...two...one..."

The whistle blows and Colton takes off down the field. He's going against Olsen and damn if Olsen isn't fast. He may be slightly faster than Colt. I count to three in my head before I take a few steps back and launch the football down the field.

Brady's ball manages to make it to the 45-yard line before Olsen catches his pass. Meanwhile, mine surpasses his, reaching almost sixty yards when Colton snatches the ball out of the air.

"Fuck yeah!" I shout, running up to Colton to high five him. "Great catch, Colt!"

"Thanks, Pace. But what about that pass? You definitely threw deeper than Brady."

"Reynolds, Moore. That was excellent. I liked what I just saw. Well done!" Coach praises us. He turns to Brady. "Mr. Thomas, you may want to try to take an extra step back and make sure you are following through during the throw. It could make the difference in yardage." Brady isn't pleased with Coach's comments judging by the way he's staring at me with his brows frowning and angry eyes on full blast.

"Let's do a slant route next. Sanchez, Calloway, you're up."

I get in the ready position, waiting for Freeman's signal. Coach blows the whistle and Lambert snaps the ball. I catch it and step back, ready to throw it to Sanchez. As the ball is about to leave my hand, I feel a shove in my back forcing the ball to go over Sanchez and in the direction of the cheer squad. I see Sadie up in the air, in some sort of stunt, and the ball is aiming right for her. *Shit!*

As if it plays out in slow motion, I watch the football smack Sadie in the side of her head causing her to stumble and fall down. Thankfully the group who was holding her up caught her before she could smack into the track. I hear what sounds like fighting behind me, but I ignore it, racing to where Sadie is sitting on the ground. I push through the group of people to make my way toward her.

"Excuse me, guys. I need to get through." I squeeze my way through until I'm in front of her, squatting so I'm at her eye level and I can make sure she's not seriously injured. "Sadie, I'm so sorry. Are you okay?" I reach for her chin, gently lifting it to look at me. Her gorgeous steel blue eyes meet my jade ones, and a small smile crosses her face. I let out a small sigh, relaxing a bit.

"I'm okay," Sadie says. "I got hit on the side of my head. May have a little bruising but nothing serious."

"Are you sure? I feel so terrible-—"

"Can you fuckers move out the way?" Brady rushes through the crowd of people to get to where Sadie and I are sitting. He shoves me to the side before reaching for Sadie's hands and pulling her up.

He takes her face into his hands. "Oh my God, babe. Are you okay? You're not seriously hurt, are you?

"I'm fine, Brady. It's just a small hit. May have a bruise but I'll be fine," Sadie tells him.

"Sadie," I stand up so I'm standing next to her. "I'm so sorry. I got shoved in the back and it overthrew my pass. I feel terrible."

Brady turns to face me, anger all over his face. "You should feel terrible. That pathetic pass nearly took out my girlfriend!"

Girlfriend? Did he just say Sadie is his girlfriend? I could have sworn there was something happening between us at the party. The feelings, the spark I literally felt when our fingers touched. Is Sadie straight and I just misread the signals?

Sadie looks at me. "Payson, I'm okay. I promise."

I nod my head and turn to walk away when Sadie reaches out to grab my arm. "Payson, wait."

I look at her, taking her in for a moment.

"I'm glad you're okay, Sadie."

I turn and walk back to the field to finish out today's drills with a sadness I hadn't expected in my heart. What am I doing? I said no girls this year. Senior year is dedicated to football and school. I can't let this distract me from the path I have laid out for myself. I'm just going to have to forget whatever was felt between us and focus on my future.

Chapter 4

Sadie's POV

"**B**rady, I said I'm fine!" I push him away from me with a slight force.

"Are you sure, babe?"

"Yes! Can you please just get back to your football drills so I can get back to my squad? We still have a lot to cover before I call it a day."

"Okay. I'll see you after conditioning ends and give you a ride home." Brady leans forward to kiss the top of my head before jogging back to the field.

I'm not sure why I'm feeling irritated with him. Maybe it was because of their interaction I saw when they bumped into each other. I'm not sure what was said but Payson looked a bit flustered. It could also be the way he was so rude towards Payson, who was clearly feeling guilty for hitting me accidentally in the head and making sure I was okay.

I didn't miss the sad expression cross her face when Brady told her I was his girlfriend. Now she's going to assume I'm straight. I mean, I am straight...right? I have a boyfriend. I care about him a lot, but if I'm being honest with myself, I think I'm scared to face the truth. Brady is handsome but he doesn't bring out feelings the way Payson has recently. He doesn't make me feel the butterflies with one look or stare at me like nothing else exists in the world. With Brady, it feels like I need to prove myself worthy of his time and his attention. He can deny it all he wants but I have caught his eye wandering on more than one occasion. Truthfully, I may have secretly looked at the same girls too but I can't be attracted to girls. I mean I *am* attracted to girls but this is something I have to keep hidden, locked away from everyone in this town. Only one person knows my secret and I trust her with my life to not say a word.

I just fear my secret getting out there, more importantly for it to get back to my mother. She has never approved of the LGBTQIA community. As a devoted Christian, she says it was never in God's plan for two men or two women to love each other and get married or for a person to change their gender completely.

"Alright, everyone!" I clap my hands together and face the squad, getting their attention. "I promise you all, I'm absolutely okay." I give them a warm smile. "Why don't we get back to stunting? I want to get everyone accustomed to the basics before we can perform the more simple stunts."

After three hours of cheer camp with the freshmen, I'm a hot, sweaty mess. My curls are probably frizzed out. There's sweat caked to my face, and in other places I'd rather not even go into.

"That is it for today. I appreciate everyone coming out and enduring this nasty hot weather. We will be here again tomorrow. Make sure to bring plenty of water with you. I'll see you guys then!"

I watch as everyone gathers their things and head towards the stadium exit that leads to the parking lot. I'm gathering up my stuff when I notice a blond-haired girl sitting on the bleachers. She's one of the incoming freshmen who made the JV squad.

"You're Thea, correct?" I ask her. I'm making sure I note each new face and remember their names, so they feel welcome as well as a part of the squad.

"Yeah, that's me."

"Do you need a ride home?"

"Uh, no thanks, Captain. I'm just waiting for my brother to finish up with football. Our cousin, Payson, is giving us a ride home."

"Oh, yes! Colton's little sister. He had mentioned you yesterday at the party." I sit down beside her. "I hope you enjoyed the first day. It wasn't too difficult, was it?"

She shakes her head. "No, it was equally challenging but also a lot of fun. I can't wait for tomorrow."

I raise an eyebrow at her. "You're not just saying that because I'm the captain, are you?"

"What!? No! Definitely not!"

I let out a small laugh. "Okay, good."

"It's just..." She sighs. "I used to do competitive cheer growing up so I know how this stuff can be."

"Why don't you still do competitive cheer?"

"I had to quit it. The coach I used to have was amazing. She made us challenge ourselves, but she also kept things fun. She was the sole reason I fell in love with the sport. Then, she had to move to a new state due to her job and we got a new coach. The new coach was awful though. Total b-i-t-c-h. It no longer felt like cheerleading, but more like boot camp or something. I don't know. Eventually it just sucked the joy I had for it, and I quit. That was about two years ago."

"I'm so sorry to hear that, Thea. Whoever the new coach was sounds completely awful. Any coach who can take away the love of a sport from an athlete should never be allowed to coach."

"I agree."

"What made you decide to try out for high school cheer?"

"For starters, I missed cheering. It was just something I enjoyed. It was my little escape from everything, ya know?" I nod in agreement. It's the same reason why I have cheered for as long as I have. "Then there's the state competition you guys do. I miss competing. The adrenaline of performing a routine in front of judges and all of those people exhilarates me. And we cannot forget cheering on the sidelines at games. Football is huge in my family, especially with Colton and Payson. Football is their life."

"Is that the only reason?" I nudge her shoulder and nod my head towards the field. I've seen her glancing there a couple of times during our conversation.

Her face turns slightly pink. "There may be a guy…"

"Mm-hmm. I could tell when your eyes kept going in the direction of mister tall, bronze and handsome. Does he know you like him?"

She lets out a sigh. "He knows of me but not that I like him. He would never fall for me, though."

"What? Why? You're gorgeous and you're sweet. What's not to like?"

"He's one of my brother's best friends. He would never see me as anything more than Colton's little sister. Not to mention, I'm a freshman and he's a junior. There's too much of an age gap for him to see me—oh shit! I mean shoot!" She jumps up quickly. "Colton and Payson are walking this way. Can you do me a favor and just never bring up my little crush on Zealand? Please?"

"I promise you; your secret is safe with me."

At that moment, Payson and Colton stop in front of us.

"What's safe with you?" Payson asks.

"Thea is. I didn't want to leave her sitting and waiting by herself."

"Thanks, Sadie. I appreciate that," Colton says. "Thea, are you ready to go?"

"Yeah. See you tomorrow, Captain!"

"Bye Thea!" I turn to face Payson. "Hey, can I speak to you for a minute?"

"I actually have to get these two home, and head home myself. I got to shower and help my mom tame my little brothers. But I can text you later."

"Oh. Yeah. Of course."

"Do you need a ride home?" Colton asks me.

"I have a ride home. Thanks for—"

"Piss off, Reynolds. She's got a ride with me. Ain't that right, babe?" Brady comes up beside me and wraps his arm around my shoulder, giving Payson and Colton a smug look.

I remove Brady's arm and glare at him.

"He was just being nice and simply asking. You don't need to be so rude." I grab all my stuff. "I'll meet you at your truck."

"C'mon Sadie. I was just teasing. You don't need to be a whiny...Sadie...Sadie!" Brady yells for me but I ignore him and storm off to the parking lot.

I find Brady's black Ford F-150 and stand by the tailgate, waiting for him to come out of the stadium so I can get in. As I'm waiting for Brady, I spot Thea, Colton and Payson getting into the yellow Jeep, the very one Payson had given me a lift in just yesterday. I vividly recall every detail of that shared little moment in the driveway before Brady's call brought me back to the reality of my life.

Brady finally emerges with Nathan and Chad flanking his sides. Thankfully, Nathan and Chad head towards Chad's car which means Brady and I will be alone. I need to have a few words with him without his friends intervening.

"What the hell was that, Sadie? Didn't you hear me calling you?"

"First off, you're not my father so don't you dare speak to me as such. And secondly, what was with the asshole behavior towards Payson and Colton? Colton was just making sure I had a way home since I waited with his sister. Payson already felt horrible and was only making sure I was okay—"

Brady interrupts me with a chuckle. "Sadie, do you really think that butch ass tomboy was only concerned with you being okay?"

"Yes! I really do. I could see the concern all over her face."

"Please. If you had heard what she said specifically about you before drills, you wouldn't think that."

I swallow hard from a tinge of nervousness about what she may have told Brady. Was it in regard to yesterday?

My curiosity is getting the best of me. "What did she say about me?"

"I had assumed she was trying to hit on Colton and asked her if she was supposed to be over with the cheerleaders. Then she got bitchy and said something about her only place on the cheer squad is under a cheerleader with them riding her face, more specifically you. I think she has the hots for you."

I let out the breath I didn't realize I was holding in.

"Don't be silly, Brady."

"I'm stating facts, babe. I am a guy and when she said that it could only mean she wants you. Unless she was saying it to get under my skin. I just didn't think she knew who I was since she's the new teammate from Cali that Coach has been talking about."

"I still think you're ridiculous to suggest such a thing." Even if my heart might have taken an extra happy beat. "And she wasn't flirting with Colton. That would be kind of incestual considering they're cousins."

"Why does it seem like you know so much about her?"

"Colton brought her to the party yesterday and we met. We talked a little bit before Lydia started acting out of line."

"Are you two friends? Because no way in hell can you be her friend."

I'm taken aback. "Brady, we barely talked for ten minutes. I don't know that much about her to call her a friend. And you can't tell me who I can and cannot be friends with!"

"You can't be her friend, Sadie!" Brady runs his hands through his dark hair. "You hear me? You absolutely cannot be her friend."

"Why? Why do you dislike her so much? You were rude to her when she came to check on me and now I'm not allowed to be her friend?"

"Because she is going to take my position from me!" He yells.

I held my hand up in front of his face. "You can lower your voice when talking to me."

"Sadie, she plays quarterback. Coach informed me that before school starts, they are going to hold tryouts for the starting position. I'm going to have to go against her for the spot that I've earned and held the past two years!"

"Brady, a little competition wouldn't hurt."

"You didn't see her throwing game out there. The bitch has a good arm, hell better than mine. I give her that. But no way in hell am I going to lose my spot on the team to a *girl*. I don't even know how they allowed her to be on the team. Girls have no business in a sport played by men."

"Wow, Brady. What a complete sexist thing for you to say. What about guys in cheerleading?" Nothing irritates me more than when people think girls can't do the same things as guys. I think it's pretty admirable of Payson to play one of the most challenging positions on a football team.

"That's different. There are only two reasons guys are on the squad. One, they are gay and two, for their strength to lift and toss you girls around."

"Hate to break it to you, *babe*, but only three of the guys are gay. Most of them are straight, including Marcus."

Brady has never been a fan of Marcus and our friendship. I think it's the whole alpha mentality Brady has. He can't stand it when other guys are around me. Marcus and I would never cross the friendship line, though. He really is a great friend plus he has a girlfriend who attends Greystone Academy in the next town over.

"Are you fucking serious right now?"

"He's a friend and only ever will be. I'm not ending that friendship over your own insecurity."

"I am *not* insecure!"

"Really? Because you're sounding like you are. You have nothing to worry about with Marcus. I promise you."

"Fine," he grits out.

"Also, if I want to be friends with Payson, I'm going to be. You don't get to tell me to do anything. If you think that, then we can end our relationship right here, right now."

Brady quickly walks up to me and wraps me up in a hug. "What? Babe, no. Please don't say things like that."

I pull out of his arms and distance myself from him.

"I don't like this side of you, Brady."

I look around the parking lot and notice that just about all the cars are gone.

"Look, can you just take me home? It's been a day and I need to get home to shower and prepare for tomorrow."

"Yeah, of course." He nods. "You know I love you, right?" He leans down to give me a kiss. I give him a quick peck in return before muttering, "Love you, too." We get in his truck and ride in silence on the way to my house.

We pull into my driveway behind my mother's car. I'm about to get out of the truck when Brady stops me.

"Sadie, wait." He reaches across the seat to grab my wrist gently. "Look, I'm sorry for being a dick back at the field and for saying the things I said to you."

"I appreciate the apology, Brady. But I meant what I said. If you think you can control me, control who I want and choose to be my friend, then we will be over."

"Understood. Can I call you later?"

"Yeah. I'll text you when I'm done. But I really do need to go."

Brady kisses my hand and releases me. I get out of the truck and walk up the walkway to the front porch. Brady is already pulling away and speeding down the street before I even reach the door. I think back to yesterday and how Payson ensured I was safely inside before she left. How different Brady and Payson are from each other in regard to me.

Before I think any more about it, I step inside. I take off my sneakers and head upstairs to my bedroom, locking the door to keep my younger siblings out in case they are home. Hannah likes to raid my closet and Isaiah likes to pull pranks when I'm not paying attention.

I strip down and walk into my en suite bathroom to take a shower. I open my shower door, and turn the water to steaming hot, just the way

I like it. I stand under the falling water, letting the heat relax my muscles and melt the stress away. Once I feel relaxed enough, I turn the water down to a warm temperature before I wash my hair and scrub my body down.

When I'm finished showering, I go through my skincare routine before throwing on some comfy clothes. I hop onto my queen size bed and snuggle under the fuzzy, soft throw I keep at the foot of my bed. I grab my cell phone and pull up my text messages. I contemplate sending Payson a text but decide to message Jenna instead.

Hey. Wanna come over and hang out with me? I could use some of my best friend's advice.

She reads it quickly and responds back.

Yeah. Give me 5 minutes and I will be over.

I unlock my bedroom door and head downstairs to the kitchen. My mom is washing her hands at the kitchen sink when I walk in.

"Hey mom. What are you up to?" I ask. "And where is everybody? The house is so quiet."

"Oh, I'm just tending to my garden. Pulling weeds and all that other fun stuff." She gives me her warm smile. "Your father is still at the office. He won't be home until after five. Hannah and Isaiah are hanging out with their friends. They will be home for dinner though. What are you up to? How did camp go?"

"Just grabbing some water while I wait for Jenna to come over. I hope you don't mind. Camp was good. I think it went well. I just hope the freshmen are taking it all in okay."

"I'm sure you're doing a wonderful job, sweetie. As for Jenna coming by, it's fine with me. I'll be outside, working on those flower beds if you need me." She pats my arm before she heads back outside to work on her gardening.

I grab myself a yogurt cup and a bottle of water. I'm spooning the last bit of the yogurt into my mouth when I hear the doorbell ring and Boscoe starts to bark. It's his way of letting the family know we have company.

"Coming!" I yell, rushing through the foyer to the front door. I see Jenna's gorgeous face peeking into the small windows that run along the side of the door. "Boscoe, move your furry butt. It's just Jenna!"

Boscoe is standing in front of the door, his tail wagging. I push him to the side and open the door, blocking Boscoe from running out. Jenna comes inside quickly and gives Boscoe the attention he so desperately feels he needs before she faces me.

"Alright. I'm here. What did you want to talk about?"

I look around to make sure my mother isn't around. "Let's go up to my room."

"Ooh. It's *that* kind of conversation."

I nod in response. Jenna knows I can't openly talk about anything that my mother considers unholy or goes against God.

We make our way to my bedroom, and I shut my door to ensure we have some privacy. Jenna plops her booty on my bed, and I take the bench seat at my vanity.

"Is it safe to talk now?" She laughs.

"Should be. My mom's outside gardening but I wanted to make sure we have extra privacy for what I want to talk to you about."

"Alright, girl. Well, I'm here now. Start spilling."

"Okay, okay." I let out a small laugh then take a deep breath. "There's this new girl in town. I know people talk so I'm not sure if you heard about her or her family."

"Are you referring to the family who recently moved from California?"

"That would be the one. Anyways, I don't know much about the family except the oldest is Payson and she's around our age. I met her yesterday at Lydia's pool party."

"Ugh," Jenna rolls her eyes. "I cannot stand that bitch, nor do I trust her. I'm telling you Sadie, that girl is trouble and is a mad hater. You need to watch your back with her." Jenna has never liked Lydia for as long as I can remember.

"Yeah, yeah. I know how much you dislike her."

"Hate. It's hatred that I feel towards her. Not dislike. No, no, no, *hate*."

"Look, you know how I feel about the word hate. How about...strongly dislike?"

"Fine. I *strongly* dislike Lydia. Better?"

"Yes. Now may I continue with my troubles?"

"You may proceed," she says as she moves her hand in a circular motion for me to continue.

"Okay, so Stacey and I were laying out by the pool at Lydia's party. I went to the bathroom and when I came back, Payson and her cousin, Colton, were sitting on the chair I was using. Colton was all into Stacey, so Payson introduced herself and I don't know, Jenna. There was this moment when we looked at each other and everything around us seemed to just disappear for a few moments. I've never experienced anything like that, not even with Brady. Oh and when we went to shake hands after she told me her name, there was this tingly sensation going through my hand, like a spark or something. I think she felt it too because she flinched and pulled away quickly the same time I did."

I told Jenna everything that happened at the party, from Lydia's interruption to afterwards when Payson dropped me off. I also filled her in on what happened at cheer camp today, how rude Brady was being and our whole conversation at his truck before he dropped me off.

"He then sped off, not even making sure I made it inside like Payson did. I don't know. Why am I comparing the two of them?"

"Okay, first off. Brady can kick rocks. That boy, and I cannot emphasize enough on the boy part, is so damn insecure. He's delusional if he can't admit to that." She rolls her eyes. "As for this Payson chick, she sounds like a chill girl. Clearly, she sounds like someone who's confident about who she is. Plus, she plays football? Complete badass in my opinion. From the sound of things, she really seems like she cares about your well-being. I think I like her. And judging by the way your eyes sparkle when you talk about her, I think a part of you does too."

"What are you talking about? They did not sparkle. Nobody's eyes sparkle." I give her a pointed look.

"Right, so I'm just seeing things?" She quirks an eyebrow.

I nod my head at her. "Yes, you are."

Jenna grabs one of my throw pillows and chucks it in my direction.

"C'mon Jenna. I really need your honesty about this whole situation." I give her the best puppy dog eyes I can muster up. "Please?"

"Alright, but remember you asked for the truth. I don't want any crocodile tears if it hurts your feelings." She sighs before she continues. "Truthfully, I believe Brady needs to go. I think it's time you two called it quits. You guys have been together for almost two years, but lately you just haven't seemed so happy with him. Not sure if anyone else has noticed and told you, but I have noticed. Plus, I don't like how one sided he is with you about things. He gets his balls all in a knot whenever anyone shows an ounce of interest in you but has the audacity to let other girls feel him up or flirt with them? Like what is with that? I'll tell you what that is. A big ass red flag."

I had no idea she felt this way towards Brady or noticed anything about our relationship.

"Look, Sadie, I don't want to hurt your feelings or upset you, but I wouldn't be surprised if he has cheated on you or is cheating on you. I have seen —"

"No." I shake my head, refusing to believe he would hurt me in such a way.

"Sadie…" Jenna gets off my bed and to me. She crouches in front of me so that she is looking me in the eyes and places her hands on top of mine. "I know that no matter what I say, you're not going to want to believe me. And that's okay. The only way you are going to know for sure is by seeing it yourself. I just need you to make yourself more aware when you're around him."

I know Jenna means well and quite frankly, she isn't wrong. Obviously, I haven't been paying enough attention.

"Okay, enough about him. Let's talk about Payson."

"What's there to talk about?" I glance towards my bedroom door, making sure I don't hear my mom outside of it.

"Well, obviously you are feeling her. Right? I mean, you're clearly bothered by the fact she seemed to have brushed you off when you wanted to talk to her."

"I mean, yeah. She went from being worried and caring to just unbothered. How does anyone do that? I feel like I messed up with her and I don't know why I feel this sadness in my chest over it."

Jenna smiles warmly at me. "I think it's because you have actual feelings toward her. I believe you got yourself an actual girl crush."

I feel my cheeks warm a bit. I have never had an actual crush on a girl I physically knew. This is so new for me, an exciting yet terrifying feeling.

"I…maybe…sort of…feel some kind of way about her. I just don't know what to do. This all feels like some sort of punishment from God. How can I have a boyfriend but have some crazy emotions about another person at the same time? Let alone a girl?"

"Sadie, it's not a punishment. You are experiencing natural feelings, specifically your own. No one but you know what you are feeling. It's a part of being human. Not God's punishment."

She makes a valid point. "Do you think I should reach out to her?"

Jenna shrugs. "What's the worst that could happen? She doesn't reply back? You don't need to admit or bring up your feelings. Just check on her."

I pull my cell phone out of my sweat pocket and pull up the text I sent from her phone so that we could have each other's number. I hesitate for a moment before I type out what I want to say. I hit the send button before looking up at Jenna.

"I guess we will see what happens."

<h1 style="text-align:center">Chapter 5</h1>

Payson's POV

I'm lying in my bed, resting after I showered away all the sweat from the day, when my cell phone dings with an alert. I grab my phone from my bedside table and see a text from Sadie. I contemplate whether I should read the message or not when another text comes in, this time from Colton.

Thanks for giving Thea and I a ride home. My mom says she appreciates you taking Thea since she was running behind. I will need you to take me again tomorrow, if that's ok.

Not a prob. I got you. Anytime you guys need a lift, just let me know.

Before I think it over, I send Colton another text.

> Sadie texted me. Not sure if I should read it. What do you think I should do?

Why don't you just, idk read it? I don't see any harm.

Sadie is a great person and I thought you two were hitting it off? Ya know, potential BFF's?

> I may have misread her ?

What do you mean by that?

> I mean, I thought she was into me and I may have been flirting back with her.

Payson Christene Moore! What happened to focusing on senior year and football? No girls, remember?

> Don't you dare use my govt name. Only my parents can do that. (:p) And yeah, that was the plan. Or is the plan. But dude, have you seen Sadie!? She's stunning.

Is it the plan or was it the plan?

& Yeah, I know she is. Not going to deny that but so does the vast majority of the guys in this town. There is also one other teeny, tiny issue. What was it?

Oh..yeah.. She also has a BOYFRIEND! Ya know, the douchebag you're up against for starting QB?

> Yeah, well I could have used that tidbit of info in advance there.

Pace, I had no clue you were feeling any sort of way towards her. Had you, idk, said something, I could have told you. Save you some trouble. Sadie isn't into girls. She's dated guys as long as I've known her.

> I just, idk. What should I do? I feel so embarrassed for misreading her and I don't want to make an ass out of myself.

Just read the text. She reached out to YOU right? Just see what she says and reply back. No harm done in that.

Okay. Guess he isn't wrong there. I exit out of our conversation and pull up Sadie's text.

Hey. It's Sadie, in case you didn't save my #. I just wanted to check and make sure you're okay.

Huh. I'm not the one who got knocked in the head by a football going I don't know how fast and she's asking if I'm okay? This girl is really something else.

> Yeah, I'm ok but are YOU ok? I mean you were the one who got hit.

The text bubbles pop up fairly quick before her response comes through.

> Yeah, I'm fine. I'm fairly tough. Lol But I wanted to make sure you weren't beating yourself up over it. I'm assuming that's why you left so quickly and didn't want to talk?

Shit. How do I answer her? Do I be honest and risk embarrassing myself while also potentially making her feel uncomfortable because I assumed she was into girls? Or do I just go along with what she's thinking?

> Look, Sadie. Imma be real w/ you & I hope you don't take it too personally. I thought there were signals comin' from you. I thought you were into me bc I was feelin you. Ya know? When Brady said you're his gf, I felt dumb. I was embarrassed. I misread you and I apologize for that. I'm not tryin to get involve in any drama. I'm sry if that comes out rude. That is not my intention but I hope you understand.

Honesty is the best policy. At least that is what everyone says and they ain't wrong. Whoever they are. I watch as the text goes from delivered to read. Then the bubbles pop up. Stop. Pop up again. The anxiety of what or how she will answer my text has my heart slightly racing. Then her response comes through.

Ok. I understand

Fuck! What does she mean she understands? Is she upset with me? How do I even respond back to that? Before I can even think about it, my mom calls for me to come downstairs and I end up leaving Sadie on read.

Chapter 6

Sadie's POV

I t's finally Friday, the official last day of cheer camp for the newbies before a weekend off. Then next week we will start having normal practices with the full JV and varsity squad altogether. I have been busy working out routines, stunts and where I'm placing every cheerleader for games and our competition routine on paper to help me be prepared. It's been the one thing to keep my mind busy this week.

After Payson's text on Monday, I decided that it was best to just let things go. I wouldn't reach out to her. I would just simply try to ignore her, if only it was easy to do so. I glance her way during her drills, watching her own the field. She never glances back so I assume she's avoiding me just the same. She never replied back so I took it that maybe this is where we stand. I'm not going to lie, it kind of stings a little.

And if that wasn't enough, Brady has been extra moody and unbearable. We have argued and fought more than I ever remember us doing in our entire relationship. He says he's stressed out now that there is a possibility of losing his spot on the team. He's afraid if he doesn't get to be a starter, then he would be letting his father down. His father used to be in the NFL before a career ending injury took him out. I personally think his dad is just trying to live vicariously through Brady and it's putting unnecessary stress on him. That topic was actually one of our arguments we had this week. However, nothing takes the cake like what he pulled the other day.

Brady and I went to the outlet mall after we finished with football and cheer. I wanted to get a birthday gift for my sister so I was browsing in one of her favorite clothing stores, trying to find her a cute outfit. Brady decided to wait outside the store on one of the benches. I glanced out and saw some girl sitting next to him. He never once pushed her away until he happened to look back in the store and saw me staring at them. I stormed out of the store and walked away. He caught up to me and tried to say he was just being nice, but I called bullshit. Then he just got angry and defensive before abandoning me at the mall.

I called Jenna and explained to her everything that happened. She came to the mall right after her art class ended. We grabbed some ice cream, sat at a table in the food court and just had some much needed girl talk. She helped me pick the perfect outfit for Hannah before taking us home.

Brady did text me later that night, apologizing for snapping at me and leaving me at the mall. I didn't have it in me to accept his apology or forgive him even though I could hear my mother's voice in my head preaching to me the importance of forgiveness. *"Be kind and compassionate to one another, forgiving each other, just as in Christ God forgave you."*

I just don't see how I can forgive him for leaving me alone at the mall. What if some creep had tried to kidnap me or worse? He doesn't understand the dangers a young woman like me face when we are alone. I'm just grateful that Jenna was close by and could get to me.

A whistle blows from the field and I'm back to the present. I rub my hands down my face and sigh. I'm ready to go home to shower and crawl into bed with a good book.

"Sadie? Are you okay?"

I turn to see a concerned Stacey looking at me.

"Yeah, Stace. I'm okay. I think I'm just burned out from the week."

"Would you like me to wrap up camp for you?"

"You don't mind?"

"Of course not! I got this. Why don't you go take a walk around the track or something. Help clear your mind a bit."

I pull Stacey into a hug. "Thank you. You're the best, you know that?"

"Remember that next time I may need a favor." She gives me a wink before she faces the newbies.

"Hey everybody, listen up! Let's run through the cheers one more time, then we will call it a day."

I leave Stacey to take over and walk around the track, making sure to keep an eye on any flying balls that may come in my direction. I end up walking three laps before I head back to the stands to grab my things. All the cheerleaders have already left for the day. I grab my phone to text Jenna, to make sure she is still able to give me a ride home.

> Hey. I'm all finished up here. Let me know when you're headed this way to get me. & Thanks again for getting me.

> I'm running slightly behind but I'll be there asap. Should be like 20 min tops & girlie, it's no trouble! I got you. That's why we're besties. Xoxo

> It's ok. I can do a few more laps around the track or something. See ya when ya get here. Xoxo

I place my cell phone into my leggings pocket, pop in my air pods and step onto the track. I start out walking, breathing in the summer air as I go. Then I start to pick up my pace and turn my walk into a jog. I'm about to go for a third lap when one of the football coaches waves me over. He's very handsome for a guy with salt and pepper hair. I think this is the coach that everyone calls the silver fox and I can see why. I pull out my airpods as I approach him.

"Just wanted to let you know we are about to lock up the gates. Everyone has pretty much gone home. You have a ride?"

That's when I look around and notice the football players have all left and the coaches are putting equipment back into the school shed.

"Oh...um, yeah. My friend is picking me up. She said she was running a little behind."

"Okay. Just want to make sure you get home safely."

"I appreciate it, Coach. I'll go grab my bag and head out to the parking lot. She should be here soon."

"Have a great weekend, Miss Adams."

Right. Forgot there for a moment people know who I am.

I double check that I have everything in my bag and head towards the exit to the parking lot. I pull my phone out just as Jenna sends another text.

> Im coming! I didn't forget you. Just got stuck at the train tracks and this train is taking 4ever!

I let out a small laugh and tell her it's okay and that I will be waiting for her to get here as soon as she can. As I look up, my heart almost stops, and all the air leaves me.

Brady's standing at his truck and he's not alone. He doesn't see me since he's across the parking lot, his back towards me. He has a girl pressed up against the side of his truck, and he's feeling her up and making out with her. She has her legs wrapped around his waist, practically humping him in broad daylight! I can't tell who the girl is from here, but I recognize the white BMW convertible parked next to Brady's truck. The only person in our school whose daddy splurged on a fancy new car for their 18th birthday was Lydia.

For a moment, I feel like I can't breathe in any air. My heart is racing while my throat feels like it's trying to swallow it down. I can feel the tears start to burn in my eyes. I finally snap out of the moment and turn around to make a dash for the bathroom when I end up colliding into Payson.

Payson grabs my arms to steady me. "Whoa, hey…Sadie? What's wrong? What happened?"

She looks me over, checking for any signs that I'm hurt. When she doesn't see any, she looks me in my eyes, almost pleading for me to tell her what's wrong. I want to tell her, but I can't. I know the moment I say those words, the tears are going to flow and Brady doesn't deserve my tears.

"If you can't tell me, can you show me?"

I nod my head and point my thumb behind me. Payson's eyes follow and I know the moment she spots them. Her face morphs into one of anger. Payson pulls my bag off my shoulder, grabs my hand and drags me towards her Jeep nearby. She tosses our things into the back seat before opening the passenger side door. She nods for me to get in, but I don't. I'm not sure if I should since we have been ignoring each other all week.

"Sadie, get in the vehicle. Let me get you out of here."

I wrap my arms around my waist, trying to keep myself together. I don't look at her, keeping my eyes pointed at the ground.

"Sadie, please get in the Jeep," she pleads.

I shake my head no but Payson doesn't accept it. She backs me against her vehicle, grasps my chin and forces me to look at her.

"Listen to me, and listen to me closely, princess. You are going to get in my Jeep and let me get you away from here. Understood? You don't have to use your words, just nod yes or no."

I stare into her eyes for a moment then nod my head up and down slightly.

"Good girl."

Oh, Lord, dear heaven. She just called me a good girl. She's activated the praise kink. Payson backs up some, ensuring to block my view of Brady and Lydia as I get into her vehicle. She shuts the door and circles to the other side.

"Did you have a ride home?"

"Um, yeah," I sniffle. "My best friend is on her way."

"Message her and tell her you got a ride home."

I pull out my phone and text Jenna.

> Hey, Payson is giving me a lift home. Will explain later. BTW, you were right about Brady.

> Ok. This slow ass train is still going. I'm sry. You better call me later. I need to know what I'm right about.

> It's ok & I will. XoXo

I slip my phone into the cup holder and fasten my seat belt. Payson gives me a small smile and the butterfly sensation begins in my belly. Payson backs out of her parking spot, making sure to avoid the direction of the action and drives us off. When we didn't make the necessary turn to go to my house, I decided then and there whatever happens, let's just see where it leads.

Chapter 7

Payson's POV

I know I said I was going to give Sadie a ride home, but seeing what she saw, I could think of only one place better suited to help her release everything she's feeling. Wreck-It-Rage. It's one of those rage room facilities where you pay to just smash the hell out of things. It's a great way to get out every feeling you have locked inside. Uncle Richard took my brothers and I here a few times when we would come for summer visits. It helped us deal with our emotions while dad was deployed. All the anger and worries melted away after you took that first swing and heard the sounds of glass crashing around you.

I pull into the parking lot of the gray building and park near the front entrance.

"What is this place?" Sadie questions. It's the first time she's spoken since leaving school.

"It's one of those rage room businesses."

"Rage room? What is a rage room?"

"You're joking, right? Please tell me you're joking."

"Sorry to break it to you, QB. I am not," she whispers.

"Alright so basically you pay to get a bat, or some sort of object, and you go into a room and just break everything."

"On purpose?"

"Yep. Now, let's go!" I'm trying to get her hyped or perk up but it's not helping. "Sadie, this is going to allow you to let go of all those feelings you're holding back. I promise you; this is going to help you feel better."

She doesn't say anything. She just sits there with her arms crossed in front of her, looking out the window.

"Alright, princess. You asked for this."

I hop out of the Jeep and circle around to her side. I open her door and unbuckle her seat belt.

"Payson, what are you doing?"

"Helping." I smirk at her. I grab her waist and slide her towards me, making sure her head is outside of the vehicle so as to not hit it on the door frame and hoist her over my shoulder. I shut the door and walk to the front entrance.

"Oh my gosh, Payson put me down. You're going to hurt yourself or mess up your throwing arm!"

"Awww. Is my little cheer captain worried about me?" I chuckle lightly. "Relax, princess. You're not going to hurt me. I'll have you know I do lift outside of football and FYI, you're light."

I set her down when we reach the door, her body sliding down against mine and I can't help the slight shudder I get feeling her body against mine.

She's glaring into my eyes. "Don't call me princess."

"Why?" I ask her, staring back into her blue eyes, "Isn't that what your name means?"

She looks at me quizzically. "What do you mean?"

"Sometimes, when I get bored, I look up people's names. See if it matches who they are. When you look up the name meaning of Sadie, it's Hebrew for princess."

Her face goes soft. "Oh. I had no idea. I just assumed it was your nickname for me since I'm the mayor's daughter. Everyone has called me the town's princess since my dad was sworn in and I just get so offensive about it. Like they think I'm spoiled with lavish gifts and I'm not."

"So, don't call you princess? Got it." I give her a moment before I reach for her hand. "C'mon. Let's go inside."

I pull Sadie into the doors and approach the man at the counter.

"Welcome to Wreck-It-Rage. How can I help you?"

"Hey. I need one room for two people for thirty minutes. And two protective suits."

"Alright. I just need to have you both sign the waivers first," the man behind the counter states. He hands me a clipboard with the waiver forms for us to sign. I'm already familiar with it so I sign my name and pass it to Sadie.

Sadie takes a few moments to look over it before signing and handing it to the gentleman.

"Thank you. So, for the two of you for a thirty-minute session will be $80. How would you like to pay?"

Sadie's eyes bug out when she sees me handing the guy my debit card.

"Wait! I have money in my bag. Just let me go get it and I'll pay for my half," Sadie says.

"Nah, I brought you here. I got it covered." I pay the man and wait for him to return with the protective gear we will need.

"Here you go. You have room number two. Make sure you have your gear on before entering the room. There is a wall by room one lined with various weapons you can choose from. Just make sure you are aware of the other person in the room with you when swinging. Enjoy and let your rage fly." He gives us our protective gear and I thank him. I lead Sadie over to the bench by the front windows and show her how to put on the gear before heading to the weapons wall.

"Pick whatever you want, whatever draws you in," I tell her. I reach for the sledgehammer. It's my favorite. I watch Sadie's eyes move all around the wall before settling on the baseball bat. She lifts the bat off the rack and smacks it against her hand a few times.

"Ah. Good choice. You're ready to unleash your inner Harley Quin." I give her a smile. I'm trying to get her to lighten up, see that sparkle in her eyes and smile spread across her beautiful face.

She shrugs. "I assume everyone just picks this."

"Not everyone. Mine was this," I lift the sledgehammer slightly. "My uncle preferred the golf club. So, are you ready to head in because I'm itching to smash some shit."

"Yeah. Just lead the way."

We walk down the hall a little bit to the second door with a number two on it. I open it, allowing Sadie to enter first. She walks in looking around at the graffiti walls and the various items around the room for us to smash.

"So, we get to smash everything that's in this room? And we won't be punished for it?"

I chuckle. "That's right. Everything in here is placed for us to break. Great way to let out your anger or stress. Want to go first?"

She stands against the closed door, the bat hanging by her side. "You can go first."

"Alright." I walk around the room for my first target when I spot the old computer monitor. I raise my sledgehammer over my head and slam it down on the computer a few times until the monitor is broken into several pieces. This is exactly what I needed after this week, dealing with Brady and his goon of friends constantly messing with me during conditioning, trying to get under my skin.

"Whoo! I needed that. Alright, Sadie. Your turn."

"I think I'll pass," she says softly.

What do I have to do to get this girl to release what she's holding back? Then an idea pops into my mind.

"Awe, c'mon, princess. Don't be shy with me now." Yeah, I may be a bit of an asshole since I told her I wouldn't call her a princess. Judging by the ugly glare she is giving me right now let's me know it may just be the only way I get her to let loose.

"I thought I told you to not call me that," she grits out.

"You seem to need a push there, . What's the matter? Afraid you may break a nail?" I'm taunting her but I need to get under her skin, make her get so angry she just unleashes her fury.

"Are you for real right now?" She bites back.

"At this moment, yeah. I am. So, what are you going to do about it, princess? Are you going to just hang out by the door and let me smash everything in this room by myself? Are you seriously going to pretend you didn't see Brady make out with that girl at his truck, practically dry humping her? I mean, for all we know he could have actually been fucking her. Not hard to do if she was in a skirt or tiny shorts." Sadie is now giving me the death glare, her nostrils flaring in anger. I'm definitely hitting the button to make her burst. "Are you seriously going to act like it's not eating you up inside? Make you feel like you never mattered to him?" I know it's a low blow, but I will say anything to get a reaction from her that isn't the distant, sad shell of a person in this room.

"How fucking dare you," she seethes. "Of course, I saw them. It was why I was going to go to the bathroom before I bumped into you. It is taking everything inside of me to not break down, to not shed a single tear for that asshole!"

"You're right. He doesn't deserve your tears. So instead of crying, lift that bat and break some shit. Pretend it's Brady's face if you have to and go mad. Use his betrayal to fuel the anger."

Sadie's eyes dart around the room before zeroing in on her target. She heads for a 32-inch TV and swings the bat right into the screen, causing the screen to crack.

"Hit it again, Sadie. Smash it!" I need to keep her motivated, so I let the roles reverse. I'll be her cheerleader, pepping her to keep going.

Sadie swings the bat over and over until the TV no longer looks like one. She's breathing heavily, some strands of her hair coming out from under her hard hat.

"Pick another object. Like, the vases." I point to the table aligned with a few colorful glass vases.

Sadie walks over and gets into a baseball stance. She swings the bat and smashes the vases in one full swing.

"YES!" I shout. "Hit something else."

Sadie finds a laptop sitting in the middle of the room. She raises her bat over her head and slams it onto the laptop, over and over until the laptop is left in a million pieces. Her breathing is rapid and heavy from the exertion of swinging.

"How are you feeling now?" I ask her.

"I feel...somewhat...better," she pants out. "Mmm, not good enough for me." I eye the giant wooden spool table with plates, bowls and teacups on it and point to it. "You see those? Throw them at the wall."

"What? No way! They are so pretty and look expensive!"

"You know what else is pretty and expensive? The car of the girl who is doing your boyfriend right now."

Sadie clenches her jaw before she lets out a scream. She grabs one of the teacups and throws it at the wall, pieces dispersing onto the floor. I grab some of the bowls and chuck them against the wall myself. We repeat the process, alternating turns until we have run out of dishware. Sadie then picks up her bat and goes wild around the room, hitting anything and everything she can. I stand back against the wall and watch her, seeing the fury and pain at the forefront as she slams the bat against her targets.

My cell phone vibrates in my pocket, so I check my phone and make note that we have another ten minutes before our time is up in the room. I have a few texts from Colton, but I will respond to him once I get home. Right now, Sadie is hurting, and I need to be here for her.

"I'm sorry I'm holding you up. You probably have other plans and instead, you are here wasting your spare time on me."

I look up and see Sadie looking at me and my cell phone. I quickly pocket my phone and walk over to her.

"I don't have any other plans than what I'm doing with you right now, at this moment." She briefly looks at me before turning her eyes downward.

"You don't need to look after me, Payson. I'll be okay."

"Are you really going to stand here and lie to me, Sadie? You're not okay. The way you demolished most of this room is proof of that. That's why I brought you to this place."

She glances at me before sighing.

"You're right. I'm not okay." She looks around the room then back at me. "I'm hurt." She removes her safety goggles, rubbing her hands over her face in frustration before putting the goggles back on. "I feel like the biggest idiot in the world."

"Sadie, you're not an idiot. I promise—" I start to say but she cuts me off.

"Why me? What did I ever do to deserve to be cheated on?"

"You did *not* deserve to be cheated on. No one ever does. Trust me—" I try to continue but she keeps going on her rant.

"I mean, we hadn't been on the greatest terms this week. But if he was unhappy, he could have just said something. We could have ended things amicably. Right?"

"Of course. It's not hard to do—" Another attempt to get her to refocus. But again, she keeps ranting and I'm starting to get frustrated.

"I'm pretty understanding. At least I like to think I'm an understanding person. It wasn't like I was happy either, but I chalked it all up to stressing about being captain and running two whole squads this year. Heck, Jenna even noticed! She even told me there were signs. She told me to keep my eyes open and aware. I didn't listen to her, though. Why didn't I listen? I didn't do anything but be blinded like a...gosh, I'm so freaking stupid!"

Tired of hearing her degrade herself, I rush her. I place one of my hands on her midsection and push Sadie back against the wall. I grab her face in my hands, and I slam my mouth down onto hers, kissing her soft lips. Lips that taste like cherries. Damn I don't want to stop. She starts to kiss me back but then stops, forcing me to pull back and look into her eyes, eyes that are glossy with unshed tears.

Fuck. What did I just do!?

"Shit! I'm sorry, Sadie. I shouldn't have kissed you like that but every time I tried to say something, you cut me off. I don't know why but kissing you felt like the only way I could get you to stop talking so negatively about yourself. I mean, do you hear what you are saying? You're far from stupid and you're certainly no idiot." I take a step back, allowing her some space to ensure I'm not making her feel uncomfortable.

"I want you to listen to me and listen closely." I point a finger at her heart and stare into her eyes. I want her to fully grasp the truth and sincerity of my words.

"Understand this, Sadie. You are way too good for Brady Thomas. You have to know that. If anyone is the stupid one, it's him, not you. If he couldn't see what he had in front of him, then he never deserved you at all. He, and any other person who would do you wrong, never deserve someone so dedicated, loyal, honest and most of all, beautiful like you. It's their loss."

There's a moment of silence between us. Sadie's eyes bounce back and forth between mine. I'm waiting anxiously, my heart racing. I expect her to yell at me, push me away or say something about not being into girls. But what I didn't expect was for her to pull me into her and kiss me again.

Chapter 8

Sadie's POV

I was taken back when Payson pushed me against the wall and started kissing me. But wow, the girl can kiss. There was no tongue, but it was still one of the best kisses I've ever experienced. I started to kiss her back before my mother's voice made itself present in my head and I stopped, causing Payson to pull back.

I thought I messed up the moment until she started rambling. I couldn't help but find it adorable. As soon as she started telling me how I was deserving of someone better than Brady, that I was beautiful, I caved. I wanted her to kiss me again, so I grabbed onto her protective suit and yanked her into me.

I pressed my lips with hers, wrapping my arms around her neck to pull her closer. I slowly moved my hands up toward the base of her skull, just trying to get as close to her as possible. I slip the tip of my tongue into her mouth, wanting to deepen the kiss, craving more of her. Payson opens for me, allowing our tongues to caress each other while feeling her lush lips against mine.

The moment I let a moan slip out, Payson snatches my wrists from her neck and pushes my arms above my head. It catches me by surprise and if I'm being honest, it's turning me on. I can feel my panties getting damp. One of her hands holds my wrists in place while the other slowly glides down my arm, slightly brushing the left side of my breast before gliding up towards my throat. For a moment, I think she is going to wrap her hand around my throat, but she doesn't. She moves it up to the side of my face and holds me in place. Her thumb caresses my cheek and, at this moment, for once, I feel cared for. I feel wanted.

Payson pulls back slightly and presses her forehead against mine. She releases my wrists and places her arms on either side of my head, caging me in. Her eyes are closed, and we are both quiet aside from breathing heavily after that intensely passionate kiss. Payson opens her eyes and looks like she wants to say something when there's a knock on the door.

"Room Two. Your thirty minutes are up."

"Thank you!" Payson shouts back so the guy hears her. She picks up the bat I had dropped when she kissed me, along with her sledgehammer. Just like that, the bubble I allowed myself to get lost in bursts. Reality comes dousing back on me and I can feel the panic setting in.

What am I doing!? I just made out with a girl! The kiss was amazing, but still! What were you thinking, Sadie! You are just as bad as Brady! You haven't officially ended it with him and here you are making out with another person!?

"We should get these back on the wall and head out. I'm sure our families are wondering where we are."

I clear my throat, trying to keep the panic down. "Um, yeah, we should get going."

I follow Payson to return the weapons on the wall and the goggles and hard hats. We toss the protective suits in a hamper like basket by the front desk and head out to Payson's Jeep. Payson opens the door for me, holding it open until I'm seated. She hops in the driver's seat, and we head out.

"Are you hungry?" Payson asks. "I can stop somewhere and get you something to eat before I take you home.

"No, I'm not that hungry. Thank you though," I tell her. It's not a complete lie. From seeing Brady making out with Lydia to releasing all my emotions then making out with Payson, I'm drained more than anything.

We ride in silence, apart from when I need to tell Payson where to turn. She pulls into the driveway and turns off her vehicle before reaching in the back to hand me my bag. I'm about to open the door when she stops me.

"Sadie, wait. Can we talk about what happened back there?"

"Talk about what?" I'm purposely feigning dumb right now, hoping to avoid any discussion about me kissing her.

"That kiss. Look I know when I kissed you, that was on me. I shouldn't have crossed a boundary with you, and I am sorry if I was in the wrong for it. But when you made the move to kiss the second time? That was...I don't know what to make of it. What did that kiss mean for you?"

I swallow the lump building in my throat. She had to ask that question. I'm sure she's confused, just as much as I am. But what do I tell her? I avoid eye contact with her, knowing what I'm about to say may hurt her. I don't want to cause her any pain, but I'm too unsure of where my head is at.

"It was a mistake, Payson. I was lost in my feelings and when you said those things to me, I just, I don't know. It made me feel some sort of way. I kissed you in the heat of the moment and I shouldn't have done that to you. I'm sorry."

I quickly get out, slamming the door before Payson can say anything. I dart towards the front door, quickly making my way into my house and head to my room. Dropping my bag by my door, I crawl into my bed. I pull my fuzzy throw blanket around my body and release the tears I have been holding back since practice ended. My heart feels like it's been trampled on over a hundred times. I lay there and just cry, until I have no more tears left. The heaviness of a post cry session weighing me down, I close my eyes and drift off to sleep.

Payson's POV

I watch as Sadie makes it safely into her house before I head home. I keep replaying our kiss over and over, thinking how incredible it was. I have kissed many girls in my life since coming out in middle school but none of them matched Sadie's. It was hands down one of the *best* kisses I ever experienced. There is no way that kiss she gave me was a mistake.

Then again, she did see her boyfriend cheating on her and I know the feelings she is experiencing when you catch someone you care about with someone else. You're hurt, angry, confused, and it makes you feel worthless. You start questioning yourself. How can someone you feel strongly for not feel the same way about you? How can someone you devote your heart and soul to pretend to love you only to mess with other people behind your back? What did I do wrong?

Maybe Sadie was telling me the truth. Perhaps it was a mistaken moment. I can't be upset with her for it. So I'll cherish the kiss we shared and lock it away as a memory.

I like Sadie. She's an incredible person and I don't know if I could stay away from her if I tried. No matter what I feel for this girl, I will just have to repress those emotions and be there as a friend.

Chapter 9

Sadie's POV

My alarm goes off, annoying me to wake up and get my day started. It's the first day of school, my official *last* first day of school. Hello senior year! I get out of bed and drag myself to my bathroom, getting myself together and ready to start the day. I make sure my outfit looks nicely put together and the little makeup I normally wear looks polished. I throw my backpack over my shoulder and pocket my cell phone before heading downstairs for breakfast. Mom has this tradition of making a big breakfast spread for our first day of school. I enter the kitchen and am instantly hit with the smell of coffee. Nothing smells more heavenly than brewed coffee beans in the morning.

"Morning."

"There she is!" Dad exclaims. "There's my soon to be high school graduate."

Dad gives me a big bear hug. He pulls back to look me over with a smile, one that beams with so much pride. It's strange to see him at home, considering he's hardly ever here. He's usually up before we are and gets home just in time for dinner, sometimes it's later.

"Dad? I'm surprised you're still here. Aren't you going to be late for work?"

"I moved my schedule around so that I could go in a little late today. It's not every day your little girl is a senior, embarking on her final year of youth before you have to let her loose into the real world."

"Hey! I'm your little girl too, ya know. And I only have a couple of years until I'm a senior," says Hannah, my thirteen-year-old sister. She's rocking the outfit Jenna helped me pick for her birthday.

"You're both my little girls. Sadie just happened to be the first one." He gives me a quick wink before he kisses the top of Hannah's head.

"Isaiah James Adams, you need to be getting ready for school!" Mom yells from somewhere in the house. Mom comes into the kitchen and gets to work. She pours Dad's coffee in his thermos, making it the way he always likes. She helps him straighten his tie and makes sure he has everything he will need in his briefcase.

"Shall we tell her?" Mom asks Dad as she inspects his attire, ensuring nothing is wrinkled or out of place.

"Tell who what?" I ask.

"I think it would be better if we showed her," Dad says.

"What are you two getting at?" They are being really weird and cryptic and it's too early in the morning.

"Why don't you go out to the driveway and see for yourself," Dad says. I'm not sure why the driveway but I hurriedly walk to the front door. I pull open the door and step off the porch, gasping at the sight. The most beautiful, red Pontiac GTO sits in the driveway with a big white bow on the hood.

"Oh...my...gosh. Is this a joke? Please tell me this isn't a joke?" I squeal. I look back at my parents who are standing on the porch with smiles upon their faces.

"Not a joke, Sadie. The car is all yours. Your mom and I had a long discussion about it. It's your final year of high school and with being captain, you're going to be pretty busy during the school week. We felt it was time for you to finally have your own set of wheels. Now, there are some rules, but we will go over them this evening. I have to get to the office and prepare for a few meetings."

He gives mom a quick kiss before giving me a hug and kisses the top of my head.

"Have a good day, sweetheart. Just, please be careful driving. I love you and I will see you when I get home."

"Love you too, Dad." I say. "Thank you so much for the car! Both of you! I *love* it! You guys are the best!" I hug my dad and squeeze him as tight as I possibly can.

"You're welcome." He glances at his watch for the time. "Oh, I gotta get going. Can't be late to my meeting with the chief of police."

Dad gets in his car and drives off to work while I head back inside to eat my breakfast. After I finish eating, I put my dirty dishes in the sink and grab my backpack.

"You're going to need these," Mom says. She's holding a key and car fob in her hand. "Promise me, Sadie, that you'll be super cautious when you drive. Signal for every turn. Look both ways before entering an intersection. Not everyone slows on yellow and the last thing I need—"

"Mom, Mom, Mom... Calm down. I promise you I will be safe. I remember everything from driving school."

"Please don't cut me off. You know how much I dislike that."

"Sorry, mom. It won't happen again."

"Yes, well, again, just be careful. I'm a mother and worrying about you and your siblings is always on my mind, day and night. You'll understand one day when you're married with children of your own."

She gives me a smile that has a twinkle in her eye. Sometimes I get the impression if I don't get into college, she's expecting me to walk down the aisle and start popping out babies the moment I graduate. Most likely with Brady. The thing is, I'm not sure if I want to be a mother someday. Kids are cute and I don't mind them but what if I fail at being a mother? My mom isn't so bad, but she doesn't express her love in ways I have seen other mothers do. Mothers who aren't so hellbent on always looking "perfect" or brush you off instead of listening to you when you have something to discuss. I'm so grateful for Jenna's mom for being there for me when I needed my mother most.

What if I fall in love with a girl? Obviously, for certain reasons, I wouldn't be able to make her a grandmother unless it's through adoption or in vitro fertilization. Even if I did do that, she would disown me the second I tell her I love another female.

"Let me pray over you before you leave."

She raises her hand and places it on my forehead. She whispers a prayer, for God and his Angels to watch over me on my journey to school, to protect me from all harm and to ensure my safety to and from school. We both say, "Amen," together before she hands me the keys.

"You better get going. Wouldn't want you to be late."

"Thanks, mom."

I grab the key to my brand new car and set out for school. I drive across town to Bellwood High School, pulling into the student parking area and park in an unmarked spot. Students who drive to school have assigned parking which means I'm going to have to stop by the front office and get a parking tag.

As I walk across the lot, I spot Payson pulling into her spot over by the giant Oak tree. I automatically stop to watch her and am unable to move. It's been about a week since she took me to the rage room, and we shared a kiss. One very hot, steamy kiss that I can't get out of my head. The one that leaves certain fantasies to play out when I'm lying in my bed and I force myself to not touch the small sensitive bud pulsing with need. It's my own sort of punishment for thinking sexual thoughts about another girl. My mother's voice would pop in and start with how homosexual sex is sin, and they are destined to go to Hell as they should. So I try to think of Brady and his toned body when he's shirtless and his six pack is on display. I figured if I could think of him in the sexual sense then maybe I can get myself off but it doesn't work. I have to wonder, is it because he cheated? Is it because I'm not as attracted to him as I am to Payson?

After I told Payson the kiss was a mistake and I took off, I've been avoiding her texts. At practices, I made sure to avoid looking at the field; not looking at her or in her direction was no easy feat.

Payson gets out of her vehicle, along with Colton and Thea. She is dressed in tight, black skinny distressed jeans, rocking a white tank with a red plaid flannel tied around her petite waist. She is also wearing a white baseball hat backwards and damn, I have never found her hotter than I do at this very moment.

"What are you staring at?" a voice says from beside me, spooking me out of the gaze.

I turn to see Lydia standing with Christina flanking her side.

Lovely. Just who I wanted to see this early on the first day of school. I look around to see if Brady is nearby as well. His truck isn't here yet which means I still have a chance to avoid running into him.

"I'm not staring at anything."

Lydia looks in Payson's direction and then back at me.

"Right and I'm blind as a bat." She starts to laugh with Christina as Jenna appears by my side.

"Blind as a bat and probably filled with all sorts of diseases like one too," Jenna tells her.

This shuts Lydia up quickly, but Jenna isn't done yet. She never is.

"How about the two of you make your way down to the clinic. I heard they have some free testing going on. Wouldn't want to catch anything the two of you may be spreading. We've already dealt with one pandemic, don't really feel like going through another. Toodles!"

Jenna finger waves them before she links her arm in mine, and we walk towards the school entrance.

"Thank you for that, Jenna. I was not expecting to run into Lydia already. I'm not ready to confront her about Brady."

"Girl, what is friendship for? I got you. You know that."

"Yeah, I do."

"But you do realize you're going to have to stop avoiding Brady and confront him. You can't just keep ignoring his messages and dodging him in public."

"I know. But you know I'm not a confrontational person. It makes me feel like throwing up at just the idea alone. I'm just not sure how to go about it."

"You can't be serious right now. You literally caught him with Lydia's legs around him, fucking him in broad daylight—"

I place my hand over her mouth. "Shhh, keep your voice down! I don't need the whole school to know my business!"

I look around to make sure no one overheard us then start picking up the pace. I really need to get inside before Brady shows up. Good thing Jenna can keep in step with me.

We enter the school, making our way through the crowd of students. I tell Jenna I need to go to the front office and get my parking tag and tell her I will see her at lunch. I approach the front desk where Mrs. Colbeck, the school secretary, is seated.

"Good morning, Miss Adams. How can I help you?"

"Morning. I need to get a student parking tag.""Give me one second." She reaches into a filing cabinet drawer, flipping through the file folders before finding what she's looking for. She hands me a clipboard and pen.

"Just fill in your name, student ID number and information about your car."

"Oh, um, I just got the car today and don't know the tag. May I run out really quick and check it?"

"Of course," she smiles warmly back at me.

I rush out to the parking lot only to stop when I notice Brady pulling in. Shoot! I don't want to talk to him, and I don't want him to see me. I do probably the most childish thing I can think of and creep alongside all the parked cars. I make my way across the parking lot to where I can see my car's tag. I type out my license plate number into the notes of my phone before checking for Brady's location. I spot him talking amongst his fellow football teammates so I quickly dart back across the parking lot to the office without him noticing me. I fill out the form and hand it back to Mrs. just as the late bell rings.

"Would you like me to write a note for your teacher, Miss Adams?"

"Uh, yes please. I'm so sorry."

"It's no trouble at all."

I am not sure if she is usually this nice or if it's because I'm Mayor Adams's daughter but I'm taking the handout. I hurry out of the office to get to my first class once I have the note in my hand.

The first two classes go by fairly quickly. I make a stop at my locker to drop off my books before heading to my third period class. As I'm walking down the hall, I spot Brady at his locker, talking to Chad and Nathan.

Great! Now how do I avoid him catching me in the halls?

I duck my head, keeping my face looking down and speed walk down the hall, ensuring no one shouts my name that would draw his attention. I finally make it to Ms. Steinhall's room. There are about three other kids already here which means I'm either really early or everyone is running late. I make my way towards the back of the classroom and pick the seat closest to the window. I pull my phone out and start scrolling through my Instagram when a text pops up from Brady.

> Sadie. Where are you? Can you plz talk to me.
> Are you even at school today? I just need to see
> u. I miss u.

I roll my eyes and hit ignore. If he truly missed me, why was he so wrapped up with Lydia?

"Yeah, right," I mutter under my breath.

"Yeah, right what?" asks a familiar voice, one belonging to the one person I haven't quite managed to get out of my mind lately.

I look up to find the most beautiful pair of green eyes staring down at me.

"Oh, um. Nothing important," I say as I quickly close out of Instagram and put my cell phone away.

"Do you mind if I sit here?" Payson asks, pointing to the desk beside mine.

I shake my head no, and Payson sits down next to me.

I cannot believe I'm going to have Payson in English class with me. Did I wake up into some Twilight Zone or is this my punishment for kissing a girl?

"How have you been?" Payson asks.

"Okay, I guess. Just been super busy with cheer."

"Yeah. I have to say, I'm impressed. You really got those freshmen in shape quickly."

My mouth drops open in surprise. She's been watching me during her practices?

"You might want to close your mouth there, cherry pop. I wouldn't want you to catch some flies," she smiles at me.

I quickly shut my mouth and sit up a bit straighter.

"You-you mean you have been watching my practices?"

"Well, yeah. In between drills and all of that. Kind of hard not to," she says. There's a smirk on her face before she bites on her bottom lip. My eyes gaze at the motion for a second, thinking back to our shared kiss before the screech of a chair snaps me out of the memory.

"I'm sorry. I'm just surprised, I guess. I mean, I figured since, you know, I mean..." I honestly have no idea how to word it.

"You mean since you said it was a mistake and then ghosted me?" Payson answers for me. I guess she knew what I was saying after all.

"Yeah," I answer softly.

"I'm going to be real with you Sadie. What you said? It did hurt. You not answering my texts? That hurt a little too. But then I sat in my room, thinking back over everything that happened that day and I couldn't be upset with you for running."

"Look, Payson, I—" but before I can apologize for what I said or try to explain myself, the bell rings and Ms. Steinhall comes rushing into the classroom.

"Sorry, sorry. I'm a bit late! My apologies!" She sets her things down on her desk before she faces the class. "Good morning, everyone! In case you don't know who I am, I'm Ms. Steinhall and I'll be your English 12 teacher for the semester."

"You don't look old enough to be a teacher," says Chad. "But you certainly look old enough for a good time."

Ew. Then again, I shouldn't be surprised because it's Chad Turner. He's one of the biggest playboys in school and Brady's best friend. Makes me wonder if he knew of Brady and Lydia's little rendezvous.

There are smacks of high fives from some of the other guys in class sitting close to him.

"Thank you, Mister…"

"Turner. But you can call me Chad." He gives her one of his flirtatious winks.

"Thank you, Mr. Turner. I appreciate that. Yes, I am young. I'm only 25 years old. I have a few years of teaching experience, but I can guarantee you all will be able to have the knowledge you need to get your English credit to graduate. However, I do *not* tolerate unwarranted sexual comments from misogynistic little boys such as yourself. So, if you do not want to be expelled from my class and unable to graduate with the rest of your peers, I would suggest you keep your little pervy mouth shut. Do I make myself clear?"

The classroom is silent, all eyes on Chad. I don't think I've seen anyone be able to put him in his place. Chad's face reddens as embarrassment settles all over it.

"I asked if I was clear, Mr. Turner. I need a verbal response from you."

"Crystal clear, Ms. Steinhall," he grits through clenched teeth.

"Good. Now that we got that out of the way, let me take attendance and we will get started." We go through attendance and over classroom rules before Ms. Steinhall talks about the various topics that will be covered over the semester. There are moments where I would glance over and catch Payson staring back. Once, I typed out a message on my phone, asking her if I had something on my face. She shook her head no before returning her focus back to the teacher. The class passes by fairly quickly and soon it's almost time for lunch.

"Alright class. We have about five minutes before the bell dismisses you all for lunch. What I'd like for you all to do is find a partner, and please choose your partner wisely. This is for a class project you will be doing here that counts towards 50% of your final grade. When you have picked your partner, please see me so that I can write your names down."

I feel a slight tap against my leg and turn to see Payson leaning in towards me.

"Want to be my partner?"

"What? Are you sure?" I asked her. Not that I have any objections to being her partner, but I really wasn't expecting her to want to be mine.

"Of course. I mean, I barely know anyone, and I don't want to get stuck with someone who makes me do all the work."

"How do you know I won't do that to you?" I raise an eyebrow. I'm teasing her though. I would never allow someone to do my share of the work.

"Because something tells me you are not that kind of person. I mean, you offered to pay for your half with the rage room. Remember?"

"Fair enough," I tell her. I reach my hand out to shake hers. "So, partners?"

"Partners."

We shake hands as if we were making a deal. The moment our skin touches, that tingly sensation shoots through my fingers but Payson doesn't drop my hand this time. I'm not sure if she didn't feel what I did but she hasn't pulled away, keeping her hand on mine.

The bell rings, breaking the moment and Payson drops my hand.

"I'll let Ms. Steinhall know we are going to be partners for the project," Payson informs me.

"Thank you. Do you want me to wait for you? I can walk with you to the cafeteria." I'm not sure if she knows where to go or if anyone has been guiding her around the school. Not sure I like the idea of anyone showing her around if I'm being honest.

"You can go on to lunch. Colton's meeting me after class so we can walk together."

"Oh. Okay. I guess I'll see you at lunch?"

"Yeah, I'll find you."

I give her a smile and head out the door. I walk the long halls and go down a small flight of stairs that lead to the cafeteria when I see Jenna is waiting for me by the doors.

"About time! Girl, I'm fucking starving!"

"Calm down. I had to walk a little further this year. I got Steinhall and her classroom is like 2 miles away."

"Oh, how is she? I have her as my last class, but I heard she's pretty cool."

We walk into the noisy cafeteria, picking the a la carte line over the traditional lunch line since it's shorter. We each grab a bottle of water and a round, deep dish pepperoni pizza for lunch before heading to our usual spot. We have always picked the round table closest to the backside of the cafeteria where the windows are.

"You're definitely going to like her. Chad made a comment about her being young and basically doing her and she managed to shut him right up. I didn't think it was possible that anyone could embarrass Chad."

"Oh yeah. I definitely think she is going to be my favorite teacher."

We sit there talking about our morning classes when I feel an arm drape across my shoulders. I smell the spicy, woodsy scent of his cologne and know exactly who is touching me.

"What do you want, Brady?" I turn to face him, giving him my best, I don't want to see you face. I'm just not sure the message is conveying.

"What do I want?" He chuckles for a moment before turning serious. "I'm your boyfriend, Sadie. I have been reaching out to you, trying to get your attention wherever I can but what do I get? Nothing! Nothing but silence and the cold shoulder. It's like you're avoiding me for some reason."

"Oh, no, there is definitely a reason," Jenna says before she takes a sip from her water bottle.

I narrow my eyes at Jenna, warning her to not say anymore.

Brady looks back and forth between Jenna and I before settling his chocolate brown eyes on me. "What does she mean by that? Why are you avoiding me?"

I remove Brady's arm from my shoulder. "This isn't the place or time, Brady. Just give me some space, please. I have a lot to think about."

"A lot to think about? I have been calling and texting you over the past week. I tried to find you in between classes so I can talk to you in person. I really thought you ditched the first day but then I was like, not my Sadie. She wouldn't miss school, especially senior year. Plus, your mom would have a whole bitch fit if you did that. Then I get a text from Chad about how you two have English class together, along with what's her name so I knew I would finally be able to get your attention at lunch. So no, Sadie. I'm not going to go anywhere. We are going to talk right here, right now!"

I glance around to make sure nobody close is listening to us.

"Brady, please, I really don't want to talk to you right now—"

"Hey!" someone shouts and the whole cafeteria gets quiet. Payson appears with Colton, Zealand, Rhett and Jeremiah behind her. "What's happening here? I may not know what exactly was said but I'm pretty sure I just heard Sadie say to leave her alone. The lady even said please. So why don't you go find your little fan club to take selfies with or whatever it is you do."

Brady stands up and gets close to Payson, leaning his face so he's eye level with hers.

"I don't know who the hell you think you are, but it's none of your concern what is going on between *my* girlfriend and me," Brady seethes.

Payson looks at him, her brows furrowed, arms crossed and jaw tense. She backs away from Brady just a bit before glancing in my direction. "Is that the truth? Is he still your boyfriend?"

God this is bad. So bad! I need to just woman up and talk to him, to both of them really.

I lower my head and give a nod. "Y-y-yes." I say softly, "I haven't talked to him yet."

"Are you for real right now?" Payson asks.

I avoid her hardened stare, not willing to answer her.

"Un-fucking-believable!" Payson drops her arms to her sides. "So, you're telling me after *everything*, you're still with this asshole?"

"Hey!" Brady shouts, stepping towards Payson but Zealand and Jeremiah step in between them, forming a human barrier.

"You better back it up, Brady and calm down," Zealand says. "You gotta chill, man. You really want this to get back to Coach?"

Brady points at Payson. "That bitch needs to keep her nose out of business it doesn't belong in!"

"Nah, It's fine Z. Not much else to say here. It's not worth anyone getting into an altercation or messing up *my* chance on the team," Payson says. She goes to walk away but stops to say one more thing. "Oh and uh, Sadie? You need to fucking pull your big girl panties on and tell him. Tell him about the predicament you caught him in. Because he ain't worth it. No one deserves to be treated like that, especially someone like you." She nods to the guys. "Let's go boys!" She walks away to get in the lunch line with her cousin and his friends.

"What the fuck does she mean by that?" Brady asks, turning to me. "What predicament?"

The volume in the cafeteria has gone up some, but those closest to us are whispering, listening in on what's happening. Of course, they would be. The star quarterback and the town's are clearly on the fritz.

"Like I said, I don't want to talk about this. Not now and definitely not here," I look around us, noting those listening in. "Brady, I just need time to think things through—""She caught you and Lydia by your truck, making out and practically fucking in broad daylight, dumbass. In case you may have some amnesia or forgot but it was that last Friday of cheer camp. You know, the day she asked me to give her a ride home since you told her you couldn't due to some family function. I had no clue Lydia was family. Incest a kink of yours, Thomas?"

"Jenna!" I exclaim. I can't believe she just freaking told him! I wanted to do it when I was ready to, away from school where it won't get plastered all over social media.

"What? Look, I love you and you're my bestie, but Payson is right. You needed to tell him that you know what he did. I know how you are about confrontations but avoiding it til you were ready was never going to happen. Let's face it. I ripped the Band-Aid off for you. He knows you know now so you can proceed to take out the trash. I'll take my thank you later." Jenna gives me a sympathetic smile before she gets up to throw her trash away and leaves the cafeteria.

I drag my hands down my face.

Brady sits down in the chair beside me, taking my hands into his. "Sadie, it's not what it looked like. I swear! I'm not sure what you saw, but you got it all wrong, babe!"

"You must think I'm stupid, don't you?" I remove my hands from his and look at him, remembering the way he was so passionately kissing her, gripping her, and grinding on her. I feel the anger seep in and use it to give me the courage to do what should have been done. "There's only one person in this school who drives the very car that was next to your truck. I know who I saw and what I saw that day, Brady. If you're so unhappy with our relationship and you want to be with her, then Brady, you are all free to be hers. I won't stand in the way of your happiness."

I go to stand up, but Brady grabs my wrist and pulls me into his lap.

"No. You don't mean that, Sadie. I'm telling you, whatever you saw you got it all wrong."

I search his face, seeing the pleading in his eyes. He really doesn't want me to dump him or believe what I saw. But then I glance over the top of his head and spot Lydia at the table where she typically sits. I see the jealousy in her eyes before she turns to talk with her friends.

"I don't think I am." I get up from his lap, grab my tray and dump what was left of my lunch before heading to the girls' room where Jenna texted me she would be if I needed her. And right now, a hug from my best friend is just what I need.

Chapter 10

Payson's POV

The final bell rings to end the school day. Thank God! Now it's time for my favorite part. Football practice. I drop my books off at my locker before I head to my Jeep to grab my football gear. Colton's waiting for me since he left his stuff in my vehicle too.

"Are you ready for football practice?" Colton asks.

"You know I'm always ready." We do our little fist bump handshake. "If football was a chick, I'd marry her in a heartbeat."

We both start to laugh when Sadie walks by, going across the parking lot towards a red car. Brady is behind her, begging from the sounds of it.

"Sadie, will you please just fucking talk to me!?" he pleads with her. But Sadie ignores him, picking up the pace until she reaches the car and gets in quickly. Brady attempts to open her door but Sadie is quick to lock it so he can't get to her.

Brady pounds his fists against her window, asking her to just hear him out.

"Should we go and intervene?" Colton asks me as we both watch from where we are standing.

"Nah, man. Let those two deal with their situation," I tell him. "Besides, I'm already on Brady's shit list as his competition for QB. I don't need to put myself into their problems and add more fuel to the fire."

I couldn't believe she didn't dump his ass over him cheating on her. Why would she stick with him, especially seeing him in the act with her own eyes? Did he convince her it wasn't him? Did he say something to make her believe that he's innocent?

I may not know much about Sadie or her relationship with Brady, but I do know that she deserves to be with someone a thousand times better. Someone who worships the ground she walks on. Someone who would never for a second think of or look at another girl. Who would be stupid enough to do that to her?

We grab our bags and start walking towards the football stadium. Coach sent out an email to the team we are to meet on the field before practice starts so no one can get changed until afterwards.

"What do you think the meeting is about?" I ask Colton.

"Dunno. We've never had one before a practice."

"Interesting. I guess we will find out soon enough."

We walk in silence for a moment before Colton speaks.

"So, did you hear?" Colton asks.

"Hear what?"

Colton points his thumb in the direction of Brady and Sadie. "According to the rumors circling around school, Sadie dumped Brady at lunch."

"Are you sure? Because she admitted they were still together, and she never confronted him."

"Apparently it was shortly after your little standoff with Brady," he says.

We make our way around students leaving school and go through the entrance to the field.

Colton pauses a moment before speaking. "Can I ask you something without you potentially taking my head off?"

"Depends on what you want to ask, Colt."

He stops walking in the middle of the track and takes a moment to look around before facing me.

"Do you have feelings for Sadie?"

Well, damn. Out of all the things I could think of, I was not expecting him to ask me that.

"What makes you think I do?" I ask nervously.

"You two have only known each other since the pool party, but you seem...I don't know. You tend to have this vibe when you mention her. Like your face lights up a bit and you smile all big. Then there is the whole situation with what happened at lunch. You were ready to defend her. So, I have to ask. Do you?"

Colton was always pretty good at reading me. I guess it's just the bond we have since we are pretty close. I lick my dry lips, trying to consider how to answer him. If there is anyone I can trust with this and word not get out, it's him.

"Look, I wouldn't say I have feelings per se. It's just, I don't know. There is something about Sadie, though. I can't shake her. The first time we met, and we physically touched, it was like electricity shot through our hands. I know how crazy that sounds but I'm pretty sure she felt it too because we pulled apart the moment we both felt it. When I'm around her, I get so caught up in her beauty, her eyes, her smile. It's like I'm a moth and she's the flame drawing me in. But that kiss—"

"YOU TWO KISSED!?" Colton shouts and I punch him in his shoulder.

"Dude, shut up!" I quickly look around to make sure no one heard anything. When I see the coast is clear, I punch him again for good measure.

"Ow! Dude, easy on the shoulders. I need those to be in top notch condition. I got balls to catch!"

"Sorry, not sorry," I taunt. "And for your info, yes, we kissed. It was after she caught Brady. She was really upset, trying to keep herself together so she wouldn't break down right there. So, I took her to to help her get her feelings out. She started rambling on and on. I couldn't get a word in, so I kissed her to, ya know, shut her up. But when she kind of stopped, I realized I made a mistake. I apologized and gave her my honest opinion, you know, how she deserves better than Brady. Then she pulled me back in and kissed me!"

"Wait a minute! So, you're telling me you kissed her and she then kissed you?" He pauses for a moment. "Was it good?" A slow smirk crosses his face.

"Colt!"

"What? The people want to know. And by people, I mean me." He gives me one of his infamous goofy grins. "So, was it good? Terrible? I don't think she would be terrible, but then again, Brady was hooking up with another girl."

This time I smack him in the back of the head.

"Ow! Seriously Pace?"

"Hey, it wasn't your arms. Plus you deserved it," I tell him. I think back to the kiss for a moment, relishing the memory. "Truthfully, it was probably one of the best kisses I've ever had."

It was more than the best. It was one of those deep, passionate kisses that made you question all the other ones before and damn if I wasn't craving another taste of Sadie's perfect lips. I think if we had had another thirty minutes in that room, I would have done a whole lot more than what we did. But knowing there are also cameras in there, I wouldn't want anyone seeing Sadie coming undone and naked but me. What can I say? I'm a greedy bitch.

Colton waves his hand in front of my face. "Where'd you go there, Pace? Fantasizing about that kiss?"

"Shut up," I chuckle. "I haven't stopped thinking about it since then. But what's the point? She's straight, right? Every time I think about it, I chalk it up to being in the moment. Sadie was upset and just kissed me purely because her emotions were running high. She even said it was a mistake and ran away from me. I tried reaching out a few times to talk about it but when she didn't respond or let alone read my texts, I just backed off. I haven't tried reaching out to her until earlier today in English."

"Are you turning her gay?" He says it jokingly, but it grates my nerves whenever people say things like that.

"You *can't* turn someone gay! They are either gay, but they are afraid to come out, or they are curious about the same sex, so they want to test the waters. Unless you're like *Miranda* and do it solely for the attention from the guy you want," I snarl.

Miranda is my ex-girlfriend back in California and someone I try to avoid thinking about. She claimed she was bisexual, which I wasn't bothered about whereas some lesbians avoid bi chicks like the plague. She liked me and I was the one who fell in love with her. We dated for almost a year before I caught her having sex at a party with one of my football teammates who was also one of my friends. When I confronted her about it, she came clean and told me that she only used me to see if she could truly be with another girl. She realized she mainly preferred dick and was going to break up with me. That was until the guy she cheated on me with said how sexy it made her, seeing her make out with me made him want to be with her even more so she used our relationship to get a guy. That shit fucking broke me. Since then, I've been avoiding girls and not showing any interest in anyone. At least that was until I met Sadie.

"Sorry, Pace. I didn't mean to stir up those feelings or upset you. I just, I don't know. I think maybe Sadie could have an interest in you. What if she is in the closet?"

"I don't know Colt. What I do know is I don't want to fall for someone who is going to just use me as an experiment on whether they are straight or gay *again*."

The coaches blow their whistles and wave for everyone to go sit on the 50-yard line.

"Look, why don't you talk to her best friend?"

"The dark-haired girl with the tawny skin she was sitting with at lunch?"

"Yeah. Her name's Jenna Altwood. She lives next door to Sadie and they have been best friends since preschool. If anyone knows Sadie the best, it's her. Why don't you talk to Jenna and see what she says?"

"I don't know...I'll think about it. Okay?"

We make our way to the center of the football field and sit with the rest of the guys. Once everyone has arrived, Brady showing up last and looking thoroughly pissed, Coach Watson blows his whistle signaling for everyone to quiet down so he can speak.

"Good afternoon, everybody. I hope you all enjoyed your first day of classes. I will try to keep this quick so you all can get into your pads for warm-ups and then we can start running some plays. Now, as you all know, Bellwood High has acquired their first female football player, Payson Moore."

The majority of the guys hoot and holler for me as I raise my hand and wave it around. The ones who don't are clearly Brady and his little cult of followers. They are the ones currently giving me the stink face.

"Alright, alright settle down!" The guys calm down, allowing Coach to continue. "Since we have Miss Moore on our team, we need to go over a few new rules. Miss Moore and I have already discussed how things were done with her previous school's team and we feel we can apply some of those changes here. In regard to away games. If, for any reason, she must change before a game and the girls' locker room is unavailable, Payson is allotted the visiting team locker room first. Once she is fully dressed, she will step outside and the rest of the team can change."

"What!? How the fuck is that fair? She's a girl. She will waste like twenty minutes!" Za'darius shouts.

Coach glares at him. "Language, Mr. Olsen."

I turn to face Za'darius who is definitely team Brady.

"Hey Olson! I can be changed and fully padded in four minutes flat. How long does it take you to get ready there, huh, pretty boy?"

Some of the guys snicker and Za'darius gives me the middle finger. I turn back around, giving him my back.

"As I was saying, if need be, Miss Moore is to go first. Nobody will be allowed in until Miss Moore has exited the locker room. For halftime and post-game chats, every male athlete is to remain clothed from the waist down. You may remove your shoulder pads and jerseys, but that is it. Once Miss Moore has exited the locker room, you're welcome to shower and change or remain sweaty until we return home. This is clearly to protect both Miss Moore and the rest of you. Do we understand the new rules?"

"Yes, Coach!" We all shout in unison. I'm so glad this all got cleared up. I hate that Coach had to do this but it's what is best to prevent any uncomfortable and potential risks. We don't need anyone catching a rape case or sexual harassment charges.

"Good. You all are dismissed to the locker room to get changed. You have ten minutes max. If you exceed ten minutes, you will be running laps, one lap per every minute you are late. Your time starts now!" We all quickly get up and dart towards the locker rooms.

I head straight to the girls' locker room in search of my locker. Once I find it, I quickly undress. I throw my flannel, pants, ball cap and tank top in the locker. I pull on my practice pads over my boxer briefs and strap the shoulder pads over my muscle shirt. I snap the straps under my armpits and pull the strings to ensure they are nice and tight. I'm so glad I'm part of the itty bitty titty committee. I don't know how any busty chick who plays football would make it work. *Does it suffocate them?*

I shake my curious thoughts aside, pull on my white cleats and lace them up. All that's left now is to pull my hair back. I grab my bag looking for my scrunchie, but I don't see it. I look under the bench, around the floor and even in my locker. I grab my pants, checking the pockets and fuck, no hair tie. How am I going to show pretty boy up with all this hair in my face?

"Excuse me?" I hear a soft, feminine voice speak. I turn around and am met by a pretty cute girl. She's on the short, petite side. Probably about 5'2". Her chestnut brown hair is short with beach waves in it, falling to her shoulders. Her eyes are a blue-gray which pop with her sun-tanned skin.

"Uh...hi."

"Hi. Are you looking for one of these?" She holds up a hair tie and I could just about hug her but I won't.

"Yeah. I can't seem to find mine and I need to get to practice."

"Here. You can have this one. I always carry extras in my bag. You never know who might need one." She blushes slightly and I wonder if she's flirting with me.

I reach for the hair tie and take it from her.

"Thank you. I appreciate it. What's your name? I'm new to this school."

"You're welcome. And I'm Willa. Willa Voss. It's nice to meet you."

"I'm Payson Moore. New QB."

"Wow, QB huh?" Her eyes roam over my body before returning to meet my eyes. "Color me impressed. Never met a female QB before. I'm assuming they got rid of Coach's pride and joy?"

"Brady is Coach Watson's son?" I ask. No way those two are related. They look nothing alike.

"No. He's just Coach Watson's favorite player and kisses his ass to appease Brady's dad, Russell Thomas."

"Whoa, hold up! You're telling me that Brady's the son of *the* Russell Thomas, a former NFL star quarterback?"

"From what I hear, yeah." She checks her phone. "Shit, I got to get to volleyball practice. It was really nice meeting you Payson. Hope we run into each other soon."

She gives me a wink and brushes past me. I watch her as she exits the locker room, taking note of the nice peachy bottom and how they look in her volleyball shorts. I'm an ass girl so I definitely appreciate a plumpy rear end. I hear a locker slam and turn in the direction of the noise only to see Sadie glowering at me before she quickly grabs her poms and darts past me out of the locker room.

What the hell was with that? Did Sadie just get jealous of me checking out another girl? I don't have time to think about this. I pull my hair into a low ponytail, grab my helmet and head out the same way Sadie did. Maybe Colton might be right about Sadie being in the closet.

Chapter 11

Sadie's POV

I don't know what came over me. Seeing Payson totally check out Willa just brought about a sense of jealousy I didn't think I would feel over another girl. I can't fault her for looking at Willa. I haven't really given Payson any indication that I am girlfriend material for someone who is so confident in their sexuality, not afraid to be their authentic selves.

I'm too afraid to seek out that part of myself, too afraid of my mother disowning me and keeping my siblings away from me. There's also the fear of embarrassing my father. What would the town think if the mayor's daughter was seen dating a girl? I could never cause that kind of scandal to ruin the image my mother has made our family out to be.

Practice got away from me, so I didn't have time to grab a shower afterwards. I'm heading to my car, ready to go home to eat dinner and knock out some college applications when I see Willa standing by Payson's Jeep. Payson is leaning against the driver's side door while Willa is clearly being flirtatious. She keeps leaning into Payson, brushing a hand along her arm or finding some way to touch her.

I can feel the ugly green monster crawling up, ready to unleash her claws and remove Willa's hands from touching any part of Payson. I'm unfamiliar with this feeling and once I realize the jealousy that's sizzling under my skin, I end up snapping myself out of it.

What am I doing? *Jealousy is a sinful desire of the flesh. The Devil is at work so the moment you feel it, you must confess it and ask God to forgive you.* I can hear my mother say. I say a small prayer, confessing my jealousy and asking for His forgiveness. As soon as I whisper, *amen*, I feel a presence behind me.

"Sadie."

Either this is my punishment for feeling jealous or it's a sign that I just need to work out this situation with Brady so I can move past whatever feelings Payson is stirring up in me. I take a deep breath before I turn around and face Brady. He's standing before me, with a sadness in his eyes and hair dripping wet from his after-practice shower.

"What Brady?" I ask, exhausted from avoiding him.

"May I walk you to your car?"

I glance around the parking lot. I take one last look towards Payson and Willa. Payson takes Willa's cell phone from her hands, punches in something then hands her phone back to her. My guess? Payson just gave Willa her cell phone number which can only mean that Payson is interested in her. I'm not sure why that stings my chest, but maybe this is God answering my prayer, a way of saying I just need to get over whatever girl crush I have on Payson and focus on fixing what Brady and I have.

"Yeah, Brady. You can walk with me." I manage to offer him a soft smile.

We walk towards my car in silence. I'm not sure if Payson sees us, but it is what it is. If Payson wants to pursue Willa, no matter how much that makes me unhappy for some reason, I have to let Willa have a chance because Payson deserves to be happy.

"So, can we please talk about what you saw? I'm sure it looked bad and hurt you. For that I am so sorry, Sadie, but if you just let me explain, you'll see it was all Lydia, not me."

I unlock my car and toss my cheer bag along with my poms into the passenger seat. I leave the door open so I can sit in the driver's seat, facing Brady.

"Alright, Brady. Tell me what happened."

"Wait. You're really going to hear me out?"

"Yes. I'm tired of avoiding you, of you begging me to hear you out. So, here's your opportunity. Let's hear it."

He takes a deep breath.

"Okay. I did have a family thing. My dad and uncle had some meetings set up with some college football scouts. My dad's trying to get some of them to come out to some of our games for the season to watch me play. And we are not talking about some small schools. We are talking about big name colleges like Notre Dame and Ohio State."

It makes sense. His dad was a pretty famous quarterback in the NFL until he sustained a career ending injury. I've always felt Brady's dad put too much pressure on Brady to be a top-notch quarterback in hopes he gets drafted to the NFL. I think it's his dad's way of reliving his glory days vicariously through his son.

"I came out to my truck after stopping by Coach Watson's office to let him know what was going on. Lydia was parked beside me, a little too closely. I asked her if she could move so I could get in my truck and didn't risk scratching up her BMW. You know those cars are not cheap and I didn't want to have to pay for any damages or for it to get back to my dad."

I nod to let him know I understand and to continue on. So far, all sounds reasonable.

"She gets out of her car on her side and comes to stand between me and my truck. She then starts touching me, telling me she would move her car if I gave her a kiss. I assumed she meant on the cheek or something.

So, I leaned down to kiss her on her cheek but then she wrapped her legs around me and started making out with me."

"Why didn't you, I don't know, tell her no? Why didn't you push her away?"

"Because Sadie, I was running slightly behind. My dad was already blowing up my phone wondering why I wasn't there. I figured I would give her a quick kiss then she would move, and I would get to leave. And I tried to get her off me, but she was latched onto me like a leach. I didn't want to shove her off because I didn't want her to hit her head on my truck and for me to catch a lawsuit. Her dad would not hesitate to go after my dad over his daughter."

I guess that makes sense now that he explained it but something keeps nagging me.

"Why would Lydia want you to kiss her?"

"I don't know, Sadie. Probably because she has had a crush on me since 8th grade? Look, Sadie, Lydia is jealous of you. She wants what you have, and she will do anything to ruin us. She practically has and you're falling for it! She wants us to break up so she can have me."

Jenna has mentioned to me about being cautious around Lydia, about her hating on me. I just always ignored it because I like to give people a chance. Everyone deserves the opportunity to be treated with kindness and compassion.

"Brady, that sounds very authentic but what I saw...I mean, you two were practically humping each other—"

"You said you saw us, right? I mean, Lydia probably saw you walk out of the stadium and that's why she did that. To make it look like we both wanted each other. I told you Sadie. Lydia is out to ruin us to have me to herself."

I cover my face with my hands, taking a moment to let what he says sink in. She very well could have seen me and jumped Brady, grinding herself on him so I would have to break up with him. I mean, I pretty much did so at lunch, didn't I?

"Sadie, please," he begs. "You have to know I would never do anything to hurt you in that way. You have to be crazy to think I would want someone like Lydia. She's nothing compared to you."

I sigh heavily. "Okay, Brady."

"Okay? Okay? What do you mean okay?"

"Okay. I heard you out. I—" I stop speaking. Do I really want to try to fix us? I think about Payson, the jealousy and all the influx of emotions she stirs within me. The fact I don't think I can ever give her the authentic me, to openly date her the way Willa can makes me confirm that I'm making the right choice.

"I will give us another chance. But you have to stay away from Lydia if what you say is true. It's the only way we can work through all of this."

His sad, puppy dog eyes turn to glee and a smile crosses his face. He reaches down, pulling me up into his strong arms, squeezing me in a hug.

"Oh baby. That makes me so happy to hear." He reaches down as if to kiss me but I pull away.

"I stink, Brady."

"I don't care," he chuckles.

I hold my hand up in front of his face, stopping him from kissing me again.

"I also need to get home before my mom has a panic attack, thinking something happened to me since I drove in my car today. Plus, I may have just forgiven you for what you did, but it's going to take me some time. I hope you can respect that."

Brady backs up slightly. "Of course, babe. Anything. I'm just happy you're giving us a second chance. Can I call you later?"

"Um, yeah. Call around seven?"

He nods in agreement before pecking a kiss onto my lips. I close the door and buckle up before I look out my window and give Brady a small wave. He takes two fingers to his lips and blows me a kiss before I drive off to head home. I glance in the rearview mirror as Brady stands in the parking lot, watching me drive off. I'm not sure what to think of our situation but somehow, I feel like this is one decision I may regret later.

Chapter 12

Payson's POV

I made it to English class a bit early today, wanting to try to talk to Sadie before class starts. After Willa and I exchanged numbers after practice last night, I happened to spot Brady talking with Sadie. I'm not sure what they could have discussed but there's been rumors of the two of them being back on.

I'm sitting at my desk, anxiously waiting when a text comes through on my phone from Willa.

> Hey. Just wanted to tell you that you look really good today. <3

I'm not quite sure what to make of Willa. She's cute with a great ass. She's definitely blunt and straightforward and it seems she is clearly into me, but I'm not sure how to feel about her. To be honest, she doesn't make me feel the way Sadie does.

A chair screeches beside me, pulling me from my thoughts, and it's as if the Goddess herself appears when I'm thinking of her. I turn to look at Sadie, but she doesn't glance in my direction. She's busy unloading her supplies from her bag onto her desk when her pen rolls off and onto the floor. We both bend down to pick it up at the same time, our heads knocking into each other.

"Ow!" I say, a little bit louder than I intended.

"Oh my gosh, Payson! I'm so sorry! Are you okay?"

I rub the spot on my head where we collided for a minute. It hurts just a little bit but it's nothing compared to some of the hits I've taken out on the field.

"Yeah, I'm fine," I tell her. "Are you okay?"

"I'll be fine. Nothing like some of the bumps and bruises I get in cheerleading."

Sadie gives me a quick smile before she flips her notebook open. I'm about to ask her about the rumors going around school but Ms. Steinhall stands to begin class. We go over today's lesson and take what feels like hundreds of notes. I constantly glance over at Sadie, but she doesn't pay me any mind. I can't help but wonder if Brady said something about staying away from me.

I pull my phone out under the desk where the teacher can't see it and send Sadie a text.

> Hey. R U Good?

I hear her phone vibrate but I don't know if she actually looks at it. A few moments later, my phone vibrates in my lap.

Yeah. I'm ok. Why do you ask?

Idk. You seem to be avoiding me today.

I'm not avoiding you, QB.

I'm about to ask if she is certain when Ms. Steinhall gets our attention.

"Okay everyone. I want you to get with the partners you selected for your upcoming class projects and push your desks together, so you are side by side."

Well, this couldn't be more perfect timing. We have a whole half hour before the class dismisses for lunch, so I get thirty minutes of talking to Sadie.

The classroom fills with loud screeches of desks and chairs sliding across the floor, everyone moving their seats to be beside their partners. Thankfully, Sadie and I only have a few inches to move.

Once the room is finally quiet and everyone is settled, Ms. Steinhall begins.

"You and the partner you have chosen are going to be writing a ten-thousand-word novella. In case some of you don't know what a novella is, it is a short story. You must figure out what genre of fiction you both want to write. Do you want murder mystery, science fiction, or perhaps romance?"

Some of the girls make noises of excitement while some of the guys mutter things like gross.

"If you choose romance, think about what type of tropes, or kind of theme you would like to present in your story. Are the characters enemies to lovers? Is it a forbidden romance? Once you have settled on the kind of story you both want to write, then you must plot and plan out how you want your story to go. What's the conflict? How will it be resolved? And so forth. BUT and here is the big BUT—"

Chad and some of the idiots he surrounds himself with start laughing only it's short lived when Ms. Steinhall glowers at them.

"You and your partners are each going to be the main characters. You may write them in first person or third person point of view. But your story must convey two main characters, written by each of you. This assignment will be due at the end of the semester. If you have any questions, feel free to see me at my desk, otherwise you all may begin planning."

The room fills with voices, our peers speaking with their partners and chatting about the assignment. At least, most of them do.

"So, what type of story would you like to write?" Sadie asks.

I seriously have no clue. I don't like to read, unless of course it's a playbook. Other than that, books are just not my thing.

I shrug as I answer her, "I have no idea. I'm not much of a reader."

"Okay, what about movies? They're like books, just giant visual ones. What's your favorite genre?"

"I like action, certain horror films and comedies."

She gives a slight giggle and man, what a sweet sound it is. Makes my heart seem to flutter just hearing it.

"Okay. I'm not sure I can write scary. Not sure I'm funny enough for a comedy either."

"Do you read?" I ask her.

"Yeah, I love to read. I have a bookshelf loaded with books. My TBR is like a mile long."

"TBR?" My eyebrows furrow in confusion. "What's that?"

"Oh, it's like bookworm talk. TBR stands for to be read. I have like hundreds of books that I want to read, and it never feels like there are enough hours to find the time to sit down and read them. Plus, Booktok never helps. They share a book that sounds intriguing, and I have to get it, causing my TBR list to get even longer."

"What kind of books do you like to read?"

"Oh, um, the romance kind." Her face starts to turn a shade of pink, making me wonder why she would be blushing.

"Romance kind? What kind of romance?"

"Uh...the kind that may... or may not...have some spicy content in them..." She says sheepishly. Her face is getting redder by the second and then it dawns on me after a moment why she is blushing so hard.

"Wait! You're telling me you read books that have sex scenes in them!?" I whisper shout as to not draw attention to us.

Sadie covers her face with her hands, nodding her head yes before peeking through her fingers.

"Well, now. That takes me by surprise there, cherry pop. I didn't think you had a naughty side to you."

She looks at me with puzzlement. "Cherry pop? That's like the second time I've heard you call me that."

Shit! I sit up a little straighter, trying to figure out how I could possibly explain the small nickname I've given her. I lick my dry lips and let out a quick breath. I look around the room to ensure no one is eavesdropping on us.

"God you're going to think I'm weird," I let out a small chuckle. "But when we first met, and we were in close proximity to one another, you smelt like cherries and vanilla. Not sure if it's a body wash or what but it smelt really good. And then when we, you know, your lips tasted kind of like cherries. So, Cherry pop just kind of came to fruition."

Sadie doesn't say anything. She just bites her bottom lip before reaching into her bag and pulls out a small tube of what looks like ChapStick. She hands it to me and right on the side of the tube, it says *Revlon Kiss Lip Balm Sweet Cherry.*

"It's my favorite lip balm and I love that it has a slight taste of cherry to it."

I hand it back to her where she pockets it into her bag.

"Does it, you know, bother you or weird you out that I call you that? Because if it does, I'll stop."

"What!? No!" Sadie says a bit too loudly when the closest group turns to look at us. She gives them an apologetic smile, whispering, "Sorry," until they turn back around.

"I mean, it's completely okay. It's way better than being called a princess." She rolls her eyes as she says the word.

I chuckle at her hatred towards the nickname, but I get why she is annoyed with it. She is absolutely far from the princess type. She's caring and kind and sometimes I wonder if she even has a single mean bone in her body.

Sadie and I discuss ideas for our project. We decided on a romance novella since Sadie seems the most comfortable with that genre. I had her explain to me more on what tropes are and who knew there were so many of them! The way she goes on and on about the books she reads makes me even more curious about picking one up. Leave it to the pretty blonde cheer captain to make me want to start reading.

We are actually enjoying ourselves, talking and laughing a bit. There are moments when we bump elbows or our hands brush each other, leaving a spark of heat at the touch. At one point, while we jot down some ideas on paper, I leave my hand close to hers just to enjoy the warmth of her skin next to mine. Sadie doesn't pull away, which makes me want to ask her if she is feeling some sort of way about me.

My phone vibrates in my pocket. I check it only to see a text from Willa. Sadie must have glanced at the name before she quickly pulls away from me and it's as if her entire demeanor changes.

"I'm sorry." She says quietly and now I'm unsure what happened.

"What are you sorry for, Sadie?"

"I...um...just...you know..." she stutters out, unsure of what to say. "No. I don't know. I need you to explain it to me."

If this is where she is going to tell me she's sorry for showing any interest in me, if it's proof of jealousy towards Willa, then I'll know. I'll know without a shadow of doubt, Sadie Adams is into me.

"Nothing. It's nothing."

I call bullshit. No way was she so comfortable with me a second ago and now one text from another girl and she's pulling away from me?

"You're lying to me, Sadie," I whisper. "I'm trying to understand what's happening here. There is something between us. I can feel it and I think you feel it too. So don't tell me it's nothing."

Sadie looks around us, her leg bouncing with nerves. She lowers her head so that she can whisper to me, so that no one can hear what she has to say.

"Payson, there is nothing between us but what I can only hope will be a wonderful friendship. That is all we are and all we can ever be." She refuses to look at me as she continues talking.

"Besides, I'm with Brady—"

"Hold up!" I say, cutting her off. *So, the rumors are true?* She is giving that cheating asshole a second chance?

"You better be fucking lying. Are you serious right now, Sadie? He cheated on you! You and I both saw it as it happened! There is no excuse for what he did or for how he hurt you." I can feel my anger boiling up within me, making my temper flare. I need to calm down before I make a scene or say something I could regret later.

"We talked last night, and he explained it all to me, about what really happened. I just...I had it all wrong."

She cannot be serious right now. There is nothing that would explain his innocence, not how I saw it. He was clearly mauling that girl's face and humping her like a dog in heat.

"Sadie, he's just saying whatever he can to save his own ass."

She doesn't say anything. She just looks out the window, her hand resting under her chin. I hear the slightest sniffle and fuck, she's trying not to cry in class. I don't want to be a dick, but she has to see Brady is lying and he's just going to continue to cheat on her.

I lean back in my chair, resting my hands on top of my head. I take a moment to calm myself before I talk to her again.

"Listen to me, Sadie." She refuses to look at me, so I gently grab her wrist that her chin is resting on, using my other hand to turn her to look at me. I can see the glistening of the tears in her eyes, the ones she's holding back like a dam so as to not let them fall.

"I don't trust or believe him, and I hope with every cell in my body that you do the same. I can tell you over and over he's lying but I also have to accept the fact that you are not going to believe me. You may think I'm saying things because I have to fight him for the quarterback position. That I'm just trying to screw him over. But I'm not. I like to win fair and square. And who knows. Maybe I am wrong and maybe he was being truthful about what he told you last night. But the Brady I see at practices? He isn't someone who..." God I don't want to break her heart. The only way to prove he has a wandering eye is for her to find out herself. "Just be careful, Sadie. Protect your heart because it's way too beautiful to be crushed by someone who could give two shits about hurting you. I don't know or understand what's between us, and I sure as hell hope you figure it out. Until then, I'll be on the sidelines, waiting to see how this plays out."

Sadie's lips begin to quiver, and I think she may cry but then the bell rings to dismiss us. She shakes herself from the moment before gathering her things up quickly. My phone goes off and once again, it's a text from Willa. I don't answer it and glance up to see Sadie with a somber look on her face, staring at my phone.

"Seems like Willa really likes you. Maybe you should give her a chance," She grits out before storming out of the classroom.

I sigh heavily, looking up to the ceiling before I grab my things and head to lunch. I really need to talk to someone about this situation because fuck me.

Chapter 13

Sadie's POV

It's been a few weeks since that day in English when I had to tell Payson I was giving Brady a second chance. I was afraid to tell her, worried she would be completely upset with me and just stop talking to me, cutting me off altogether. I mean, feelings wise, it would have been the best option, but the selfish part of me, the part that enjoys being around her, couldn't handle that idea. She makes me laugh and smile and I have never felt so appreciated by anyone like I do when I'm around her.

Brady and I have been working on us, although sometimes it feels like I'm the only one who's actually trying. Sad thing is, I'm not even putting in that much real effort. We were doing great for that first week. It felt like how it did when our relationship first began but then he fell back into old habits. Getting agitated easily, wanting to hang out with his friends more and starting arguments with me even more than before. He claims I don't trust him when he did nothing wrong in regard to Lydia. I tell him I do, but then again, do I really?

Sometimes my mind goes back to that day and the kiss he had with Lydia in the parking lot. It seemed too heated on both their parts for it to be only Lydia's doing but maybe that is my assumption. Maybe it was just my own mind playing tricks on me, giving me an excuse to break up with Brady because of what I was feeling for the girl who was making me question myself. *The Devil is at work here.* Something my mother would say if she knew.

Brady's side of the story also keeps going through my mind and I tell myself that is why I'm giving him another chance, a chance to prove himself and show me he was truly the innocent one in all of this. Yes, he's been a jerk towards me, but it's got to be because he's stressed out with football. His dad keeps questioning why he is sharing the spotlight with a girl as a quarterback and how she's showing him up, proving Brady is unworthy of the Thomas name and being scouted. I couldn't believe his dad would say such things to his own child.

Coach Watson hasn't officially declared who the starting spot goes to. He's been alternating them throughout every game, ensuring they both get some rest time to keep them healthy for the season or so he says. Payson and Brady both bring their own strengths and so far, it has worked in our school's favor. We are one of only three undefeated teams in our area. Our next game is this Friday night against our biggest rivals, Wimbleton High Wildcats. Knowing this is going to be a battle of who stays undefeated means this game is going to be even bigger and more intense. The quarterback is like a general on offense. They command how they will get past the defense to score points and having our best quarterback in charge will be significant in us winning.

Payson has been really good at keeping herself composed. She hasn't given any indication she's stressed about the upcoming rivalry game but I do wonder if she is keeping it all inside, afraid to show a hint of vulnerability or weakness.

We have been working hard on our class project in English class. We came up with two amazing characters and a plot I think Ms. Steinhall will appreciate. Payson and I were in agreement that neither of us would talk about Brady or any relationships with anyone else while we were working together if we wanted to be partners. Which, in all honesty, I was perfectly okay with. I don't think I could bear to hear about Payson dating anyone. Yeah, I know I care a lot for Brady but I also have these feelings toward Payson too, feelings that for some reason, I can't let go of.

I haven't heard any rumors of Payson and Willa dating. However, they do text each other quite often. I've caught her name popping up on Payson's cell phone a few times when she's left it on the desk. The jealousy I feel whenever I see her name makes me want to just claw the eyes out of the girl and I hate myself for it. Sometimes I have to take a deep breath and say a silent prayer to reel the envious monster back. I keep reminding myself I have no place or say in that matter. Payson is free to talk to whoever she wants.

Sometimes, it's hard when I can sense Payson's gaze on the side of my head as I'm jotting down notes. Or the coquettish smile she occasionally gives me in class while Ms. Steinhall drones on about the day's lesson. It's not just any smile either. It's the kind of smile where the dimple makes an appearance and the butterflies set flight within your stomach when she glances your way. When she lets her hand linger next to mine as she's writing her part of the project, the warm, soft skin touching mine always sends a tingly sensation through my body. I get tempted to want to cross our pinkies but that would just cross the friendship line we established.

I will never understand why she brings about the feelings she does in me or why I cannot see her as just a friend. Why does Willa talking to her make me feel insecure and want to claim Payson even more? Especially when I am the one still dating another person. A person who makes me question my worth and doesn't make me happy like he once did.

The other day while hanging out with Jenna at her house, I brought up my mess of a love triangle. At least that's what Jenna likes to call it. She said that I'm just clinging onto Brady for the sole purpose of clinging to the heterosexual daughter my mother dreams me to be. How I'm always trying to appease my mother out of fear of rejection or abandonment.

Maybe there is some truth to what Jenna says. She knows my family and what they are like outside of the public eye. Especially my mother. She's like one of those Stepford Wives but for Jesus.

Jenna and I enter the cafeteria like we always do, her arm linked in mine. We grab a tray and wait in line to grab our lunches. I'm waiting for the others to move forward when I feel the sharp jab of an elbow in my ribs.

"Ow! Jenna, seriously?"

"You may want to pay attention over there." She nods her head in the direction of the table where Brady is sitting with some of the guys from the team. A pretty girl with fair skin and wavy, fiery hair is talking to Brady. She's a bit too close and I don't miss the way Brady's eyes look her over.

"Is he for real right now?" Jenna asks. She must have caught him checking her out too. We move along with the line, grabbing our lunch before we make our way towards Brady and the girl. Just as we approach, the girl raises her hand and slaps Brady across his face before spitting on him.

"You're a real piece of shit!" She yells at him before she storms off. Some of the guys, "Ooh," as Brady takes a napkin and wipes his face.

"Shut the fuck up!" he tells them.

Nathan taps him on the arm.

"What!?"

"Your girl is behind you, dude."

He turns around to see Jenna and me looking at him, taken aback to see us standing there.

"What was that about?" I ask him.

"Yeah, Thomas. Why did the pretty girl just bitch slap you like the dog you are?" Jenna says sarcastically.

Oh my gosh, Jenna! I don't need her sass to make Brady more upset than he already is.

"It was nothing. Just some crazy bitch trying to hit on me, and I told her no. Told her I have a girlfriend. Guess she didn't like being told no."

"Really?" I ask him, uncertainty in my voice. If that is the truth, then why could he tell her no but not Lydia?

"Yes really. You know I only got eyes for you babe." He smiles at me before he leans down and gives me a kiss. "C'mon. Sit next to me."

He sits on the bench seat and pats the spot next to him at the long table. "C'mon you ass wipes, move down so my girl can sit," he tells some of the jocks who eventually scoot themselves down.

I look at Jenna, wondering if she is going to sit with us. She is not a fan of Brady's and would rather eat trash than be near him. Her words, not mine.

"I'm going to go sit with Rebecca where all the wonderful, creative people are," Jenna says. "No hard feelings?"

"That's okay. Wait for me after lunch?" We usually walk to our classes after lunch since they are beside each other.

"Of course! Talk to you later!" she says. She gives Brady a nasty look before she heads to the table where the art students are sitting.

"She really doesn't like me," Brady states.

"Yeah, well—" I start to say before Brady's phone vibrates on the table, stopping me. I glance down at the text message on his screen.

We need to talk. ASAP.

I look at the name attached to the message. L.J. Brady snatches the phone off the table before he puts it in the pocket of his jeans.

"Whose LJ?" I ask. I mentally run through all the guys he hangs out with, all the football players on varsity but none match to the initials.

"Uh, a family friend who works with dad. We all call him LJ. He must have some news for me. I'll just contact him after school."

Okay. Not completely unusual.

"Oh, what news—"

"What are your plans this evening?" Brady asks me, effectively cutting me off and changing the subject.

"Um...well, I have to get home and work on my English project. Other than that, nothing—"

"Cool. How about after school, I'll follow you home and we go do something. Like a date." He gives me a warm smile, something I feel like I haven't seen him give me in so long.

"Okay. I mean, I will have to run it by my mom before she leaves for Wednesday night bible study.'

"Perfect."

After school, Brady followed me to my house so I could drop my car off before he took us back to his place. We decided to play video games in what I call the theater room. There's a huge comfy sectional that makes a U shape in the center and a projector above that points to a 200-inch screen that comes down at the push of a button. There are two square ottomans that when you push them up against the sectional, it makes for a nice little day bed. It's perfect for snuggling and watching movies.

After a few rounds of Mario Kart and Madden, to which I somehow managed to beat him in with no idea how, Brady decides to watch a movie. I think I bruised his ego.

"I'm going to go to the kitchen and grab us some drinks and popcorn. Why don't you pick the movie?"

Brady leans down and gives me a quick kiss, leaving me with a warm smile before heading to the kitchen. I grab the remote for the projector, scrolling through all the movie options.

I hear the buzz of a text alert. I look at my phone, thinking it's mine but no one has texted me except for Jenna which was at the end of school. I go back to scrolling before I hear the buzzing go off a few more times. I spot Brady's cell phone laying on the couch beside me. I stare at it, contemplating if I should check to make sure it isn't the coach or his dad needing to reach him. The screen lights up and I glance at the name.

LJ.

Brady said he would contact him later, but he's been with me after school and there's no way he could have contacted him while he was at school. Seems kind of important so I reach over to read the message. There are a few messages and missed calls from LJ, along with messages from several other people, more specifically other *girls*.

My stomach knots and I start to feel queasy. My heart begins to pick up the pace as I slide the phone to unlock it and go into his messages. Texts upon texts of different girls sending Brady pictures of their breasts as well as full out nude shots. I browse through some of them, reading his texts in response, to see if he ever mentions me but nope. Nothing but him replying back with all the ways he would like to fuck them, seeing their lips around his cock or sliding his cock between those with the biggest breasts.

A text comes through as I attempt to exit the current conversation I'm reading and I accidentally open it. What I see makes me want to vomit. A text message with a picture of three different pregnancy tests; two have double lines and then a digital one that says pregnant.

> Since you won't answer my calls or texts,
> maybe this will get your attention. What are we
> going to do about this Brady?

"What are you doing?"

I jump up off the couch and turn around to see Brady, popcorn in one hand and two sodas in the other. I should have listened better for the sound of him returning but I couldn't hear anything over my pulse beating loudly in my ears. I hold his phone up so he can see the message I just saw.

"What am I doing? Really? How about what have you been doing, Brady?" The anger is thrumming through my body and I allow it to overcome me, preventing the angry tears that want to be released.

"Who is LJ really, Brady? Because unless what we learned in health class is wrong, two guys can't physically have a baby together."

"What the hell are you talking about?"

"Who is she? And be honest for once with me!" I yell at him, pleading with him to be truthful. How could he do this to me? To us? How could I have been so blind?

"Why the fuck are you going through my phone? I thought you trusted me?"

"I thought I could! But judging from the messages from Shelby, Alicia, Danielle…and God only knows the others I didn't go through, I can't! I was so stupid to even give you a second chance. So, I'm going to ask you again. Who. Is. LJ?"

At that moment, Brady's phone begins to ring and low and behold, LJ is calling. I answer the call, putting it on speaker.

"It's about fucking time you answer me!" the voice snaps and I go still. I know that voice. It's a voice that I have known all through my years of school, a voice that I have stood beside on the sidelines, cheering on our team at games with. It's the very voice of the girl I caught with my boyfriend in the school's parking lot before school started.

"Lydia!?" I gasp.

"Sadie!? What the hell are you doing—"

"What am I doing? That's rich coming from you. Shouldn't I be asking you what *you've* been doing with *my* boyfriend?"

Lydia laughs. Laughs!

"Oh, you mean the boyfriend you have somehow seem to have forgotten about, especially anytime that Peyton chick is around?

"Her name is Payson! And she's just a friend."

"Hmm...could have fooled me. You two looked like you were getting pretty cozy there at my pool party before I came to interrupt your little moment."

"You have no idea what you're talking about Lydia."

"Sure, Sadie. Whatever you got to tell yourself to sleep at night. I've been sleeping like a baby, especially on all those nights Brady dicked me down—"

"Enough!" Brady shouts. He snatches the phone out of my hand and hangs up on Lydia. He tosses the phone onto the couch, his back towards me and his head hanging low. After a minute he turns to face me, crossing his arms at his chest.

"Sadie, look—""No!" I shout at him. I feel the tears welling up, but I'll be damned if I let him see me cry over this, over him. I should have listened to Jenna and Payson. They warned me about him, how much of a tool he was but did I listen? Nope.

Gosh, I'm so freaking stupid!

"Sadie, let me explain—"

"*No*! There is no way to explain yourself out of this!"

"She's lying! *If* she is pregnant, it's not mine. She's just using me to come between us, Sadie! I told you that she is jealous of you. Of us being together!"

My phone alerts me to a new text.

If I know Brady, which I do pretty well (smirk face emoji) he is probably trying to lie his way out of this. Just wanted you to know the evidence is in the due date. It puts my conception date around the time of the pool party and he forgot the condom. Whoops!

Oh and btw. I won't be able to cheer due to my condition. You understand, right?

Attached to the message is an ultrasound. Lydia's name and date of birth along with how far along she is at the top. I go into my calendar to see when the pool party was and count. Sure enough, it lines up. Another message comes in from Lydia; this time, it's of the screenshot of their conversation from that day and a picture of what Lydia wore to convince him to start the stupid argument he purposely pulled on me just so he could go have sex with her.

"There is no lying your way out of this one, Brady."

I quickly grab my things and head for the front door with Brady hot on my heels.

"Are you really going to sit there and believe Lydia over me? Sadie...*Sadie*! Damn it, would you just stop so we can talk?"

I whip around and jab my index finger into his muscular chest.

"There is *nothing* to talk about! Because we are done, Brady. Done! Don't come begging and pleading for me to take you back or hear you out. I was a fool for doing so before, I'm not going to make the same mistake twice. Good luck with *your baby* and Lydia!"

I storm out of Brady's house and quickly jog as far away from him as I can before he thinks to jump in his truck to come after me. I cut through a neighbor's yard to make it to the other block as quickly as I can.

The tears I forcefully held back stream down my face. The betrayal, the anger and all the emotions of feeling unworthy to someone I had given my heart, not to mention my virginity to, overwhelm me and I don't realize where I'm at or where I'm going. I'm in my own world of hurt until a voice calls my name.

"Sadie?"

Chapter 14

Payson's POV

I'm heading to my Jeep after spending the afternoon hanging out with Colton at his place. He needed some help with his math so since there is no practice on Wednesdays, I decided I would come help him out. I was about to get in when I spotted curly blonde hair quickly jogging down the sidewalk. I would recognize that golden haired beauty from a mile away.

"Sadie?" I ask.

She stops and looks around before her eyes fall onto me and that's when I note the black streaks from her mascara running down her cheeks. She's been crying and just a moment ago, she was jogging like she was trying to get away from something or maybe someone?

The thought makes me uneasy, and I quickly go to her. Looking her over, I make sure there are no visible markings on her. If someone laid a hand on her, I will not hesitate to seek them out and make them pay for it.

"Are you okay? Are you hurt?" I ask her, needing her to tell me what's going on.

She sniffles and attempts to wipe the tears away from her eyes.

"Oh my gosh, I'm a hot mess," she exhales. "I'm sorry. Um, where am I exactly?"

"I was just leaving Colton and Thea's house. I'm about to head home. Do...do you need a ride?"

She looks around, glancing over her shoulder. For what, I don't know. Is someone chasing her?

"Yes, I actually could use a ride home. Thank you, Payson."

I nod to her and open the passenger door for her to get in before going to the other side and driving us to her house. Sadie is quiet the whole way. She doesn't make a sound. She just stares out the passenger window, hands trembling and her right knee bouncing. Something is wrong and has her visibly upset which has me worried.

I pull up in front of her house instead of pulling in the driveway when I notice Sadie's red GTO. How come she wasn't in her car since I recall she drove to school today?

"Do you want to tell me what's going on?"

She shakes her head no, not making eye contact with me.

"Sadie, something happened, and it has you really upset. I'm worried about you. You can talk to me, tell me what's going on—"

"Would you like to come in?" She interrupts me. Her eyes go wide before she blushes slightly. "I'm sorry, that was so rude of me for cutting you off." She closes her eyes and shakes her head for a second. "My dad is stuck at the office. My siblings are probably at their friends' houses and my mom is still at Bible study. Jenna has an art class she teaches after school and I'm not sure I want to be alone at the moment."

"Are you sure? I mean, wouldn't you rather have Brady? I don't want this to cause problems for us if he were to find us hanging out together." I'm surprised that wasn't her first choice, being he is her boyfriend.

"No! Absolutely not!" She firmly states.

Okay...Maybe this has something to do with Brady. I want to ask but we made a promise to keep whatever personal business to ourselves if we wanted to be friends.

"Will you please come inside? I could use a friend," she asks.

"Yeah, of course," I tell her.

Sadie gets out and walks up the walkway to her front door. I send a quick text message to my mom telling her I may be home a little later. I tell her a friend really needs me right now and she gives me the okay as long as I'm back before curfew and she will place my plate in the microwave for me.

I lock up my Jeep and jog up to the door as Sadie holds it open for me. I step inside, closing the door behind me, taking a look around. It's a really beautiful home. Cream colored walls with weathered oak floors and trim. The entryway walls are covered in family pictures. I look at a few, enjoying how adorable a small Sadie was in some of them.

She clears her throat, getting my attention and nods for me to follow her up the stairs. She leads me to her bedroom which is at the front of the house. Her walls are painted off white which takes me by surprise. Sadie must have noticed too.

"What is it?" She asks.

"I was kind of expecting the walls to be...red." I shrug. "Cherry red seems to be your favorite color."

"I think my mother would have had a heart attack if I painted my room in red." She lets out a soft chuckle. "I'll be right back. I'm going to freshen up and change really quick. You can sit anywhere you want." She gestures around the room before disappearing through a door that must lead to a bathroom.

I waltz around her room, taking in everything. It's done in white and blush pink with hints of gold here and there. Two windows face the front yard. There's a vanity in between them with a blush pink bench that sits across from her queen size bed. To the left of the room there's two bookshelves going from floor to ceiling surrounding a window and a bench seat underneath. Books upon books fill almost all the shelves. It takes me back to when we started our novella project, how she mentioned she likes to read books with sex in them.

Curiosity gets the best of me as I look through the titles and spot one that catches my attention. It's got a cute cartoon-like cover on it with a really pretty figure skater and some hockey player. I notice there are little colored tabs sticking out. So, I open the book to one of the tabs and begin reading. I choke on my spit as I read out the scene on the page.

"Reading anything interesting?"

I turn around to see Sadie leaning against her door frame to her bathroom. She scrubbed away all the makeup and changed out of her clothes. She's wearing the tiniest red cheer shorts with a white cami tank top that has cherries all over and lace that goes along the straps as well as the hem and top. She looks ethereally beautiful like this, fresh face with not a lick of makeup on.

She nods to the book in my hand, making me realize she asked me a question.

"Oh...yeah. I saw the cover and thought it looked interesting til I went to one of these tab things and started reading. How does a book with a cartoon on the front have vulgar porn like scenes inside?"

Here I thought this was some cute romance story, not something from PornHub. Guess you really can't judge a book by its cover.

Sadie laughs before she walks over to me and grabs the book from my hand.

"This was a great hockey romance. One of those BookTok books I had to get. What's nice is my mom assumes it's a cute romance story but has no idea the things that are inside of them. That's why a lot of romance books I buy have the discreet covers. If my mother saw the ones with half naked men or people on the covers, she would keel over."

"What's with all the tabs and stuff inside? I didn't quite peg you to mark up a book."

"The tabs mark my favorite scenes or quotes."

I give her a sly grin, realizing she must mark up a lot of the sex scenes. Seems like Sadie has a bit of an erotic side to her, which makes me wonder if she would ever want to re-enact some of them. Fuck. The idea alone turns me on, wanting to pick a book at random to find a scene and play them out with her.

What am I saying?

"What? What are you smiling at me like that for?"

"No reason."

"Riiight." She laughs softly before she replaces the book back on her shelf. She goes over to her bed and sits on the edge.

"Are you okay now?" I ask. She seems to be in better spirits, but I don't know if she's just masking it temporarily until I leave.

She lets out a small sigh before pulling her knees to her chest, wrapping her arms around her legs and resting her chin on top.

"Honestly? No." She glances at me, and I can see the glistening in her eyes, like she may cry again. I go to her and crouch down so I can look at her.

"I meant what I said earlier. I'm here for you. I'll listen. Whatever you need, Sadie. I'm here for you."

"I can't...we made that promise."

The pieces start to click together. This must have to do with that pompous asshole and why she refused to have him here.

"This has to do with Brady, doesn't it?" I ask her. She nods her head, hiding her face behind her knees.

"Fuck what we said about that promise, Sadie. We aren't in school, are we?"

She shakes her head, keeping her face hidden behind her knees.

"So, spill. What the fuck did Brady do?".

"We were hanging out at his house, having fun for once. He went to get us snacks to watch a movie and his phone kept going off. I checked his phone to make sure it wasn't his dad or coach but what I saw...I'm such an idiot."

"What did you see?"

"Texts upon texts from different girls. I read some of them, to see if maybe he told them he was taken. News flash: he didn't. He just responded to them. Some I think he may have actually hooked up with. Then there was this LJ. He told me at lunch it was his dad's associate but when the text came through, clearly LJ is not a man because LJ sent a picture of three positive pregnancy tests. That's when Brady caught me going through his phone. I found out LJ just so happens to be Lydia Johnson."

What. The. Fuck.

I stand up and begin pacing back and forth. If there is one thing I cannot stand, it is a cheater. It makes my blood boil, especially seeing how wrecked Sadie is over it.

"Why am I unworthy of love?"

I stop my pacing and glance at Sadie. I'm not sure I heard her right.

"What did you say?"

"Why am I unworthy of love?" she says, louder for me to hear.

"Are you fucking serious right now, Sadie? Unworthy? If anyone is unworthy, it's Brady's dumbass. Not you!"

Sadie shakes her head.

"You don't get it."

"Then explain it to me so I can."

Chapter 15

Payson's POV

Sadie looks up at me from her knees, eyes glistening with tears. The sight of her like this, so vulnerable, makes me want to go to her and encase her in me.

"My dad, he loves me for sure. He loves all of us. But his career as mayor takes up so much of his time. He's hardly home or around to actually spend time with us. I miss our family trips, family dinners. I miss having him home and snuggling next to him watching tv when the world feels too much for me. Or when I'm dealing with something personal. It's his words of wisdom that help get me by. I can't wait for his term to end but I'll be a sophomore in college somewhere when that happens. Since dad is always gone, it just makes things with mom harder. She tries to show she is this happy wife blessed with a beautiful family to everyone in public, but behind these walls, she's something completely different. I've heard arguments with my father at night when they think we are asleep. She yells and screams, saying she feels like his job is a mistress. I think she's just stressed out, feeling like a single parent running the house, cooking dinners. Even when my siblings and I do things to help out, it's never enough. Sometimes I question if dad works so much because he's tired of her complaining all the time when he is home. She's never happy when he is around. She'll fake it in front of my siblings and me and in public but when it's just the two of them, it's always fighting that ensues. I think my dad sleeps on the couch in his office and not in their room."

"If your mom is so unhappy with things, why doesn't she divorce your dad?"

Sadie lets out a short laugh.

"She won't because it's against the word of God. That God's intent is for no one to get divorced and anyone who divorces, it is because they are corrupted by the Devil."

"What is she in? Some religious cult?"

"I wonder about that myself sometimes. Dad never pushes Christianity on us. Said he would rather leave it up to us and what we want to believe in, that we should be focusing on our education and finding ourselves. That really set my mother off. He told her if or when we wanted to commit to the church, we would come to her, to just give us time. But I won't. At least not *that* church. How can a church who are all praise of God and Jesus, about spreading love and kindness also be so hateful towards people because their lives are considered sinful or different? It's why I never go, because I don't think I would be welcomed. I'm too broken, cursed to be worthy of the church."

"What does that mean?"

"I need to confess something to you, something nobody else knows about me except Jenna."

"Should I be in black gown, and shouldn't we be in a box? I mean, correct me if I'm wrong but that's how confessionals usually work right? Hold on."

I make my way to the door beside the bathroom door and sure enough, it's a walk-in closet with all of Sadie's clothes. The girl has everything so nice and neat. Clothes hang in rainbows which makes this next part easy. I spot some of the dresses she has hanging and pull a flowy black summer dress off the hook. I throw it over my clothes and walk back out.

Sadie belly laughs so hard she falls over on her bed.

"What? Does it make my butt look big?" I turn around to show my rear end. Sadie laughs a little more before she finally calms down. At least I got her to laugh. That has to count for something. I go over and pull Sadie up off the bed and walk her over to the bench seat between her bookshelves.

I have her sit on one side. I grab a couple of her books and neatly stack them up to create a barrier before I sit down on the other side. I hear the soft giggle of Sadie and my heart melts just a little at the sound.

"Alright. Now we have our confessional booths. Let us begin."

"You're ridiculous but okay. I'll play along." Sadie sighs. "Excuse me, Father, for I have a confession to make."

"Yes, child. What must you confess?"

There's a pause and I wonder if Sadie is rethinking telling me.

"I think God hates me and makes it impossible for me to be loved because I'm a sin."

"How are you a sin, my child?"

"You see, for a few years now, since sixth grade, I've sort of started looking at girls the same way I would view boys I liked. Maybe even more than I liked boys. I'm not sure why or how to explain it. I really thought something was wrong with me. As I've gotten older, those feelings continue to occur but as of recently, they are even stronger now, particularly towards this one girl."

Hold up. Wait. Is Sadie confessing that she is into girls?

"My ex-boyfriend and I, we had been in a bad spot for the last six months. I found out it's because he's been cheating on me. I allowed him to take my innocence in hopes that it would prove that I am straight. I think he wanted to have sex more but I always found an excuse to decline him so we never had sex again. Anyways, there is this girl who is new to town and I've had these feelings stir up with her. When she's around me, there are all these feelings, feelings I didn't even have with anyone before."

I push the stack of books out of the way, careful not to knock them over and damage them as I stare at Sadie, whose cheeks are tinged pink. Is she implying she has feelings for me?

"What are you saying, Sadie?" I swallow deeply, my eyes locked onto hers, heart racing, anticipating the next words to come out of her pretty pink mouth.

She licks her lips and tucks some of her hair behind her ears.

"I'm saying, Payson, that ever since the pool party, all those small moments we have shared, I have felt things for you that I have never felt towards anybody in my life. And I apologize for any hurt I have caused you when I told you that kiss was a mistake because it wasn't. I lied because I allowed my mother's homophobic voice to get in my head. I allowed her hatred of the gay community to force me to push you into the friend zone. I only gave Brady a second chance because I was trying to repress the feelings I have for you, to force myself straight so my own mother wouldn't reject me if she knew. So she wouldn't kick me out the way her parents did to her own brother." She takes a moment to swallow a lump that must have been building in her throat.

"I had an uncle but he committed suicide, you know? He couldn't take the hate they dished out. He couldn't accept how the very two people who brought him into this world, who promised him when he was a baby to always love and protect him, could just turn around and throw him out like he was trash. All because of who he couldn't help but love."

"That...that is sad and awful, Sadie. I'm so sorry about your uncle. And I'm sorry you have had to feel like you need to disguise your true self out of fear of the same fate as his. But Sadie, you're not broken or a sin. What you feel towards *whoever* is a beautiful gift that God inserts in us, and that gift is love. Love overpowers hate and love is what makes life beautiful. Just as beautiful as you."

There's another tinge of pink and God do I love making her blush. "If you don't mind, I'd like to make a confession myself."

"Go on."

"Before we moved to Bellwood, I had every intention of focusing on school and football. I told myself there would be no dating or hooking up with any girls. But then I met you and it's like I have amnesia. My no dating rule? Completely forgotten. Ever since we met, it has been your smile, your eyes, hell even your scent that I'm thinking about. I don't know why but I can't help but assume that maybe you are who I'm meant to be with. "

"What about Willa?" She tenses her jaw when she says Willa's name and I can't help the smirk that forms on my face.

"Cherry pop, is that jealousy I hear?" I chuckle.

"You two text a lot. Is there something going on between you two?"

"No. Willa tried to come on strongly at first, but I told her straight up I wasn't interested in her. She's got a nice ass, I'll admit it. You caught me staring—"

"Did not!"

"Whatever. The point is, Willa and I chat because it's nice knowing I'm not the only lesbian in this school. Just like your mom, there are homophobic people in this town. I mean we are in the south. Sometimes just having another person who understands certain things helps. I told her I would rather be a friend. Besides, I got her to fix things with her girlfriend. I told her, just be honest with your feelings. Like I am with you."

"Oh?"

"Yeah, oh. I'm crazy about you cherry pop. More so than anyone I have ever dated. You are all I see and think about before I go to sleep and when I wake up. I want to claim you as mine, especially now that I know you do feel something for me. But I also respect how hard a relationship would be with your mom being homophobic. So, if you want to explore and see where things go between us, I'm on board. We can keep it on the downlow if we have to. No one will know and word won't get out. You have my word."

Sadie doesn't say anything before she pulls me close to her and lands her soft lips on mine. Her hands cradle the side of my face, trying to pull me closer to her. I lap at her lips, wanting my tongue inside her mouth and like a good girl, she allows me entry.

I grab Sadie by the waist, pulling her toned body into my lap. Her legs rest on the sides of mine as she straddles me.

There's so much heat and passion. I can feel Sadie's confidence build with each kiss as she takes control, knowing she can be herself with me. I can taste the hint of cherry on her lips and I can't help but smile against them. But it's only for a second before our tongues are battling it out for dominance.

I pull back, needing to catch my breath but not before pressing my forehead with hers.

"I have another confession to make."

"What must you confess?"

"I'm scared."

She looks a bit confused.

"I'm scared I'm going to fall head over heels in love with you. That's how crazy I am for you."

There is something about her that's so different, no simple way to explain what it is. I'm constantly thinking about her when I'm away from her, wondering what she is doing or if she is thinking of me. She's the last person on my mind before I go to sleep and the person I'm most excited to see when I wake up. When I'm around her, I forget all the stress of football and school and I can just breathe. Kind of like the beach I would go to back in California when I needed to escape and ground myself. She's becoming my own personal Zen, my California beach. I think she really will be my undoing. I mean, I'm already throwing away my no dating policy for her. As I stare into her gorgeous blue eyes, blue as the Pacific Ocean, I want nothing more than to be closer to her.

I stand and Sadie instinctively wraps her long legs around my waist. I walk us to her bed before I set her back on her dainty feet. I remove her black dress I put on, crawl onto her bed, and prop my head up on the countless pillows that sit on it. I point my finger at her and gesture for her to come to me and Sadie obeys.

She crawls on top of me, pressing her body on top of mine and we take our time, our mouths just exploring and getting to know each other. There is so much heat between us and the desire to taste her is driving me insane.

"Do you trust me?" I ask her when we take a breather.

"Of course."

"Take those teasing things you call shorts off and sit on my face."

"What!?"

"You heard me. Remove the shorts and panties so I can taste your other lips."

She hesitates for a second before getting off her bed and makes a show of slowly removing them. She's teasing me and damn, if I'm not turned on even more but I won't be the one getting off. Only Sadie.

She crawls back onto the bed and slowly raises my shirt, exposing my toned abs. She slowly kisses up my belly, between my breasts, working her way to my neck, sucking lightly. A small moan escapes me as she hits that sensitive spot on my neck that drives me crazy and she has the audacity to smirk, knowing she found my spot. I reach out and place a finger on her lips to stop her.

"As much as I would love you to mark me, cherry pop, I want to make you feel good. Now, sit on my face while I devour you."

Sadie doesn't budge and she hesitates.

"Sadie, you don't have to do it if you don't want to. I will *never* force you to do anything you are uncomfortable doing."

"It's not that. I want to, it's just...what if I suffocate you?"

She's afraid she will snuff the life out of me? Does she know that would be the best way to go?

"You won't. I promise you. Now, get that sweet ass of yours up here."

Sadie makes her way slowly and straddles my face. She lowers herself but not completely. Guess I'm going to have to show her how it's done.

"I didn't say hover, cherry pop."

I reach up, my hands grabbing her thighs and yank her down onto my mouth. I flick my tongue over her clit, and I hear a gasp escape Sadie's lips. I glide my tongue around her entrance, slowly, moving it around, down and back up to her clit where I suck it into my mouth. The moan that comes out of her is so sexy, I feel myself getting wet in my own boxer briefs.

I pick up the pace just slightly, adding in one finger before two. I move them in and out of her pussy slowly, along with my tongue. Letting her get the feel of the intrusion. I move my tongue out, fingers still inside her and gently graze her clit with my teeth. I pull her clit between my soft lips again before flattening my tongue, lapping at her.

Sadie starts to grind my face, chasing after her release. Her moans are loud, filling her room and it's the sweetest melody to my ears. I pick up my pace as Sadie's pussy starts to grip my fingers like a vise. She's so wet that my fingers are coated with her juices.

"Oh, God. Payson...don't stop," Sadie pants out. "I'm so close!"

"Come for me, Sadie. Give me your release and come all over my tongue," I tell her. I suck on her clit, a little harder than before and Sadie's orgasm rips through her. Her grinding comes to a stop slowly before she crawls off and snuggles into my side.

"Wow...that was...incredible," Sadie pants out.

"You've never done that before, have you?" I ask.

"No, um. I'm pretty inexperienced. I've only had sex once, with Brady, and it wasn't as pleasurable. Not the way everyone makes it out to be. He also didn't like the idea of going down on me after I gave him a blow job."

Clearly Brady is selfish in the bedroom too. He likes to receive rather than give. Whatever. Sadie is his loss and my gain. I'll go down on her anytime, any day if I get to hear those moans and my name come out of her lips. I kiss her forehead as she snuggles into my side. We lay there in silence, me running my hand up and down her spine.

A door opens downstairs and closes.

"Anyone home?" a female voice yells from the entryway.

Sadie springs from the bed.

"Shit! That's my mom!"

She runs and grabs her panties and shorts, pulling them up quickly before running to her vanity to check herself over. I hop off the bed and pull her back into my front.

"You're perfect," I whisper in her ear before I kiss her quickly and dash into the bathroom. I grab the little paper cup sitting on the bathroom sink and rinse my mouth out with mouthwash. As much as I would love to have the taste of Sadie lingering on my lips, I decided it would be better to just freshen up. After all, I'm about to meet Sadie's mom.

Chapter 16

Sadie's POV

"Hey, you're home." My mother says as she enters my room. I guess she could hear me from downstairs as I made a dash to make sure I looked like I didn't just have the best orgasm of my life.

"Yeah. Sorry I meant to message you."

Of course, at that moment Payson decides to waltz out of my bathroom, full smile upon her gorgeous face. My mom looks at her and I already have an idea what is going through her head.

Payson is dressed in light distressed jeans with a basketball jersey on. Her hat is on backwards and she looks so good. But to my mother, these are flags. Flags that are probably going to lead to a lecture the moment Payson leaves.

"Who are you?" my mom asks. There's a subtle hint of ignorance to her tone.

"My apologies. I'm Payson. Payson Moore." Payson reaches her hand out to shake my mother's hand. It kind of shocks me to see her be so polite, especially knowing my mother's true feelings toward people like her. My mom hesitates at first before she shakes Payson's hand and quickly puts it behind her. I don't miss the subtle wipe of her hand on her skirt.

"Sadie and I have English class together. I was dropping her off when I asked if I could use the bathroom before heading home."

"Oh. Well, there's a bathroom downstairs off the entryway–"

"I needed her help with our project for class and I had the paper up here." I cut my mother off despite how much she hates when I do that. I knew what she was implying, and Payson doesn't deserve whatever she was going to say. "We were able to figure it out though. Thank you again, Payson."

"No problem. I'm happy to have helped." She gives me a quick wink and dear Lord, please don't let my face give us away. My heart is already racing as it is having these two in the same room.

"Allow me to walk you out," I tell Payson. Payson follows me back downstairs to the front door. I glance back to see if my mom followed behind, but I don't see her.

"I'm so sorry," I whisper to Payson.

"Don't be. It's not something I haven't dealt with before," she shrugs. "I'll text you when I get home." She pulls me into a hug, and I squeeze her, relishing her body against mine. Before Payson pulls away, she whispers in my ear.

"I'm going to be dreaming of you and those moans tonight." She gives me a wink before she's out the door and in her Jeep, driving away from me and my house along with a piece of my heart.

The next few days go by in a blur. I guess time flies when you're happy and falling for someone so amazing. Did I say falling? It's more like tumbling down a never-ending flight of stairs.

Payson and I made sure to make the most of spending time together outside of school. We went to dinner at Gary's Diner after practice on Thursday before taking a walk around Bells Lake, which is about a twenty-minute drive on the outskirts of Bellwood. I almost missed curfew that night because it got dark early, and we almost got lost. Friday, we went to the shopping mall for pizza after school and then competed against each other at the arcade center. I learned to be cautious of competing against Payson. She nearly took my head off with the table hockey puck when I was ahead by 20 points. Afterwards we went to Payson's house where I got to meet her family briefly before they left to go to Colton and Thea's house.

We spent Friday night snuggled under a blanket on the family couch watching one of those Scary Movie films. I don't recall much of what it was about because Payson and I were too busy sucking the souls from each other. I love the way she kisses me. She makes me feel desired and if I'm being honest, aroused. We almost went to her bedroom, but her family came back from their visit to the Reynolds house, and I decided I needed to get home.

The feelings I thought I felt before, when I was fighting against them, are nothing compared to being free from Brady and allowing myself to explore my feelings with Payson. She is so caring and tentative, always thinking of me and ensuring I never have to question my worth when I'm with her.

Brady has made attempts to talk to me at school since I broke up with him. After Payson left Wednesday evening, I turned my phone on only to be bombarded with so many voicemails and texts from Brady. After the twelfth missed call, I sent him a text to tell him there was nothing he could do or say to make me forgive him. I had the proof I needed to see for us to be done for good. Then I blocked him.

He hasn't had any luck though. I make sure I'm always around people to shield me away from him, but I guess luck has run out on my side today. The doorbell rang as I was about to go upstairs. I answered the door to find Brady standing before me on my front porch like someone ran over his dog. I don't understand him and why he's hell bent on talking when it looked like he never cared about me at all. His loss. Not mine.

"What do you want, Brady?" I ask in a tone laced with venom at the sight of him.

"You blocked me. I can't call you or text you, you even blocked me on your socials."

"Yes, I'm aware of that. So why are you here?"

"I screwed up, Sadie. Okay? I cheated on you and I'm sorry. It-it was a mistake—"

I let out a maniacal laugh, cutting him off. "A mistake? Really? No, Brady. A mistake is a misguided action or judgment, none of which you did when you sent pictures of your dick to several other girls or slipped it inside of them over and over, impregnating one. That wasn't a mistake, Brady. That was a choice you chose to make repeatedly. A mistake was me giving you a second chance you didn't deserve. And you can most certainly count there will not be a third chance. I learned my lesson. We. Are. Done!"

"Just like that? C'mon Sadie. Please—"

"No!" I say loudly, holding my palm out in front of his face. "You need to leave now. I have a game to get ready for just as much as you do. We're playing Wimbleton tonight and you need to focus on beating our rivals."

Before he could say another word, I shut the door on his face, ending our conversation. If there is one thing I do know about Brady, its football is a huge priority to him. So, if I have to pull the football card to get him to leave, so be it.

Chapter 17

Sadie's POV

It's a brisk October Saturday evening. Temperatures are around 57 degrees, reminding us summer is gone and fall is here. The crowd is fired up for one of our biggest rivalry games in our region. The stands are packed to the brim with students, teachers, and families. The high school band is playing music, getting everybody riled up for game time. People are decked out in school colors. Our crowd is rocking the Carolina blue, white and gold whereas Wimbleton's side is rocking their burgundy, gold and black.

"Welcome friends, family and guests to Bellwood High School Stadium! We've got one heck of a game ahead of us with the biggest rivals going toe to toe to see who loses their undefeated streak. Will it be our guests, the Wimbleton Wildcats?" the announcer asks.

Our side chants and cheers while Wimbleton boos.

"Or will it be our Bellwood Eagles? I don't know folks but I'm excited. So, let's get this game rolling!"

Wimbleton's intro music begins to play and the announcer runs through their roster as they enter the field.

That's my que. I gather up the squad and we run out to the home goal posts to get ready for our team to be announced. Stacey and Mariah are sitting on Eric and Joel's shoulders holding the banner up for the football players to run through while Marcus will set off the blue smoke bomb as soon as the music starts up for the home team.

Varsity Eagles are in our end zone with all the coaches. They huddle in the circle and I can hear Payson hyping the team up.

"This is our house! They are invading our turf and we need to send those pansy ass Wildcats crawling back to their school with a big L! So if you're with me, I need to know! Who's going to come out on top tonight!?"

"We are!" The team answers her.

"I can't hear you. I said WHO'S GOING TO TAKE THE WIN TONIGHT?"

"WE ARE!"

"WHO'S GOING TO KEEP THEIR UNDEFEATED STREAK?"

"WE ARE!"

"Hands in. Eagles on three. One, two, three!"

"EAGLES!"

The group turns, ready for battle. After that speech, I feel myself amped up. I catch Payson's eyes, peeking through her helmet, staring at me and I give her a wink for good luck.

The music starts, Marcus lets off the smoke bomb and the home fans are going wild. You can hear them screaming, chanting and stomping their feet against the metal stands.

We shake our poms as the announcer introduces our team.

"Here they are, your home team. The BELLWOOD EAGLES!"

The team charges through our tunnel, ripping through the banner and running to the 50-yard line before going to the benches. Once the team has made it through, we return to the sidelines, ready to cheer our team on.

"Step aside! Ready? Okay!" I yell for the first cheer to start us off.

"Step aside. We're coming through. Wildcats, we're after you!" our squad chants. We repeat two more times before we do jumps and kicks and turn to face the field again.

"Looks like our Eagles will start with the ball and quarterback, number thirteen Payson Moore will be starting us off tonight. Let's see what Moore and company can do."

The ball is snapped and Payson catches it. The offensive line is holding the defense back. Payson spots Colton and passes it quickly down the field. Colton catches the pass and manages to run a few yards before he's brought down.

"What a beautiful pass by Moore, caught by number eighty-two, Colton Reynolds for a gain of 15 yards. Eagles get the first down!"

The crowd cheers as do we. Our team manages to get the ball all the way down the field where we can score a touchdown. Payson passes the ball to Chad right into the end zone, and we get the first score! Eagles get the extra point and now it's Wimbleton's turn to try to score. They manage to get down to the 30-yard line in Eagles territory before Jeremiah intercepts the ball!

"Interception made by number fifty-two, Jeremiah Thompson! He's going folks... still going. Don't let off the gas, Thompson! To the thirty, the twenty, the ten, touchdown, Eagles!"

It's almost halftime and we are up by two touchdowns. Our offense and defense have been on fire. Jeremiah orchestrates the defense, making the big stops and preventing the Wildcats from making any big plays. Payson has had no trouble getting the ball to anyone open. Seeing her in her element, seeing her take charge of the team and somehow manage to get the ball to go where she needs it is absolutely amazing. Her passion, her heart, it's all out there on the field.

The refs blow the whistle, signaling the end of the second quarter and the start of halftime. The players go off to their prospective sides while us cheerleaders take the field. We finally get to run through our competition routine and showcase it for our hometown. To say I'm a little nervous is an understatement. We get into our positions and wait for the announcer to start our music.

"Adams!" I hear someone familiar shout.

I glance up to see her staring at me. She mouths, "You got this." before sending me a thumbs up. If my heart could fly away at the support and encouragement, it would.

I return to facing the ground and the music starts. We run through our routine. All our jumps in tune, flyers hitting their stunts altogether, the tumbling sequence flowing in an art of flips and leaps. The dance gets the crowd whistling and shouting and before long we end with our finale of a pyramid that ends right as the music does. The crowd goes wild, and I can feel their energy, their pride flowing through. I jump up and down, squealing with excitement at how well this squad pulled it together for its first live performance. If we can repeat this at the competition in January, we are sure to claim first place!

Everyone clears the field for bathroom and snack breaks while the marching band and color guard go out to perform for the crowds next.

Stacey and I are standing in the concession stand line when Jenna runs up to us.

"Oh my God, you guys killed that routine!" she exclaims.

"We did? It wasn't too bad?" I ask. I came up with the majority of the routine whereas Stacey choreographed the dance. It was a first for us both and I was nervous about how well we did.

"Girl, would I lie to you?"

"I don't know. Maybe?"

"Never!" Jenna exclaims and we burst out laughing.

"Who's that?" Stacey asks. Jenna and I turn in the direction she's staring at only to see Brady talking to some girl.

"I don't know and quite frankly don't care. We are broken up for good so he's free to talk to whoever he wants."

"Wait, what? When did this happen?" Stacey asks.

"Wednesday. I went through his phone and found all the messages he's been sending to all the girls he's talked to or talking to behind my back. He got Lydia pregnant which is why she is no longer on the squad."

"WHAT!?" Stacey shouts too loudly, causing a few people in front of us to turn and give us funny looks.

"Brady Thomas knocked somebody else up?"

We turn around to look at the person who asked the question behind us. It's a pretty girl around our age, with flowy blonde hair and pretty blue eyes wearing a Wimbleton High School hoodie and skinny jeans.

"Sorry, I wasn't eavesdropping. It's just, the girl he's talking to is pregnant by him," she says sheepishly.

I look back at Brady and the girl before I spot the baby bump. It's a bit more protruded like she's farther along, further than Lydia.

"Her name is Taylor and she's a junior at Wimbleton."

At that moment, a girl who looks familiar goes up to Taylor, says something to Brady which causes him to glare at her before she takes Taylor's hand, and they walk off.

"Oh, hey there's Keri! She's Taylor's cousin and the two of them are very close."

"Close enough that she would slap and spit on him in a cafeteria full of people?" Jenna asks while glaring daggers in Brady's direction. No wonder the other girl looked familiar.

"Yeah, that sounds about right. Keri is very protective of her family. She actually used to go to Wimbleton but was kicked out for beating the crap out of a kid who bullied a family member of hers. I wondered where she ended up."

I feel a lump form in my throat.

"Can I ask, do you know how far along Taylor is? Brady and I dated for two years, and I recently broke up with him because I found out about him cheating on me."

"I think I heard she's like four or five months along. She honestly hasn't even looked pregnant until the other day and the belly sort of just popped. Rumors were going around school, trying to figure out who the dad is but she never gave up a name. I'm guessing Keri found out from Taylor and confronted Brady at school if Bellwood is where she attends now. He's been denying it's his, but Taylor has never had a boyfriend. She always cared about her schooling more than dating. She attended our end of school bonfire party and caught Brady's attention. They disappeared from the bonfire later that evening. I'm sure she had no idea he was taken. He had a lot of girls all over him at the party like he was single. If she wasn't drunk, I don't think she would have slept with him. There were rumors that she was a virgin so her being pregnant was a shock to our school. I'm sorry he was so unfaithful to you."

She gives me a sympathetic look and I hate it. I don't need sympathy from anyone for having an ex who couldn't keep his penis in his pants.

I give her a hug and squeeze her. "Thank you for telling me that. You have no idea how much I appreciate it, knowing I made the smart choice to dump him."

"Oh, you made a very smart choice," she beams.

"If you will excuse me," I say and walk away from the line. I'm so overcome with emotions, the biggest one being hurt. Every time I think Brady couldn't do worse than what he's already done, I'm proven again how wrong I've been.

As I walk past Brady, he reaches for my arm and stops me.

"Hey!"

"Let go of me!" I spew with as much hatred as I possibly can. "I have nothing to say to you!" I glance around to make sure no one is watching us. I don't need to cause a scene with the town's beloved quarterback.

"What's your fucking deal?"

"My deal? I saw you talking to Taylor." Brady grimaces when I mention her name. "Yeah Brady. I know about Taylor, and I know you have two babies on the way. Not one Brady, but *two*! I can't even look at you without feeling disgusted with myself for thinking that I gave my virginity to you, thinking you were worthy of it. I loved you for two years and what did I get in return? Oh, right, I got lied to and cheated on. You made me believe that you actually loved and cared about me, but it was all just a lie. What was I even to you? Why not have the decency to just break up with me if you were not fully committed to us? Two years, all for nothing?"

"It wasn't for noth—"

"Save it Brady. I don't want to hear your pathetic lies."

I brush past him, ending our conversation. I walk until I spot Payson near the bathrooms talking to Colton and his friends. As if sensing my eyes on her, she looks around until her eyes lock with mine and she gives me her beautiful, dimply smile. One I don't see her give to anyone else.

A sense of calmness overtakes me, and it is that moment that it dawns on me. Payson is my security, my safe place. She is my peace.

Chapter 18

Payson's POV

"So, how are things with you and Stacey?" I ask Colton. They have been hanging out frequently but there hasn't been confirmation if the two of them are a couple.

"We're good. Taking our time, just enjoying each other's company, you know?"

"Is that code for sleeping with each other?" Rhett elbows Colton in his side.

"No. We literally are just taking things slow. I really like her and she likes me. We just want to play it by ear and see where things go. Not everything has to be about sex."

"Are you two going to homecoming together?" Jeremiah asks, changing the subject.

"Going tomorrow to get my tux fitted," he beams. "Y'all going solo, or do you have dates too?"

"I was thinking of asking Thea if that's okay with you Colt?" Zealand says. I'm not sure if he's joking or being serious until Colton gives him the look of death and Zealand lifts his hands. "I'm kidding, dude. Just getting under your skin. Besides, Jeremiah and I are going solo. Much more fun when we can dance with as many girls as we want."

"What about you, Payson? Are you taking Willa?" He leans in to whisper, "Or do you have a certain cute blonde you want to take?" before leaning back, waggling his eyebrows. He's the only person I trust enough to tell how things have been between Sadie and I. I also trust him not to blab about it around the school or town. I want Sadie to trust me since she has some trust issues because of Brady but I also want to protect her from the backlash her mother may reap on her. Judging by the brief interaction with Mrs. Adams, I got the vibe she is definitely not a woman I would want to cross or upset.

"Nah. Willa and I are just friends. Besides, she said she is taking her girlfriend."

At that moment, I feel the hairs on my neck rise and the sensation that I'm being watched. I look around until I spot the steely blue eyes burning their gaze into me. She's dressed in her Carolina blue, gold and white cheer outfit paired with a long sleeve under her shell and leggings that cling to those beautiful, toned legs. Her hair is in a high ponytail, held with a sparkly bow that matches her uniform. Light makeup is dusted upon her face, showing off her natural beauty.

"Excuse me fellas," I tell them, and I head in her direction. When I get close enough to her, Sadie grabs my hand and drags me behind her, pulling me to where I don't know. But wherever it is, I'll follow her anywhere like a lovesick puppy. *Lovesick?* The L word alone makes my palms sweat. No way can I be falling this hard for this girl.

We go through the stadium entrance and out to where the parking lot meets the sidewalk. Sadie pulls me around the side of the brick building, into the dark shadows where she surprises me by shoving me against the brick wall before pulling my face to hers. Her soft lips greet mine and

I'm suddenly encased in her cherry vanilla scent. Sadie bites down on my bottom lip, tugging it gently into her mouth and I let out a soft moan.

"Shhh. We don't need anyone to hear us." Sadie whispers against my lips. I grab Sadie's wrists into my left hand and spin her around, forcing Sadie's back against the wall. I hold her wrists above her head, which causes Sadie's chest to heave. Clearly this move has an effect on her. I take my finger and gently run it along the side of her face, feeling the sparks that ignite between us tingling at my fingertip.

"Does this turn you on, baby girl?"

"Y-y-yesss," she whispers back.

I continue tracing my finger down her side, gently brushing the side of her breast and down to her midsection, causing Sadie to squirm in my hold.

"Are you wet for me, cherry pop?"

Before she can answer, I dip my finger under the band of her skirt, feeling the soft silk of her panties as I reach for her pussy and stroke her gently. I run my finger from the bottom, slowly up to her clit, feeling her arousal coat my finger. As I brush her clit on the way back from pulling my finger out, Sadie lets out a soft gasp. I keep my eyes focused on hers as I suck her wetness from my finger.

"Mmm...so sweet and wet for me."

Sadie takes me by surprise and leans forward to kiss me. The fact she is willing to kiss me while I have the taste of her on my lips does something for me. This time I kiss back with a fervor of want and need. Our tongues battle it out for dominance and God, do I wish we were somewhere private right now. I want to make Sadie moan, quivering from orgasm after orgasm and come all over my face.

Our heated moment gets interrupted by the speakers overhead as the announcer gives a two-minute warning that the second half of the game will begin soon.

I press my forehead against Sadie's, relishing in our moment.

"What are you doing to me?" I whisper to her.

"I don't know. I could ask the same question."

We give each other a sweet kiss before we head back through the stadium entrance and back to the field. Sadie gives me a hug, but whispers in my ear, "Win the game and I may have something special planned for you later. Go kick some Wildcat butt for me."

She pulls back with a devious smile and gives me a wink before darting back to the track where the rest of the squad is gathering.

Damn. How am I supposed to play after hearing that?

"Well, well, well. If that isn't the most disgustingly adorable thing I ever did see."

I turn around only to come face to face with the long-haired brunette who kicked me out of her party over the summer.

"Excuse me?"

"You and Sadie. You two make quite a cute pair. Too bad she's just using you."

I feel my heart drop in my stomach. Using me? Sadie wouldn't use me. She's not that type of person.

"I'm sorry, I-I don't know what you're talking about. Sadie and I are just friends." I start to walk away from her, not needing her ignorance to distract me from the game. "Right. Like I didn't witness your whole make out sesh out front. Gross, by the way."

I stop dead in my tracks, feeling knots grow in my gut. Lydia just saw Sadie and I make out? This could get ugly. Lydia would completely rat Sadie out and then everyone would know, including her mother and potentially making Sadie's life hell.

I turn around to face her. "What do you mean she's using me?" I cross my arms, bracing for whatever Lydia has to say.

"What? You can't tell she's using whatever feelings you have for her to piss off Brady? To get under his skin? Wow. You must be in deep if you can't see what's happening. I mean, she had a confrontation with Brady right before she took off with you for your little rendezvous sesh. He watched you whisk her away. The guy was practically envisioning all the ways to murder you when he saw the direction you two were headed. That's when I stepped in. I told him he needed to focus on the game and to forget about her. He knows where the two of you ran off to. That little spot you were just in? It's Brady's spot. The perfect little sneak away when he wanted to make out with Sadie or get his dick sucked. Sadie, of course, refused to do anything sexual with him after she gave her virginity to him. So, I happily took advantage of the opportunity. That's how he's managed to have an undefeated home record. My blowjobs gave him the relief he needed to pull out the wins."

"If this is your way of offering to give me head, I decline."

"Ew, gross. Completely not interested. But if you don't believe me, look for yourself." She points over to the sidelines.

Brady is saying something to Sadie. I'm not sure what they are saying to each other but the moment she moves away from him, Brady looks upset.

"Poor guy. Pretty sure Sadie just told him about the two of you making out. It's okay. I'll make sure he forgets all about her," Lydia sneers before she walks off back to the bleachers.

I jog back over to the benches as the timer on the scoreboard quickly ticks down to signal the second half. Brady spots me and the look he is giving me is pure hatred. Could Lydia be right? Is Sadie just using me to get under Brady's skin for how badly he hurt her?

Chapter 19

Payson's POV

Second half begins with Wimbleton in possession. Our defense holds them back and before long, it's a turnover on downs.

"Moore, lead the offense down the field and get us ahead. I want to knock Wimbleton off their high horse," Coach Watson says.

"Yes Coach!" I shout, excitement thrumming through my body. I shove my helmet on and jog out onto the field. We got sixty yards to get into the endzone and I know the perfect play to call.

"Alright boys. Time to send these pussies home crying. Eagles play on three. Three!"

Our huddle claps and we go to the line.

"Eagles...Eagles..." I look to my left and right, ensuring my line acknowledges which play I'm calling. When I see all their nods, I call for the ball.

snaps the ball to me, and my linemen make the proper blocks. I look for and spot him running down the field and throw the ball in his direction. It lands in his arms beautifully right before he's taken down by a Wildcat defender. We just gained twenty yards, moving the chains, and claiming our first down.

We managed to get down to the 10-yard line but their defense upped their game and we had to settle for a field goal. Our punter takes the field to punt the ball and defense takes over. I remove my helmet and drop down on the bench, realizing my hair tie broke. Now my hair is a hot mess from sweating, and I need to do something with it.

"Want some help?" I hear the melodious voice of the only girl who can make my heart skip and flutter at the same time.

"If you want."

Sadie stands behind me and the bench. She makes quick work of a french braid, tying off the bottom with one of her own hair ties before coming around and inspecting her work.

"Perfect, just like you." She says softly before giving me her beautiful white smile and walking back over to the sidelines.

I watch her walk away from me before I hear the deep chuckling of my least favorite person.

"Wow, she really is making a show isn't she? For someone who doesn't want other people to know, I'm surprised."

"What the fuck are you talking about?" I don't give Brady any of my attention. I turn my focus to the field. Defense is trying to hold the Wildcats off, but they pull a trick play and the Wildcats are now in our territory. Fuck. They are about to score if our defense doesn't hold them back.

"I'm just saying, she's doing what she can to get back at me for all the hurt I caused her. I get it. I really fucked up. Now she thinks she can hurt me too by showing affection to the new QB who's stealing my spot. Got to say, it's working. Should have known the girl has a type. Hey, maybe she will try to get with Wimbleton's quarterback next. What do you think? Want to make a bet on it?"

I let out a low growl. "I think you're a piece of shit who can't handle the fact you lost out on someone incredible and are just sour that she won't take you back."

He shrugs. "Maybe. But at least I'm not the one being used to make an ex jealous." He walks away from me, leaving me to my thoughts.

First Lydia. Now Brady. Are they trying to get in my head or am I the one blinded by my feelings for Sadie?

Third quarter becomes a challenge. Their defense started playing dirty, taking out a few of our key players and stopping our guys from getting down the field. The Wildcats score again and now there's only a three point difference. We have to beat this team. I have to show these guys the leader I am and that we can pull out a win.

You can feel the energy shift in the stadium as we are battling it out and it's starting to get to me. I'm on the sidelines, in my head. I smell her before I realize she's kneeling in front of me.

"What are you doing?" I ask Sadie.

"I can see this is getting to you and I just want to remind you of the badass QB you are. You got this game in the bag. I know it and you know it too. Bring home the win for us, Moore." She leans in like she's going to whisper a secret but presses a quick kiss to my cheek before darting away. I watch her go, giving me a smile before she looks over my head and gets back into her spot. I turn to see Brady, looking between me and Sadie. There's the slightest hint of hurt on his face before he masks it, returning to watch the game.

"Words of encouragement from the cheer Captain?" Colton asks as he sits beside me. "You know, I don't think she has done that for Brady."

Before I can ask what he means, it's time to get back on the field and get us ahead again. But I'm too inside my head and distracted. First play, I overthrow the ball, completely missing Colton and the ball goes to the sidelines. Second play, I try to hand the ball to Sanchez, but it gets fumbled, and I quickly recover it.

C'mon Payson. Get your fucking head in the game!

I glance over in Sadie's direction for some encouragement from her, but I see her glowering off to the side. I follow her line of sight only to see it's at Brady talking to Lydia by the gate. She dumped him because he was messing with her so why is she not ignoring them like usual? Or is this how she is when I'm not paying attention?

I feel my temper rising and I don't like this feeling.

I make the next play call. The ball is in my hands but before I can make a pass, I'm knocked down so hard the wind gets knocked out of me. A sharp pain shoots through my right shoulder and now I'm more pissed that my throwing arm is injured. I just hope the injury isn't too serious. I need to play. I need football like my next breath if I'm ever going to achieve my dreams.

Chapter 20

Sadie's POV

The moment the crowd gasps and the stands seem to go quiet, like someone turning the volume down on a tv, I redirect my focus to the field. Wimbleton is back on their side while our players are kneeling meaning someone on our team is hurt. But who?

I quickly scan the sidelines then the field, looking for the Carolina blue jersey with the number thirteen on it. But I don't see it. My heart is racing, hoping that it isn't Payson who is hurt.

Before long, everyone is clapping as the coaches and medic move aside and Payson emerges from the middle, clutching her right shoulder. I close my eyes and send a prayer up that Payson isn't too seriously hurt, that it's a minor injury and she can get back to playing in time for the homecoming game next week.

I watch as Payson goes to the bench, removing her pads and sits down. Colton hands her an ice pack and she places it on her shoulder, head to the sky. I can't imagine what could possibly be going on in her head at this moment. Football means something to her.

Brady went out on the field as Payson came off, but I'm not focused on the game anymore. Stacey had to nudge me to refocus a few times to do some more cheers but it's hard when all my focus is solely on Payson.

The game finally comes to an end with the Eagles taking the victory. We beat Wimbleton by a field goal in the last few seconds and our undefeated streak continues. The crowd is crazy with joy and excitement but it's hard to celebrate and share in their joy when you are worried for the person you care about most.

I grab my things and head out to my car in the parking lot. I purposely parked next to Payson's Jeep so I could tell her where to meet me for our date night. I have a romantic evening planned out but now I'm worried it's going to be hindered by her injury.

"Sadie!"

I look around for who yelled my name before I notice the Wildcats quarterback is jogging up to me. Jake Ashcroft. He used to be a neighborhood friend until his parents split. His mom moved them to Wimbleton's school district, and we have kept in touch when we can.

"Hey Jake!" I give him a warm smile and hug. He's always felt like the older brother I wish I had, even if he's older by a few weeks. "You played great out there."

"Thanks, but your team still kicked our butts," he chuckles. "Wanted to ask, the QB who got hurt was a girl?"

I feel a tinge of jealousy rise in me. "Yeah. Payson Moore. She's into girls, so–"

"Whoa, whoa, not like that. I wanted to ask because some of the team didn't believe it. I've heard of her when she was in California, and she was a big deal. It was amazing to see her play in person tonight. She's extremely talented. I just wanted to see if you heard anything about her shoulder. I hope it's not serious."

Now I feel like an idiot.

"Oh, um, no. I haven't seen the team come out of the locker room yet. But I hope it's not serious either."

He turns to the parking lot as some of his teammates yell for him.

"Sorry. I got to go but it was great seeing you, Sadie. Message me when you hear something?"

"Yeah of course."

He jogs off to meet with his teammates and I watch as they go.

"Wow. It's like that, is it?"

I jolt at the voice, turning around to see Payson standing in her game pants and tank top. Her right shoulder is wrapped in a bandage and she's holding an ice pack to it. Colton is behind her, carrying their football gear and Payson's helmet.

"Hey, you. I was so worried! How is your shoulder?" I go towards her, but she stops me with her arm held out, keeping me at an arm's distance. "Is it bad?"

"The shoulder's fine," she clips. I'm not sure why Payson is being so short with me and it's honestly making me nervous.

"Did you still want to go out—"

"No." It's a stern, flat no. I don't like the way that no sounded or how she cuts me off so harshly. "You know what I want to know? I want to know why I caught you hugging the quarterback of our rival team? Why does he want you to message him when you hear something? Huh? What exactly does he want to hear, Sadie?"

I'm not sure if Payson is jealous or possessive but I'm not liking this side of her.

"Why are you being like this, Payson?"

"Answer me, Sadie!" She says with a tone like she's admonishing me as if I'm some petulant child.

"First off, you don't talk to me like that, okay? You're making me feel like I did something wrong, and I haven't—"

"Riiight. Right, that's what they all say until you find out the whole truth." She shakes her head before turning her beautiful eyes to me. Only this time, the way her eyes look at me don't give me butterflies like they normally do. Instead, I feel like I'm the enemy and her eyes want to laser me out of existence.

"You know what, Sadie. I've changed my mind. I don't want to know. I should have kept to my original plan, but you caught me off guard, knocked me on my ass. But I should have known better. I mean, how we started should have been a sign right?" She takes a moment before she speaks again. "I can't go through this again. I'm not doing this. I can't risk being… You and me, Sadie?" she waves a finger back and forth between us, "We are done. I don't want anything to do with you. I've finished my portion of the English project and I will email it to you for you to work with and submit it. I'm not that shallow to fail the both of us our senior year. But other than that, I want nothing to do with you."

"Payson, you can't be—" I feel the tears swell in my eyes, blurring my vision. My throat swells like a golf ball is lodged in it and my heart feels like it's ready to shatter into a million pieces.

Colton opens the passenger door of the Jeep and Payson climbs inside. He tosses her bag in the back seat before making his way to the driver's side. He gives me an apologetic look before hopping in and driving off.

I stand there, frozen in place. Unable to move or think. Trying to piece together what went wrong for Payson to just completely freeze me out, to forget the beautiful few days we just had together and be rid of me. My cell phone vibrates, bringing me back to reality. I wipe away the few tears that snuck out before climbing into my car and driving home. I make a dash of getting to my room, not wanting to deal with my mother or anyone else in the house.

I close my bedroom door, drop all my things in the middle of my room and throw myself onto my bed. The tears stream down my face and I let the heartbreak consume me. I grab one of my pillows and press it into my face, not caring that I have smudged makeup from my tears or snot coming out of my nose. I scream into the pillow as my heart shatters, replaying Payson's hurtful words in my head.

How is it this hurts far worse than finding out the guy you thought you loved was cheating on you for months?

<h1 style="text-align:center">Chapter 21</h1>

Sadie's POV

The next few days after the game against Wimbleton feel bleary. Sunday, I ended up staying in my room, crying and sleeping the day away. It's the best way to spend the day you turn eighteen after having your heart broken in my opinion.

My father was actually home for once. He came to bring me my birthday breakfast in bed but when he saw what a mess I was, I feigned I wasn't feeling well. He left me to rest along with the breakfast he made but I couldn't eat it. I skipped out on eating lunch and dinner too.

I missed school on Monday and Tuesday, telling my mother I still wasn't well enough and thankfully she bought it. I'm hardly one to miss school but I knew I would need the time to myself, before having to face my friends but more importantly, seeing Payson in person.

It's now Wednesday. I showed up to school dressed in my baggiest sweatpants and an oversized hoodie. I didn't bother with taming my curls, so I threw my hair up in a messy bun. Jenna and Stacey were appalled at my appearance, but they didn't understand that I didn't have the energy to put myself together. They tried to get me to talk to them, questioning me about what was going on with me and why I hadn't responded to their texts or answered their calls. They have both been blowing up my phone since Sunday, but I refuse to talk to anyone. I know they are worried about me, but I'm so numb, so hurt, that I just want to be left alone.

I got to English class extra early so I could ask Ms. Steinhall if I could trade seats with someone in the front row. I used my absence as an excuse, claiming I wanted to make sure I didn't miss out on the new material. If Payson didn't want to see me anymore, then I was going to make it easier for her. For the both of us. No way would I be able to focus in class being near her, knowing she is a few inches away and I can no longer touch her. Thankfully, Ms. Steinhall approved, and I was able to switch my seat.

I kept my focus on my notebook, not bothering to look up at my classmates as they entered the room. The last thing I needed was to see her come through the door and give me a look similar to the one she gave me when she dumped me. But not looking didn't make a difference. It's like my body is aware of her presence when she enters any space I'm in. I made sure my eyes kept to the front of the classroom all through class until the bell rang for lunch. I quickly gather everything and make a dash out of the classroom.

Jenna meets me as usual at the cafeteria doors before heading into the noisy room. I immediately regret making the choice of coming into the cafeteria. The level of noise is overbearing, and I wish I had settled for the quiet of the library instead.

I haven't been able to eat since Saturday, so I was forcing myself to at least try to eat something, even if that means I have to see Payson, Lydia and Brady too.

"Girl, what has been up with you?" Jenna asks with concern.

"Nothing." I simply state.

"I don't believe that for one minute. You missed two days of school for someone who is anal about attendance. You're dressed like a hobo, and you didn't respond to my birthday text or answer my birthday call. I had a whole birthday serenade prepared for you and you flat out denied me the opportunity."

I simply shrug my shoulders and move along with the line. I grab some stuff I think I will be able to stomach, before paying and making my way to our usual spot. Jenna sits down across from me, eyeing me suspiciously. I'm clearly not okay and she knows it. Jenna knows me better than anyone.

"Alright. Clearly tough love Jenna needs to make an appearance." She flips her hair behind her before straightening her back in her seat. "Sadie Renee Adams, you are *not* okay. I refuse to sit here and believe that. Something is wrong and you need to start talking. Right now! Or so help me Jesus I will share that embarrassing picture from middle school for everyone to see."

I glare at her for the threat and for using my full name. She only uses it when she's being serious.

"I'm your best friend, Sadie. You know you can tell me anything. I'm here for you." She reaches across the table and squeezes my hand.

She's right. I mean, it would be nice to just express the pain I'm feeling to someone, but I know I will cry, and I'm just done with crying. I don't think I have any more tears left in me. I blow out a breath and am about to tell her when Payson walks in with Colton. I am frozen in my spot, just staring at her, at how badly I miss her. She must have felt my eyes on her because she looks in my direction before quickly looking away, greeting people with smiles as she walks past them to get into line.

The sting of her rejection, of avoiding me swells in my chest and I feel the tears building in my eyes. Guess I was wrong about not having any more tears. I grab my tray of uneaten food, dump it in the nearest trash can and make a dash to the closest girls bathroom.

Once I ensure no one is in here with me, I let the tears fall as I slide down onto the floor and let the pain consume me. A few moments later, I hear footsteps enter the bathroom. I'm about to tell whoever it is to leave when I hear Jenna's voice.

"Sadie, what's wrong? Please talk to me," she pleads.

"Payson dumped me," I mumble softly into my knees.

"I'm sorry. I couldn't quite hear you."

I lift my head and stare into her chocolate brown eyes. "Payson...dumped... me," I say between sobs.

"Wait, what!? When did this happen?"

Jenna was the only one who knew about Payson and I seeing each other. She's the only person I trusted enough to tell, the one person I knew who would support us.

"Saturday, after the game. We were supposed to go on a date. I had this whole night picnic thing planned for us at this spot where nobody knows about so we could be alone and be us. But she dumped me, and I don't have the slightest clue as to what I did wrong."

"No, there is no way she would just dump you. Tell me everything that happened."

I recount through everything, leaving out the more intimate moments Payson and I shared. She doesn't need to know about those just as I don't need to know about hers. When I get to what Payson said after I hugged Jake, I cry even harder. Her words still pierce me.

"Okay. So, something clearly changed between halftime and when she saw you hugging Jake. I don't think she would just dump you for hugging a friend. I mean she has guy friends too."

"Yeah, but you're forgetting the fact she is a lesbian whereas I was in a relationship with a guy. I'm a newbie lesbian so male friends may be an issue for her."

Jenna gasps.

"What?"

"You finally admitted to your sexuality!" She beams with such a prideful face. "Payson made me see how happy I could be if I accepted my true self." The smile I had for a moment quickly sombers. "Well up until she dumped me."

"Nope! Not happening." Jenna grabs my arms and pulls me up to stand. "Lose that face. We are going to get to the bottom of this. And by we, I mean me because clearly you are not of sound and mind."

She grabs my face so I'm looking into hers. "You are a strong, beautiful person, Sadie Renee, and you will get through this. We are going to figure this out and fix everything. You have me to support you. Okay?"

I nod my head in agreement.

"Good. Now, let's get you cleaned up a bit and get to class. After school, come over to my house. We can go from there."

The rest of the day seems to drag on and I'm relieved when the dismissal bell finally rings. I make a stop by my locker before I head out to my car when someone bumps into me roughly. I'm about to say something until I see it's Payson walking with Willa by her side. Payson completely ignores me but Willa glances back, a smirk upon her face.

What in the world?

The thought of Willa being with Payson makes me uneasy. I quickly grab my backpack and head out to the parking lot, keeping a distance away from them. I pause by someone's truck and watch as Payson opens the door to her Jeep and Willa climbs in. The smile they share before Payson shuts the door guts me.

"I don't think they're an item anymore. I mean, did you see Sadie today? My God, she didn't even bother putting herself together."

At the mention of my name, my gaze breaks from the yellow Jeep driving off to focus on the conversation I'm overhearing.

"Well after doing a little search on the tomboy dyke, I formulated a plan. Brady helped a little too. If they're not together, then this should totally fuck with her head and screw up how she plays. Coach Watson will have no choice but to give Brady more play time and put the spotlight back on him. And when this works, he'll love me and appreciate what I did for him. We can finally be together, and I'll have *my* little family."

What in the world did I just overhear?

Chapter 22

Sadie's POV

I drove home as quickly as I could to get to Jenna's house after hearing the conversation between Christina and Lydia. I pull into my driveway and shoot off a text to my parents to let them know I would be over at Jenna's helping her with an art project. A little white lie never hurt anyone, right?

I quickly cross my front lawn to the white house next door and bang repeatedly on the black door. Within a few seconds, Jenna opens and allows me to enter.

"Okay, there is no need to sound like the damn FBI is about to bust down my door. Good Lord, woman!"

"Sorry," I say, trying to catch my breath. "But I have something to tell you. I overhead Lydia and Christina in the parking lot before I got here. I think Lydia is behind Payson breaking up with me."

Jenna scrunches her face, disgusted at the news.

"Let's go to my room. I want you to tell me everything and don't leave anything out!"

We rush upstairs to Jenna's bedroom and plop down onto her queen-size bed. I repeat everything I overheard to Jenna. The more I tell her, the angrier she looks.

"That fucking little slut!" Jenna shouts. "Who the fuck does she think she is trying to ruin people's happiness?"

"You agree? You think she is behind Payson dumping me?"

"Got to be. Both her and Brady. I mean, think about it. Payson comes in and steals Brady's thunder by getting more play time than he is. I bet that shit has been eating at Brady. And let's not forget, Lydia has always been jealous of you. You have the cheer captain position, and everyone in school adores you, as they should. I mean, you are a way better human being than Lydia. You also had the star quarterback, and she has always wanted to sink her claws into Brady. I wouldn't put it past her to purposely get pregnant by him to trap him. The lengths that little witch will go to."

"She said she did some digging into Payson and found something to use against her. What do you think she meant by that?"

"Hmm..." Jenna ponders for a minute. "Isn't Payson super close to that cute shaggy haired blonde football player?"

"Yeah, Colton's her cousin but I don't have any way to reach him. And just an FYI, he's Stacey's man."

"I'm allowed to admit when someone looks good." She brushes her black hair behind her shoulder and gives me a pointed look. "But doesn't this Colton have a sister..."

"Oh my gosh, Thea!"

I scroll through my contacts to find Thea's number to call her. A captain has to have a way to send out important messages to all squad members and thank heavens Thea joined cheerleading.

"Hey, Captain!" Thea answers cheerfully after the second ring.

"Thea! Hey, are you home by any chance?"

"Sorry, I'm not. I'm over at my friend Jules's house going over some biology notes for our test next week. Why? What's up?"

"Oh. Is your brother home?"

Thea goes silent and for a moment I think we lost connection. I check the phone but it says the call is still in progress.

"Thea?"

"Um. Yeah, he is." She sounds like she is not telling me something which could only mean one thing.

"Payson is over there, isn't she?"

"Yeah, sorry. They're hanging out, playing video games. Colton's been trying to keep her mind occupied. Sorry, Captain. I really got to get back to studying."

"It's okay. Thank you, Thea."

I end the call and fall back on Jenna's bed.

"What do we do now?"

"We go over to Colton's house and talk to him."

"Jenna, Payson is there, and I don't do confrontations. We will have to find another way. Whatever Lydia and Brady said, it must be bad if she acts like I don't exist anymore."

"So? You think I care if Payson is there or not? She can fill us in on what happened. Besides, she has the right to know what those two have been up to."

I don't like the idea of going over there and confronting Payson. I don't like this cold-hearted side of her. I miss the girl before she broke up with me, the girl I met at the pool party. The girl who helped me release my emotions in a room where I could freely break things. The affectionate and loving person who looked at me as if I were the only person that truly mattered in this world.

I fiddle with my fingers and fight the turmoil in my stomach. There is no way I can do this.

I feel Jenna's soft hands touch mine. "Sadie, you won't be going there alone. I'll be right there with you. Like a buffer if I have to be. We can take my car and I will drive if it makes you feel better. But Payson has every right to know what they're doing too."

Jenna's right. Payson has always been passionate about football. So much so, it's her dream to get drafted to the NFL someday and I'll be damned if I'll allow Lydia or Brady to mess that up for her. Even if she hates my guts.

"Okay." I nod. "Let's go."

It doesn't take us long to get over to Colton and Thea's house. That's the upside of living in a small town. Jenna parks out front and I can feel my stomach somersaulting. Knowing I could come face to face with Payson, someone I was falling head over heels for, makes me nauseous.

Jenna and I make our way up to the front door. I'm about to knock when the door flies open, and Payson nearly collides into me.

"Whoa. I'm so sor—" Payson starts to say until she realizes it's me that she nearly knocked over. "What the hell are you doing here?"

"I-I-I...well we..." I have no idea what to say. The anger on her face and in her voice makes me want to crawl under a rock and hide.

Jenna steps up next to me, which makes me thankful she came along. There's no way I would have handled this on my own.

"Hey! First off, you can lose the attitude and drop the tone. There is no need to get nasty towards Sadie. Okay? She's hurting enough as is. Besides, we came here because we need to talk to you about something."

"Ain't nothing you got to say that I want to hear. Okay?" Payson looks between Jenna and me before landing her cold eyes on me. "Especially from you."

Colton appears in the doorway behind Payson. "Hey, what's going on?" He's looking a bit puzzled as he takes in the three of us.

"Nothing," Payson says firmly. "I need to get going."

Payson shoves herself between Jenna and I as she walks past us to her Jeep. We watch her pull out of the driveway and take off, clearly in need to distance herself from me.

"Let's just go, Jenna," I say somberly. This is exactly why I didn't want to come here.

Jenna latches onto my arm. "Oh no. We are not leaving until we get this whole mess figured out."

"I don't think there's anything to figure out. Payson broke up with Sadie and is solely focused on football now. She doesn't want to fix anything, even if deep down she's hurting."

"Yeah well Sadie is hurting too. I mean, look at her. She showed up to school looking like…that!" She moves her arm up and down, like a hostess on one of those TV game shows where they are showcasing a prize.

"Hey!" I state offensively. How dare she comment about how I'm dressed. Nobody wants to dress themselves up when their heart's been broken.

"Look, I have been Team Sadie since there was something going on between the two of them. I mean, I have never seen my cousin light up about anyone before. And I mean that." He gives me a sweet smile. "But Sadie, it was fucked up of you to use her just to get under Brady's skin."

"Hey, whoa hold up!" Jenna puts her hand up in front of his face. "Sadie has never and would never use people, especially those she cares deeply about!"

"That's not how it looked to Payson at the game," Colton shrugs.

"Why would Payson think I would ever do that to her? I care about her, and I thought I made sure she felt that. I mean, I had a whole romantic picnic planned for us after the game."

"After we left you in the parking lot, I talked to Payson. I mean, I was confused as hell. I even told her I felt she overreacted about you hugging that QB. But then she told me some things that happened and it kind of brought up some bad memories for her."

"What do you mean? What are you talking about, Colton?"

"Yeah, blondie. Care to elaborate?" Jenna asks.

"Listen, it's not my history to tell but the cliff notes version is, Payson was in love before and ended up getting hurt. She got played and felt humiliated and swore she would never allow it to happen again. She said she had a wakeup call this weekend and had to end it with you."

All of a sudden, I think of what Lydia said earlier and it dawns on me.

"Do you think Lydia found out about Payson's ex and used that to plant something in her head?"

"That does sound like something that skank would do." Jenna rolls her eyes.

Colton ponders for a moment. "You know, now that I think about it, I recall Brady standing by Payson on the sidelines during the game. He was saying something to her but I'm not sure what because I was getting my hand looked at."

"We think Lydia and Brady are behind the breakup, solely to sabotage Payson's focus so she messes up and Brady can get more playing time."

"But it's Brady's fault he hasn't been playing as much. He's been late to practices, sometimes he's been a complete no show. I think I overheard he's failing a class and barely passing another. I mean, I always thought Coach liked kissing Brady's ass and was worried for Payson but when he saw what she could do and her dedication to the team, he made the right call."

Jenna waves her hands back and forth in front of her chest. "Hold up! Let me get this straight. Brady isn't getting playtime because Brady isn't putting in the work yet he's willing to fuck with Payson to get her off the field just so he can get the star treatment again?"

Now it's all making sense! Brady knows how important football is to his dad and I have to bet his lack of field time has his father breathing down his neck. And I have no doubt that Lydia will do anything for Brady, even to stoop so low to mess with Payson's head to get her out of the way. All just to get Brady to be with her. *How pathetic!*

The moment Jenna's words sink in, Colton's jaw tightens. You can almost hear his teeth grind together. His hands are in fists, clenched so tight I think the veins on the back of them may pop. I don't think I've ever seen the guy show a hint of anger before.

"They don't get to fuck with my cousin and get away with it. They want to play dirty? Then we need to give them a taste of their own medicine."

"I couldn't agree more. It's time someone knocked those two off their high horses," says Jenna.

"Colton, is Payson going to be able to play in the homecoming game?" I never got to find out how seriously hurt she was but hoped it wasn't too serious.

At the mention of his cousin, Colton relinquishes his anger. "It's not too bad. She's been following the doctor's orders religiously and they believe she should be cleared in time. But Coach already said Brady is starting the game since Payson couldn't practice this week. And rumor mill is going around that a college scout is coming. Payson is hoping to be cleared so she gets to showcase her skills in case it's true."

"I can ask my dad if he knows of any college scouts coming into town. But we are going to need to get Brady out and Payson playing."

"We play Greystone Academy?" Jenna asks. Colton and I nod and a sly smile spreads across Jenna's face. "Perfect. Leave Brady to me."

I'm not too sure what Jenna's got in mind, but I trust her. If there is one thing she's good at, it's giving someone a taste of their own medicine.

Later that evening when dad got home, I was able to get confirmation about the college scout, but dad doesn't know from which college. It doesn't matter. What matters is this scout seeing the talent Payson possesses and getting her name out there to all of the scouts. Nobody deserves this opportunity more than her.

Chapter 23

Payson's POV

I'm on cloud nine right now! The doctor said my shoulder looks great and gave me the all clear to play in tonight's homecoming game! Now I just have to pass the word off to my coaches. If the rumors are true, there's going to be a college scout in the stands watching the game and I *need* to be out on that field showcasing my skills. I just hope I can convince Coach Watson to give me play time.

I missed the morning classes but made it back just in time for the pep rally. The bleachers are bathed in a sea of white, gold and Carolina blue from all the students and staff. I make my way to the senior section and spot Colton sitting with his buddies. I send him a text telling him to make room for me and head to the row he's sitting in.

"What did the doctor say?" he yells over the loudness of the crowd.

"Shoulder's fine and I can play. Just got to go tell the coach after this thing is over," I yell back. .

There's a cackle sound from a microphone being turned on and everyone in the gym quiets down as we tune in to what Principal King has to say.

"Good afternoon, ladies and gentlemen. I know we are all very excited for homecoming weekend so why don't we get this pep rally started with an amazing performance by our own Bellwood High Cheerleaders!"

Everyone hoots and hollers as both JV and varsity squads make their way to the middle of the gym floor. Some do crazy flips while the rest jog out before they get into their spots. There is a moment of silence before the music starts and the cheerleaders begin their routine. The same routine they performed for the first time at halftime last week. It's the very game where I was blinded by my feelings and allowed myself to get hurt by a girl I was crazy about. Again.

As always, my eyes spot Sadie as she does a series of backflips right into a group of male cheerleaders who put her up into a stunt. She does a few one-legged moves before she's dropped down and then tossed up into what she told me was a basket toss. My heart jumps into my throat and I keep my eyes glued to Sadie until both her feet are safely put back on the gym floor and she moves to go into her next position.

It's only then I spot her rocking a football jersey with the number thirteen on it. Sadie is wearing *my* number. For a moment, seeing her wearing my own number strikes the primal part of me, the one that wants to see her in my own jersey one day with her last name next to mine.

What the hell?

I shake my head clear of the idea. Why did I even think there could be that kind of future after she played me like a fool? Is this some sort of sick game to her?

"What's with the stink face?" Colton whispers in my ear.

"Why the fuck is Sadie wearing my jersey?"

"Principal King and Sadie thought it would be a great idea if the cheerleaders wore a football player's jersey for the pep rally to show their support."

"And how the hell did Sadie come into possession of my jersey?" I stare him down with the best glare I can muster.

"Your favorite cousin gave it to her," he replies.

"I could murder you!"

He chuckles. "It wasn't me, Pace. Thea was the one to get it to Sadie. But glad to know I'm the true favorite cousin." There's that stupid big ass grin he gives when he feels like he's won a bet. Jackass.

Before long, the pep rally is over, and I go in search of Coach Watson. I make my way out of the gymnasium and towards the locker rooms where the coaches office is located. I'm close to the door when I hear a deep, burly voice shouting from inside.

"I need you to assure me that Brady is the *only* quarterback playing tonight, Watson. You got that? Because if that little wannabe boy of a quarterback does get cleared to play and she gets even just one snap, I will have your job. That college scout needs to see my boy shine!"

"Mr. Thomas, with all due respect—"

"No! My son plays the full game, no questions asked. I don't care what excuse you have to come up with to tell that little postulant she can't play tonight. Or so help me, I will ensure you never coach in another school or sport in this district, state or country again. Do I make myself clear, Coach?"

"Crystal," I hear Coach Watson reply.

A moment later, a guy dressed to the nines in an expensive looking suit comes out of Coach's office. He's got to be at least six foot five and still in great shape. He looks like a much older version of Brady. Dark hair but his is slicked back where Brady's is long on top and hangs around his eyes. Their eyes are the only thing that would set the two apart. Brady's are brown, a trait he must have gotten from his mother and his father's are a hazel stormy gray. His eyes lock on me as he walks past me with a devilish smirk. Hard to believe I used to idolize this man when he made a name for himself in the NFL.

I give him the best dirty look I can until he passes me and disappears out of the hall.

Coach Watson appears a moment later, locking his office door before glancing up..

"Payson, how are you?"

"I'm good, Coach. Although, I'm not sure how I feel after overhearing that convo."

Coach lets out a sigh. "You heard all of that?"

"Just the last part about ensuring I don't get to play if I'm cleared. Which is why I was coming to talk to you. The doc gave me the okay."

"You have no idea how happy I am to hear that." He gives me a soft smile, but I know he isn't finished speaking. "I want to put you in. I really do. You have proven you can lead this team and get us the win. You have the heart and dedication, more than I have seen in any player out of my years of coaching but—"

"But you can't because of that asshole. Right?"

"Look, Payson. I enjoy coaching. I've been doing it for over twenty-seven years and it's honestly the best thing I've done in my life. I just can't afford to lose it. Mr. Thomas? He has money, the connections, and Lord only knows what he would do to ensure his threat is seen through. I just can't jeopardize my job. I hope you can understand that."

I do understand but it doesn't lessen the anger rising in me. I'm pissed! This situation is bullshit but I don't blame the coach. His job is on the line, and I would never ask him to risk that.

"I understand, Coach." I turn my back to him and storm out of the hall. My good mood demolished into fragments of anger and bitterness within seconds.

Once I get in my Jeep, I slam my fists into the steering wheel and yell. "FUCK!"

My phone chimes with an alert and I open it to see a text from Colton.

Did you talk to Coach?

Yeah. But he's not going to let me play.

What!? Why not?

Before I got to his office, Brady's dad was there. He basically threatened Coach that if he plays me tonight, he will make sure Watson never coaches again. He wants Brady to get all the play time bc there is going to be a scout at the game. Coach is worried he will make good on his threat. He isn't going to jeopardize his job.

That's messed up.

Tell me about it. What the fuck am I going to do?

Well...

Well, what?

Look, we may be able to get you play time. You just need to trust us. Ok?

We? Who the fuck is we?

Can't tell you. Just get your game gear and get your ass to school on time for the game. Ok?

Ok...

I don't know what Colton is up to and who he is conspiring with, but if I can trust anyone, it's my own cousin.

Chapter 24

Payson's POV

Homecoming game feels just as energetic as the game against Wimbleton. The crowd is buzzing with excitement in hopes our team will pull the win. is the other school who is still undefeated and giving them their first loss would be glorious, especially if I was the one to do it. The game has started and of course, Coach Watson is sticking to his guns. Brady is out on the field, and I'm told to sit like a dog on the bench. The other coaches questioned him after I told them I was cleared, in hopes they would convince Watson to let me play but he gave the excuse that because I wasn't able to practice this week, I had to sit out this game. Even when it was out of my control to not be able to practice. But I still showed up and did what I needed to do at practice all week unlike Brady.

Brady manages to get the team down near the end zone, but Greystone's defense holds us off to a field goal. When the kicking team goes out on the field, Colton drops down beside me. His hair is drenched in sweat and matted down. The black warrior paint under his eyes is smudged and he's smiling like he's on top of the world. I'm glad one of us is.

"I thought you said you had some genius plan."

"We do. You just have to have patience, young padawan."

"Are you going to tell me who this *we* is that you are working with?"

"Sorry, Pace. That would be a hard no."

Greystone's side of the stands go wild as their team gets the touchdown. We are not starting off too well. Colton gets his helmet on, and he heads out to the field with the rest of the offense. Brady is leading them, taking what he has always wanted; the spotlight.

This game is rough. Greystone is showing how talented of a team they are. Their defense has been ruthless on our offense, making sure our guys can't make it far. Their offense is lighting up our defense, getting past even some of our strongest defenders. The upside of sitting on the sideline and being benched? I get to study their play calls.

There's about four minutes left in the second quarter, and we are trailing Greystone by three touchdowns. We need to make big plays and get some points on the board before they do, otherwise we are going to end up in a blowout, ending our undefeated streak.

At that moment, Brady snaps the ball. He's about to throw a pass but something is off and Brady gets sacked by Greystone's biggest defender. The stadium quickly quiets down, and players drop to one knee when Brady doesn't get up. He's laying on the ground clenching his arm, his voice yelling out in agony. The medics and coaches rush out to Brady to check on him.

"This doesn't look good folks. Brady Thomas appears to be down and unable to get up," the announcer states.

The clock is frozen at the three and half minute mark and Bellwood is awarded an injury time out. Coach Watson makes his way over to me.

"Is your arm warmed up and ready to go? Because I need you to take over."

"Wait, you serious, Coach? What about the threat from Brady's dad?"

"Do you really think he can hold my job over my head when his son's arm is injured and he's incapable of playing?" He gives me a knowing look. He's right. He can't make the kid play with an injury.

"I got you, Coach!" I grab my helmet and snap my chin strap in place.

"Wait a minute folks, looks like Moore is coming in to take over for the injured Thomas. Will Moore be able to get the Eagles back on top? I'm hoping so!" The announcer calls out.

I run out on the field as Brady is helped up and taken to the sidelines to be evaluated by the medical staff. I gather my offense in the huddle, ready to take charge. I recall how their defense plays and which guys to look out for so I make a play call and inform my teammates how we are going to get down the field.

"Turner, they keep doubling up on you since you're Brady's go to receiver. We are going to have to fake them. I want you to catch the snap, hand it off to me and I'll throw the ball to Colton. Ready on three?"

Chad looks like he's about to piss his pants with this surprise call. "You want me to do what!?"

"You totally got this dude. Just call the play, catch the snap and hand it to me."

We all get into position. I'm standing to the left of Chad. He calls the play and catches the snap. He quickly hands it to me where I run it to the far right side and locate Colton. Greystone's defense has no idea what is happening. By the time they realize I have the ball, I have already thrown it down to Colton who catches it and runs it all the way into the end zone!

"Touchdown Eagles!" The announcer shouts through the speakers and our side of the stadium goes wild with excitement.

Instead of going for the field goal, we decide to go for the extra two points. I have Pitman snap the ball to me and I squeeze myself between him and Johnson as the rest of the guys push me forward, breaking the goal line. We get the extra two points!

That momentum shift changed the game in its entirety. After halftime, we were able to hold off the Wolves and managed to score two more touchdowns bringing the score 25 to 24. In the fourth quarter, Greystone got another touchdown, but the kicker missed the extra point. We were now down by five.

With a minute and a half left, we need to get a touchdown to win the game. The ball gets snapped, my offensive line is holding back the defenders, but one slips through and is gunning for me. I run to the right, scanning the field ahead. I spot Sanchez who is wide open and throw it his way before I'm knocked down. I roll out and quickly jump to my feet just in time to see Sanchez run it into the endzone.

"Fuck yeah!" I shout, fist pumping the air in excitement.

Our kicker makes the field goal and the buzzer sounds, ending the game. We did it! We won! The crowd is stomping their feet, screaming and yelling with so much pride. The marching band stands in the bleachers, playing the school's anthem. The team gathers around me and lifts me up on their shoulders, chanting my name as if I was their hero. But it wasn't just me. It was *all* of us. *We* did this together. *We* won.

Once I'm back on the ground, the team walks off in search of their families.

"You're Payson Moore, correct? The one who won the California State Championship games back-to-back?"

I turn to see two gentlemen dressed in khaki pants and wearing trench coats.

"Yeah that's me."

"Wow. It is an honor to meet you." He reaches out to shake my hand and I return the gesture. "We are from the University of Florida and just want to say, you are an incredible athlete. To play the way you did and help your team come out with the win after that first half? Impressive."

"Wow. Thank you. That means a lot."

"You're welcome. We just wanted to let you know that we got footage of tonight's game, and we will be keeping you on our radar. Keep playing like that, kid, and you'll for sure draw a lot of attention. You have great potential."

"Thank you!"

The gentlemen nod and walk off. Holy shit! I just talked to an actual college scout! He noticed me and complimented my game. What is this life?

"Who was that?" Colton appears by my side.

"The college scouts from the University of Florida. Colt, they sounded so sure of me! Can you believe it?"

"Pace, you have always had the gift for football. They would have been blind if they didn't notice." He looks over my head and gives a nod. I follow his line of sight to see Sadie and her best friend looking back at us. Sadie gives a slight nod back, a small smile on her face before they walk off to exit the stadium.

"What was that?"

"Let's just say, they are the reason you got to play tonight. My part was to ensure you got to the game."

"What? Why would Sadie and her friend help me? Especially after what I put Sadie through this past week?"

Colton shrugs. "Sounds like a conversation you two need to have." He starts to walk away, only to pause. "For what it's worth, I don't think Sadie was ever using you, Pace. I think Sadie genuinely cares about you. She proved that to me, and I think you need to hear her out." He walks off to meet our family waiting by the gate and I'm left there thinking over what he said.

The guilt settles in and I feel like shit. I know how badly I hurt her yet she still found it in her heart to put me before her pain. If that doesn't just reiterate what Colton said, I would be stupid to let her go. I need to fix this. I need to make things right with Sadie.

Chapter 25

Sadie's POV

"Wake up, bitch! We got homecoming to get ready for!" Jenna singsongs as she jumps up and down on the bed.

I grab my phone from the side table, and I could smack my best friend when I see the time.

"Seriously, Jen? It's eight in the morning!" I groan. It's Saturday morning and I was planning on sleeping in. The dance doesn't start til seven and we don't need to start getting ready until early afternoon.

Jenna grabs my arm and pulls me up until I'm sitting up in her bed. I slept over at her house last night after the game. My feelings were all over the place and Jenna suggested we have a girls' night in and I couldn't be more grateful for my understanding bestie.

"I'm sorry that *some* of us are excited to get dolled up and dance the night away."

"I'm not trying to dampen your joy, it's just...I don't know that I really want to go anymore," I say quietly.

"What? Sadie, you can't be serious. Why don't you want to go?"

I simply shrug my shoulders but in reality, I know why I don't, and it has nothing to do with Brady or Lydia. I'm so far over those two and their betrayal.

Okay, that's a lie. A part of it has to do with the possibility that Brady and I could win homecoming king and queen. The last thing I want to do is share a dance, let alone be anywhere close to him and send Lydia into a jealous rage.

"It has to do with Payson, doesn't it?"

I let out a sigh and stare into her comforter, fighting back the tears that threaten to spill because it does have everything to do with Payson.

Jenna crawls next to me and pulls me back so we are both resting against her headboard. She leans her head into mine and we sit like that in silence for a few moments.

"You really care for her, don't you?"

"Yeah, Jen. I do. It's nothing like how I felt when I was with Brady. It's so different. She has made me far happier than any guy I've ever been with. I don't know how to truly explain the way she makes me feel but it feels special, like a once in a lifetime opportunity. I guess since she still hasn't reached out, there is no chance of us talking things out. I really had hope that our plan would at least get her to talk to me, to explain everything."

"Let me ask you something, and I want you to be honest with me."

"Okay..."

"The feelings you have for Payson, are they deep enough for you to come out to your parents, more specifically your mother?"

Could I do it? Could I risk losing my family by wanting to be with a specific person?

"I want you to think about this for a second, Sadie. Let's say things between you two do work out and they are going great. Do you think Payson will want to keep the two of you secretive from everyone just to keep your mom in the dark?"

I don't think Payson would. At first, yeah but if we date seriously, which I hope we do, Payson will get tired of hiding, tired of feeling like a dirty secret and I would never want her to feel that way. Ever! And if I'm being honest with myself, I want to claim Payson as my person for everyone to see.

"No, I don't. I'm sure she would be fine with it in the beginning but after a while, she wouldn't want to be hidden. If, and that would be a big if, I can get her back, I'd have to come clean to my parents. I just...I don't know what will happen or where I would go if my mother kicks me out. You know?"

I still have the rest of the school year and summer before I can move out when I go off to whatever college accepts me. Where can I go until then?

"You don't need to worry about that. Okay?"

I look at my friend, not understanding her. My scrunched eyebrows must give away my confusion.

"I might have already had this conversation with my parents," she says shyly. "And *if* things go south, you can stay here. My parents do not mind."

The tears finally fall along with the warmth of happiness spreading through my body. I pull Jenna into the biggest hug and squeeze her as tightly as I can.

"Thank you," I whisper.

"What are best friends for?" She pulls back, quickly swiping a tear from the corner of her own eye. "Now, how about we come up with a plan for you to get your woman back?"

"Okay." For the first time in over a week, I feel hopeful. "Let's get ready for homecoming."

The limo Jenna's parents got for us pulls into the circular loop in front of the Bellwood Hotel. This hotel has been around since Bellwood first became established. There has been work done over the years to keep it updated and prevent it from collapsing as our town wants to keep it up and running since it brings in a lot of revenue.

There are around 100 rooms to rent out, a lovely dining area for eating but the best part of this place? The ballroom, located in the middle of the hotel. It has these golden pillars that are spaced out along the walls and a huge crystal chandelier built into the center of the ceiling. It kind of reminds me of the ballroom scene in the animated Beauty and the Beast minus the big windows. It's so stunning, not to mention spacious, which makes it the perfect location for our Alice in Wonderland themed homecoming.

Jenna looks stunning in her dark purple, open-back cocktail dress. From the waist down the dress poofs out a bit from the layers of tulle. The waist up is beaded and hugs her figure like a glove. She's paired it with a pair of fuchsia pink heels, the colors reminding me of the Cheshire Cat.

I went with a short strapless cocktail dress. Just like Jenna's, the bottom poofs out from the layers of tulle. Only mine is in a baby blue color. The top half is blush pink with flowers and vines all over it. Some of the floral vines go down into the blue. It's so beautiful! I've paired my dress with baby pink strappy heels and threw my hair up into a bun, the upside of having naturally curly hair. I left my makeup light tonight, only eyeliner, mascara and some shimmery gold shadow on my eyes. I highlighted my lips with a pink gloss and decided this was good enough.

Jenna and I make our way through the lobby towards the ballroom entrance when I spot a well dressed Brady staring me down. He's dressed nicely in a black tuxedo, his throwing arm in a matching black sling.

I grab Jenna's arm, stopping us in our tracks. "Hey, I'll be there in a minute. Save me a seat?"

Her brows furrow when she doesn't understand. I move my eyes to where Brady is standing, and she follows them before quickly diverting her attention back to me.

"I thought we're here to get you and Payson back together?" There's a tone in her question, noting she isn't happy about this.

"We are but I need to make peace with Brady, for good." I need to make sure there is closure between us, for him to understand that I will never want anything to do with him again. Jenna nods before she walks off into the dance and I make my way towards Brady.

"You look absolutely incredible, Sadie." His eyes roam all over me, taking in my appearance.

"Why don't you save it for Lydia? Or whatever other girl you want to sleep with tonight." I don't hold back the disdain in my voice. "I'm only here because I need to close this chapter on us. You need to know that there is not nor will there ever be an us again. No amount of begging or harassing will get me back. You understand that, right?"

Brady smiles smugly, but nods.

"I just have to ask you one thing and I hope, better yet, I *pray* you will be honest with me just this once. I think you owe me that."

He shoves his good hand into the pocket of his dress pants, glancing around the room before returning his attention to me. "What?"

"Why? Why would you hurt me like you did? Why would you just throw away two years to sleep with other girls? Why was I not good enough for you?"

He shakes his head, letting out a low chuckle. He seems hesitant and for a second, I think he's not going to tell me.

"You want the truth?"

I nod so he knows I do.

"The truth is, Sadie, that I didn't want to actually be with you. Our so-called relationship? It was all an act, a lie. A complete sham, put on by my own father. You know how he is about me getting into college and one day drafted. He told me I needed to date you because it would help my image. Who is more likely to get scouted? A playboy quarterback or the one who's seriously dating the mayor's daughter? The plan was to break up after graduation, reasoning that we were off to different schools and long distance wasn't going to work for us. Then I was going to get my freedom for another two years before dear old dad will want me to take someone else, like the daughter of the Dean or higher up, to help my image before the NFL draft. The cheating was strictly for me to have my fun while pretending to love you. I mean, don't get me wrong, you're sexy as fuck and it wasn't hard to fake being with you. But a man has needs and you weren't supplying them."

Before I can rationalize it, my hand comes up and I slap Brady's face, quickly swiping the cruel smirk off it. His eyes are wide, shocked that I actually physically harmed him. That makes two of us.

"You're a piece of shit and the worst possible human being to ever exist! I hope one day, God sends someone for you to fall in love with, only for them to do what you did to me." He needs to feel the pain of this kind of betrayal. To truly understand the magnitude of his actions.

I look past Brady to see Lydia coming out of the bathrooms, walking towards us which reminds me of something.

"What's your father think about you having not one, but *two* babies on the way?"

He shrugs. "He doesn't know about them, and I plan to keep it that way."

"Hmph. You know, it would be a real shame for word to get back to him, wouldn't it?"

His eyes go wide, the panic in them laughable. I give him the best devilish grin I can put on.

"Have a good night, Brady."

I turn and walk away from him, heading to the ballroom to find my bestie. I won't lie and say his truth didn't hurt me. It felt like a knife was plunged into my heart knowing I gave myself to him in all the ways I could only for him to not even feel anything for me. But it's freeing, having this closure, finally knowing the truth. Because now I can move forward. I deserve better, deserve someone who will love me and only me. I had a taste of that sort of thing, of that kind of love. I now know what it's like to be cared for, to have what you feel for somebody be reciprocated, and I'm on a mission tonight to get the one I want back. *If she will take me back.*

Payson's POV

I'm in my room, putting the finishing touches to my homecoming look. I decided to go with all white sneakers paired with black dress pants, tailored to my athletic figure. The matching black blazer is open, exposing the satin white tank I'm wearing underneath. It's a bit short, showcasing my toned midriff just below my belly button. My long, dark hair is parted in the middle and slicked back into a low ponytail. It's comfortable and dressy, the perfect fit for me.

I was planning on staying home tonight but Colton was very adamant that I go. It didn't help that Thea was backing him up, stating how it would be our one high school dance the three of us would get to attend together. Who was I to deny my cousins the opportunity?

I give myself a quick look over in the mirror before I head downstairs to the living room where everyone is chatting amongst themselves. Thea and her best friend, Jules are talking with my mom and aunt Charlotte while Colton is snuggled up with Stacey on the couch.

My mom breaks her conversation the moment she sees me enter the room. "Oh, Payson. You look absolutely stunning!"

"Thanks, mom."

"Come, come. Everyone get together for pictures!" I roll my eyes. Mom loves taking pictures any chance she gets.

We all get together into one big group as mom and aunt Charlotte snap photo after photo of us all. After what feels like a hundred pictures have been taken, my phone goes off. I remove my phone from my pants pocket seeing that I have a few missed calls from Willa. It's not like her to call me so I text her to make sure she's okay.

> You ok?

No. Grace has the flu and won't be able to go to homecoming. I was so looking forward to this.

> Are you dressed and ready to go?

Of course I am. I've been ready for like 2hrs. I just found out from her sister that she's sick. What do I do now? I want to go to the dance after all the money I put into dressing up but I don't want to go without Grace.

> Don't freak out, Wills. I got you. I'm taking my cousin and her friend to the dance. I can swing by and grab you on the way.

You would do that?

> Of course. Why should you miss your last homecoming because your gf is sick?

Thanks, Pace. I appreciate that. <3

"You ready to go, Pace?" Thea asks.

"Yeah, I'm ready. Do you and Jules mind if we swing by to pick up Willa first?"

Thea looks at me as if this is a bad idea. "Why does Willa need you to pick her up?"

"Her girlfriend is sick and I don't want my friend to miss her senior homecoming."

"I don't know if it's a good idea." Before I can ask her why, she turns to her best friend. "Come on, Jules. Let's go wait outside."

What was that about? It kind of feels like Thea doesn't want Willa and me around each other but that's not the case. Her and Grace had a heart to heart and worked through whatever struggles they were having. I'm happy for them and I would never jeopardize their relationship. Willa has been a good friend, especially ever since I broke things off with Sadie.

She figured out why my moods have been off lately so I caved and told her everything. She thought I was an idiot for allowing Lydia and Brady to get into my head. She admitted that she tried to help my situation when she made it look like she was interested in me after the breakup but I admonished her for that, telling her it probably caused more pain for Sadie. It was bad enough I had broken her heart as is. Willa apologized and told me that I just need to do what her and Grace did. I need to sit down with Sadie and we need to talk things out. She's not wrong. I just hope Sadie will want to talk to me.

Willa, Thea, Jules and I make it to the dance shortly after seven. Thea and her friend take off towards the bathrooms to freshen up. As if the drive messed up their perfect makeup. Willa and I head for the ballroom which is packed with Bellwood High students and staff who signed up to chaperone.

The music is loud, blaring some music from the early 2000s. I have to admit, their music is better than what is out today.

Willa grabs my hand. "Let's go dance!" She pulls me in the direction of the dance floor to an area where we both have room to move. I'm not much of a dancer, but seeing that it's helping Willa feel better, I dance with her. I keep some space between us as we jump around and act like fools. The last thing I would want is someone to think we are together. More importantly, I don't want Sadie to think I've moved on.

Sadie is it for me. She's the one I want to be with. I'm not sure if she is coming tonight. I'm holding out hope that she will though, especially since she's been nominated for homecoming Queen. I just pray I can steal a moment with her and show her that whether or not she is Bellwood's queen, she will *always* be mine.

Chapter 26

Sadie's POV

The music blares through the speakers. The dance floor is packed with bodies up against each other. Girls are grinding and shaking their butts on guys while the guys dry hump them from behind. I haven't seen Payson anywhere and I'm starting to think she chose to avoid coming tonight. I'm fidgeting with the tulle on my skirt, trying to manage a steady breathing pattern. What am I going to do if she doesn't show?

"Relax, Sadie. She's going to come. We still have time," Jenna reassures me. "And if she doesn't, then we will hunt her down."

I shake my head. "No! It has to be here in front of everyone!" I tell her in her ear, since you can't hear over the loud music.

How else can I prove my feelings for her?

Suddenly the music is cut off and there's a crackling of a microphone being turned on. Everybody turns to the makeshift stage setup towards the back of the ballroom.

"Testing, testing...can everyone hear me?" Principal King says from onstage, and everyone responds with a resounding, "YES!"

"Wonderful! I hope everyone is having a grand ol' time this evening. First and foremost, I want to thank everyone who had a hand in decorating and getting this dance together. It looks absolutely incredible!"

Everyone claps in appreciation before settling down and allowing our principal to continue.

"I'd also like to take a moment and congratulate our Bellwood Eagles football team for their impressive comeback win in last night's game against ! Way to go!" The crowd applauds loudly, with hoots and hollers from the football team being overheard.

"Alright, calm down, calm down. Y'all know that's not why I'm up here. I'm up here because it's officially time to announce this year's Bellwood High Homecoming King and Queen. DJ! Can I get a drum roll please?"

The ballroom is silent, except for the drum roll sound. Anticipation thick in the air as we all await to see who wins.

"Your 2022 Homecoming King and Queen are..." Principal King opens the envelope and with a chuckle, "I guess I shouldn't be surprised. Brady Thomas and Sadie Adams!"

Jenna screams so loud next to me, I think she might have bust an ear drum. Did I hear her correctly?

"I won?" I stare at my bestie, who is jumping up and down like a kid who got what they wanted on Christmas morning.

"Of course, you won! Now go, go, go!" She places her hands on the small of my back, pushing me through the mass of classmates towards the stage. Brady is already up there, having his crown placed upon his dark, slicked back hair.

I make my way over to the steps leading to the stage. A hand appears in front of me and when I glance up, I see Colton standing there, smiling down on me. I take his hand in mine as he helps me up the stairs to ensure I don't slip and fall. Such a gentleman.

I whisper a thank you to him before making my way to center stage. Our senior class president and my good friend, Stacey, is standing holding a tiara and sash. She drapes the sash over my shoulder and as she goes behind me to place the tiara on top of my head, I spot Payson entering the ballroom.

Relief flows through me at the sight of her. *She's here! And gosh, she looks amazing.* I find her everyday distressed skinny jeans and flannels hot, but seeing her dressed up in a pantsuit really does something for me.

My joy and excitement at seeing her is quickly snuffed out when Willa comes in with her. *What the hell?* I watch them as Brady is making his speech. I completely tune him out, my eyes laser focused on Willa and Payson. Payson is gently guiding Willa along towards a table in the back. She pulls out her chair and helps her to sit down.

Pretty sure she is capable of sitting down herself!

The envious monster inside me is making herself present, but I need to contain her. I need to focus on the fact Payson is here, and now is the time to put my plan in motion. Jenna said I needed a grand gesture to prove my feelings to Payson, so there would be no questions. Saying those feelings on stage in front of everyone was the best thing we came up with, assuming I would win Homecoming Queen. Jenna had no doubts, but I still didn't believe I could win, and we made sure to have a backup plan just in case.

I can't believe I won, though! Now, I'm about to do something I never thought I would do. I'm about to declare my heart for Payson *in front of the entire school*.

Applause from the crowd brings me back and Stacey is handing me the mic. My heart is racing against my ribs, like it may burst through my chest at any moment. My palms are clammy, the nerves settling in. Performing in front of crowds? I can handle it. About to expose my true self in front of the town I grew up in? A whole different ball game.

I clear my throat and glance around at all the faces in front of me. Jenna moves to stand right at the edge of the stage, being the beam of support I need to get through this. She knows this moment is about to change my life.

A small laugh towards the back catches my attention. Willa and Payson are quietly laughing about something when Willa's hand gently brushes down Payson's arm and I think I may just snap. Willa needs to learn that my heart belongs to Payson and maybe, *hopefully*, Payson's will belong to mine too.

I let out a breath and close my eyes, taking a moment to compose myself. When I open them up, *all* eyes are on me.

"I would like to thank each and every person who voted for me to be your homecoming queen. It is truly an honor that you would choose me worthy of this crown. But I'm afraid, I can't accept this." I remove the crown from my head and stare at the jewels sparkling in the light for a moment.

Gasps are heard all throughout the room, people murmuring and questioning me as I move forward with my speech.

"It's crazy to me how we get so worked up over nonsense titles. Whether it's Homecoming or Prom Queen, cheer captain or getting the starting spot on an athletic team. They are just titles that have little meaning when we leave here. I mean, take this crown for example. It's viewed that whoever wins it is the most popular or liked person in this school, right? But the reality is it's nothing more than a piece of plastic and fake jewels glued to it. Fake, like my relationship to Brady was."

I glare his way for a moment, ensuring he sees the vengeance in my eyes. The school needs to know the kind of person he truly is.

"This was a hard truth to find out tonight and I just want it to be clear before rumors go around. Brady faked our relationship, an idea brought on by his own father to help his image. It didn't matter that I fell in love with him or gave myself to him. Nope. Brady chose to lie to me and cheat on me with so many other girls for the simple fact he needed me to make him look good for college scouts. He needed *me* to show his *daddy* he is a good boy who follows orders instead of telling his father no. Which blows my mind because how can anyone agree to fake date somebody and never truly care about the other person's feelings? Not only did Brady sleep around with many girls, but he's about to be a daddy himself, with two babies on the way."

At this point, the crowd is losing their minds. I just hope word gets back to his father.

"Lydia hasn't been on the squad due to her pregnancy so whatever rumor you may have heard is a lie. I didn't kick her off as she claims because the truth of the matter is, Lydia quit to protect her baby she conceived when she chose to sleep with someone that I was with for the mere fact she wanted him. Lydia thinks she took my man when in actuality, she just took my problem."

There's a high pitch screech before Lydia storms off and exits the ballroom while Brady makes a dash towards me, but he's stopped when Principal King and Colton stand in front of him.

"You better see yourself out of this ballroom, Mr. Thomas," our principal sternly tells him. Brady, red faced and nostrils flaring, stares me down before he stomps off stage with the principal right behind him, both taking the same exit as Lydia.

Colton moves to stand by Stacey, pulling her close into his side and gives me a nod for me to continue. I lick my dry lips and face the room once more.

"Even though Brady couldn't find it in himself to show me a single ounce of love, there was one person who showed me what I deserved."

This caught Payson's attention, and her eyes are now on me. I make sure I'm staring into her jade green eyes as I speak, so she knows this is directly for her.

"Whenever we were together, the world around us disappeared and all I saw was them. Someone who catered to my feelings, who supported and encouraged me anytime I felt nervous. Somebody who made me feel seen and not just seen, but like I was the only one for them. This person has made me feel more like myself than I have ever felt in my entire life. But other people's jealousy cost us our opportunity to be together.

So, I'm up here tonight, in front of everybody, scared as hell, asking for another chance."

I break our eye contact as I make my way off stage. The sea of students part for me, allowing me to make my way through until I'm finally standing before her.

I take a moment to breathe in her scent, to acknowledge she's truly standing there in front of me. It feels like it's been ages since I've been able to be this close to her and I want to cherish this moment in case she rejects me. Without hesitation, I grab her face with both of my hands and pull her into me. My plush lips meet hers for a moment before I relinquish her, giving her some space but never taking my eyes off her.

"Everything I have done or said to you and felt about you has been authentically me. You were never just some strategy to get back at Brady because I couldn't hurt you like other people have. This past week has been dark and miserable for me but it's also shown me just how much I care about you and what you mean to me, Payson. I'm crazy, head over heels falling for you and I don't want to hide anymore. I want to show you off, I want to openly hold hands and shower you with kisses. I don't care who sees or knows. All I want is to be yours, if you will have me."

At that moment, I feel like a weight has lifted off my chest and for the first time in I don't know how long, I feel like I can breathe. I wasn't sure I could go through with it but *I did it!* I poured my heart out on that stage and dance floor. Now it's all on Payson.

Payson doesn't say a word. She just stands there, full of silence as I hold my breath waiting for whatever she may say. Her eyes bore into mine, probably looking for any indication this is a prank. I mean, it is completely out of character for me but I needed to do something like this to show her how serious I am about wanting to be with her.

She finally releases her breath and looks around at all the people staring at us to see what happens next. Payson shakes her head then turns and starts to walk away from me. The hope I felt earlier shatters along with my broken heart. I thought this was proof enough to show her my true feelings, of where I stand with us but maybe it just wasn't enough.

Chapter 27

Payson's POV

I'm overwhelmed with so many emotions, I had to distance myself a bit from her. The fact Sadie just came out in front of the entire school, confessing what I mean to her...*wow*. My mind is blown! This girl is as crazy for me as I am for her!

Without a second thought, I quickly turn back around and head towards the most beautiful girl I have ever laid eyes on in my life. I swiftly pull her into me, taking her by surprise. I dip her back, like those fancy moves done in the movies and I kiss the hell out of her. Everyone shouts and claps, some people whistle and others scream with joy at our display of affection. I pull Sadie back up into a standing position and press my forehead against hers.

"What do you say, cherry pop? Want to get out of here?"

She nods her head, the biggest smile that could light up the sky upon her face. I grab her hand and pull her along behind me. We exit the ballroom and make our way outside, letting the crisp night air cool our heated skins. There is a fountain in the middle of the drop off loop with a few benches placed around it. I sit down on the nearest one, pulling her to sit on my lap when she goes to sit beside me. Being away from her this past week was brutal enough, I don't want any more distance between us.

"Sadie, I cannot believe you did all that back in there. You know what this means, right?"

"Everyone in school knows my true feelings about you, *including* Willa?"

There's a hint of jealousy to that last part and honestly, I like knowing she's this bit possessive of me, even when she has nothing to worry about.

"I hope you believe me when I tell you Willa is not a threat to you or us. She's simply a friend."

"Then why did she come with you? Doesn't she have her own girlfriend?" Sadie crosses her arms; her pink lips pursed a bit.

I can't help but chuckle at her pouty face.

"Is that jealousy I hear?" I ask teasingly.

"No, I don't get jealous."

"Hmm.." I didn't think she would admit it. But I also know that after everything she went through, my girl needs reassurance. "Look, Willa was upset because her girl came down with the flu and couldn't attend tonight. I told her I was already going and that I could swing by to pick her up on the way. And I wanted to make sure she enjoyed herself as a friend. That's all. Besides, Willa knows I'm crazy about you."

"Really?" She looks at me, with unshed tears. "Because this past week felt like you despised me, like I was your worst enemy and it killed me inside."

"I know." I lick my dry lips and swallow down my pride. "I'm so sorry that I hurt you the way I did. I let Brady and Lydia get in my head when I shouldn't have listened to them. I mean, of all people, I should have known better."

"Yeah, but why did you?"

"When Lydia made the comment that you were using me, it triggered me. I had this girl out in Cali that I fell in love with. She claimed she was bisexual, and it didn't bother me because I had strong feelings for her. We were together for about a year before I caught her having sex with someone I played football with. Turns out, I was just some experimental game for her until she got the guy she wanted. She used me and our relationship to lure him to be with her."

Sadie gives me a sympathetic look. "I'm so sorry. You did not deserve to be treated like that. It doesn't feel good to be used but I can't help being happy she messed up either because I get to have you."

Sadie leans in and gives me short, quick kisses. On the last kiss, I hold her lips to mine and blow a raspberry, causing Sadie to giggle. I missed that sound more than I thought.

"Since the school knows about us, you know the word is going to get back to your parents. Are you sure you're okay with that? Because honestly, Sadie—"

Sadie doesn't give me a chance to finish talking. She presses her soft lips on mine, taking my mouth and tongue into hers. When we pull apart, I take a moment to catch my breath.

"It was the only way to shut you up," Sadie says, pulling her bottom lip in with her teeth. Sadie adjusts herself in my lap, placing her arms around my neck and crossing her perfectly toned long legs.

"Payson, I came tonight with this whole thing set in stone as long as you were here. Jenna made me realize that being with you means being honest with myself and my family. So yes, Payson, I am one hundred percent about this, about us. I could never allow you to feel like you're my dirty little secret. Besides, I want the whole town, or even the whole world, to know that I am yours."

My heart swells inside my chest. The certainty in her voice makes me want her even more than I already do.

"So if your parents kick you out?" My mind is racing for some sort of plan. I couldn't allow that to happen to her. I could talk to my family or maybe Colton and Thea could convince their parents to allow her to stay with them.

"Nothing to worry about. Jenna's parents have already stated I can take the spare bedroom if that happens. I even have a bag with my things in Jenna's trunk just in case."

She really has this figured out. All of this to show me what I meant to her.

I grab Sadie around her waist as I stand up from the bench and place her gently on her feet.

"We need to go. We need to go right *now!*""What? What's wrong?" Sadie is looking around, panicked eyes scanning for something.

I grab Sadie's hand and pull her in the direction of where I parked my Jeep.

"I need to get you somewhere alone, that's what is wrong." I tell her over my shoulder. Once we make it to my Jeep, I help Sadie in, ensuring she doesn't damage her dress. I lean in and kiss her gently, cherishing this delectable woman before quickly closing her door.

I drive us in the direction of my house. My brothers are spending the night with their friends and my parents are out on an overdue date night which means the house is empty. I grab Sadie's hand in mine, holding onto it like a lifeline. I pull her hand to my mouth, planting gentle kisses on the back of it. I was so stupid to think she could ever be like Miranda. Worst of all, I believed two people who harbored a lot of negative feelings toward the angel sitting beside me. I have a lot of making up to do, starting with getting her back to my room. I need to worship this woman and repent for the hurt I caused.

Once we make it to my house, I lead Sadie upstairs to my room. I pull my curtains shut as Sadie takes the room in.

"I need you to close your eyes and swear you won't peek," I command her.

"Okay..." she says hesitantly but does so anyway.

Once her eyes are closed, I make my way over to my dresser, pulling out the gift box I had stored in the top drawer. When you have devilish twin younger brothers, anything nice has to be hidden otherwise, bad things happen, and I would unleash Hell on them if they got their little hands on this.

I make my way back to Sadie, anticipation thrumming through me.

"Okay, you can open them." I hold the gift box in front of me as Sadie opens her beautiful blue eyes. A small gasp passes through her glossy pink lips.

"What's this?" Her eyes squinch, curiosity in her eyes.

"A belated birthday gift."

Sadie's eyes shoot up from the gift box to mine. "Payson, you didn't have to get me anything."

"No, Sadie, I did. I royally fucked up. Not only did I break your heart, but I did it before your birthday and ruined your day."

"How-how did you find out about my birthday? I never told you."

"I found out through Colton. Colton was with Stacey when she left her birthday message for you. And speaking of things I heard from my cousin, he mentioned you and Jenna being responsible for the incident that led to Brady getting hurt in the game?"

Sadie's cheeks turn a slight shade of pink. She's adorable when she blushes.

"Maybe we did? But you weren't supposed to find out. Jenna is kind of talking to the one lineman and maybe told him that if he could sack the quarterback, to hurt him, she would do something for him. I have no idea, nor do I want to know what that something is but clearly it was motivation enough. I just needed you to get your spotlight in front of the scouts. If anyone deserves to be noticed, it's you."

Seriously, how could Brady not have fallen in love with her? She's the most caring and thoughtful woman who loves beyond measure.

"Open the box, Sadie." I keep my eyes focused on her face, wanting to watch her expression when she sees the charm bracelet inside.

Her breath hitches and the whisper of "oh my gosh" can be heard in the quiet of my bedroom.

"Payson, this is beautiful! Thank you!"

I pull the bracelet out of the box and clasp it around her dainty wrist.

"Each charm on here has a certain meaning behind it." I point to the swimsuit charm first since that is the start of us.

"The bikini represents the day we met. The cheer cone and poms for obvious reasons. The baseball bat because that was your weapon at the rage room I took you to. And the cherries are for—"

"Cherry pop?"

"Yeah. That's not a corny nickname, is it?" I never asked her how she felt about it since she was so against Princess.

"I love when you call me that." She smiles at me before looking back at the bracelet. "What's this one?" She points to the heart and key charm, the charm I picked to remind Sadie she is worthy of love. This is my grand gesture.

"That one represents my heart and the key that *only* you hold. You have my whole heart, Sadie. No one else owns it but you."

Chapter 28

Payson's POV

There's a sparkle in Sadie's eyes as she looks from the bracelet then at me. I'm not sure what is going through her beautiful head, but I hope this gift makes up for the heartache I brought upon her. How stupid of me to allow two jealous individuals to get in between our happiness. I'm about to ask her if she loves it when her fingers latch onto my blazer and she pulls me right into her, forcing me to drop the gift box. Her hands move from my blazer to my stomach and she slowly moves them up my body, over my breasts and up to my shoulders where she pushes the sleeves down, making my blazer fall off. Goosebumps break out over my body as her fingers stroke along my shoulder and she stares at me with lust in her eyes.

Is Sadie trying to be the dominant one?

She leans into me and kisses me. First, it's gentle but then she gets aggressive. I tug on her bottom lip, needing her to give me more. I'm getting turned on, but I know I got to take things at Sadie's pace. I push my tongue into her mouth when she opens for me, exploring her mouth as she explores mine. She lets out a moan and it's my undoing.

I break from our kiss and pick Sadie up. Her legs automatically wrap around my waist and I walk her until her back hits my closed bedroom door. We go back to kissing each other with a hunger for more. I allow one of my hands to slide along her silky smooth thighs towards the apex and note the tiny scrap of lace barely covering her pussy. She's dripping wet and I groan. My girl is soaked just for me.

I unwrap Sadie's legs from me and she slides down my body. Once she is steady on the floor, I drop down and remove her heels. This girl may despise being called princess but she will always get the princess treatment from me.

"Turn around," I command Sadie and like a good girl, she listens. I find the zipper and slowly drag it down, staring as more of her silky-smooth skin appears. When I don't see the clasp of a bra, I let out another groan.

I step behind her and place a soft kiss where Sadie's neck meets her shoulder. I drag my lips, gently biting and sucking along her neck up to her earlobe.

"I want you so badly, Sadie and judging by how wet you are, I believe you want me too. Don't you, cherry pop?"

She moans out a yes and it's the sexiest sound I have ever heard. I push her dress off her body and hold onto Sadie's hand as she steps out of it. She turns around, allowing me to see her in her glory and damn, she takes my breath away.

"Lose the panties before I rip them off you."

"Yes, ma'am" she says and ever so slowly, pulls her panties down before letting them drop and stepping out of them.

"You are incredibly sexy. You know that?" My eyes roam all over her body, taking her in, appreciating every inch and curve. I can feel my clit swell with desire.

"And you're overly dressed, QB. Why don't you join me?"

I make quick work of removing my clothing, never taking my eyes off her as her lustful eyes follow my every movement.

"Lay on the bed, Sadie, so I can feast on you and worship you like the goddess you are."

Sadie saunters her way over to my bed before crawling on top and splaying her body out just for me. I climb over top of her, hovering above.

"Before we go any further, I need to ask you if you are one hundred percent sure you want to do this. It's okay if you change your mind. You won't hurt my feelings. I want to take things as fast or slow as you want to. But I need to know."

Sadie reaches up to press a gentle kiss on my lips.

"I want this, Payson. Show me how much you want me."

I drop my body slowly on top of hers. We kiss slowly, taking our time and savoring one another. I then work my kisses down her neck, nipping and sucking as I go. I reach her breasts, pulling one into my mouth while using my hand to massage the other. I gently bite and suck her pink nipple, relishing in the soft moans Sadie lets out. I switch to give her other breast my mouth's attention and repeat what I did before.

"Oh, God, Payson…"

I smile against her breast, knowing she's enjoying this is a boost to my ego. I crawl down her body, leaving small kisses as I go as I make my way down to her core. I flick my tongue against her clit before slowly moving it back and forth. Sadie squirms and withers, panting a little quicker. I move my mouth down and flatten my tongue, slowly licking her pussy before returning to her clit and sucking it into my mouth. I do this a few more times before I insert two fingers inside her. I slowly, teasingly move my fingers in and out while I suck and lick her swollen nub. Sadie's panting picks up the pace and her moans are getting louder with each thrust.

Thank God nobody's home.

I pick up the pace, thrusting my fingers in and out of Sadie. I can feel Sadie's walls gripping me, so I slow down, torturing her a bit. I'm not ready for her to come just yet.

"Why are you slowing down? I was so close!" Sadie groans.

"Because I'm nowhere close to being done with you."

I withdraw my fingers and crawl up to Sadie's face and kiss her.

"Sit on my face." I grab her by her waist and pull her over so she's sitting on my stomach but Sadie looks unsure about the idea.

"What's wrong? We've done this before and you didn't suffocate me. I'm still here, aren't I?"

Her cheeks blush at the memory of the last time we were in this position. "I know. It's just...what about you?"

"What about me?" I have no idea what she's asking.

"I've...never done this...sex with another girl. Shouldn't I be pleasuring you too?"

"Sadie, all I care about is bringing you to an orgasm and watching you bliss out. I'm not worried about me."

"It's just that I want to please you too." She takes a moment before she flips herself around and backs up until her pussy is above my mouth.

She's hovering above me, trying to steady herself but I'm impatient. I wrap my hands around her thighs, pulling her down to devour her. She moans, rocking back and forth, taking her pleasure.

My clit is throbbing, in need of a release and as if she could read my mind, Sadie leans forward putting her mouth on me. I feel the warmth of her mouth take in my clit, pleasure slinking its way up my torso. She lets up to slowly blow cool air on my clit and I moan into her drenched pussy.

As if my moaning encourages her, Sadie goes back to pleasing me. I feel her tongue rim my lower lips, teasing me before spearing her tongue in and out of my pussy. I do the same to her, our moans getting louder, our panting getting quicker.

I feel the tightening sensation build in my belly, so close to going over the edge. Sadie is close to her orgasm, her walls gripping my fingers. We both quicken our paces, thrusting our tongues and fingers faster and faster until we both hit our orgasms and crash down in euphoric bliss.

Sadie moves off me to crawl into my side, wrapping her arm across my midsection. We lay there together, embracing each other.

"That was incredible," Sadie whispers. She turns her head, resting her chin on top of my small breasts. "You are incredible."

I stare into her steely blue eyes, mesmerized by her beauty like always. Only this time, it seems to be more enhanced now that she has the post orgasmic glow.

"I don't think I could be happier than I am right now. With you," I tell her as I move a golden curl behind her ear.

"I love you, Payson."

My eyes widen at her words. Sadie lifts herself up, pulling herself slightly back.

"I know it may feel soon and you don't have to say it back. I completely understand if you don't. But I know what these feelings I have for you are and I —"

"I love you too, Sadie." This time, she's the one caught off guard.

"Really? You-you love me?"

I hate this doubt she has of being loved and I vow to to erase those doubts permanently.

"Yes, Sadie. I do. You are my everything. Not being with you was pure agony and after learning the truth, I knew then and there that you are my person. Yeah, football is my life and I'm not giving that up. The NFL is still the dream. I want to show little girls all over the country that they can achieve anything, especially when it's male dominated. But that dream won't be worth it if you're not standing next to me. I'm in this for the long game."

Sadie laces our fingers together and kisses me softly.

"I'm in it for the long game, too."

We lay there, holding onto each other, soaking up this bubble of peace because after tonight, life is going to change for the both of us.

I was blessed with my parents. The moment I came out to them, they wrapped me up in a hug and told me how much they loved me no matter what. Some of us though aren't so lucky.

I have no idea what lies ahead for Sadie. I'm sure word is going to spread like wildfire and get back to her parents soon. But no matter what happens, I'm going to be there for her, loving her and supporting her through whatever comes her way. If her parents cannot love her for who she is, I know mine will. And if Jenna's parents are anything like her, then Sadie will have the love and support she will ever need if worst comes to worst.

"I love you, Sadie Adams." I whisper into her golden hair.

"I'm going to love you forever, Payson Moore."

"I'm counting on that, cherry pop."

Epilogue

Sadie's POV

Seven Months Later

"C'mon Payson, can you please give me one decent photo?"

"Mom, I'm tired of photos. Can we please hurry up? Otherwise, the food is going to get cold and I'm starving," Payson pouts to her mother.

"Fine, but once you're stuffed and bloated, I want *normal* pictures." She gives Payson a pointed glare and Payson nods in agreement.

The Moore family is hosting a graduation bar-b-que to celebrate Payson, Jenna and I completing our senior year. It's a beautifully warm, sunny May afternoon and Mrs. Moore pulled out all the works. There is so much food, you could feed an army. Blue, white and gold graduation decor is everywhere. She even has one of those fancy balloon arches for a photo op set up on the back porch.

Payson and I take our seats next to Jenna and her parents. They have practically become my parents after my mother did what I was afraid she would do.

After Payson and I had made love that Homecoming night, she took me back home. I feared I was going to be interrogated when I walked through the door, but word got around at church services that Sunday. I was woken up by my mother storming into my bedroom, screeching at me to get out of bed. She asked me if the rumors were true, and I told her how in love with Payson I was and how happy she made me. My mom went on her spew of how it's against everything she believes in, against God and how no daughter of hers was going to date another girl. When she told me I needed to end my relationship with Payson, I stood my ground and told her I would not lose the love of my life because she cannot understand nor accept my life choices. That's when she told me I needed to pack my things and leave before she got back from the store, that I was no longer her daughter or welcomed in her home.

It hurt hearing your own mother wants nothing to do with you but I fought back the tears that threatened to spill. I sent a text to Jenna telling her what happened, and Jenna was over in five minutes with boxes, helping me pack as many of my things as we could. We managed to get everything I could take packed and over to her house before my mother returned.

Once I put my things into the spare bedroom that became my new room, I let the tears fall and Jenna cradled me in her arms, soothing down my pain and heartbreak. I will never understand how a mother loves their child from the moment they are born but then abandons them over something they can't accept?

My father came by later that day after finding out what happened and to my surprise, he accepted me. The relief I felt knowing my father held no ill towards me alleviated the pain of my mother's rejection. He told me that he loved me and would try to make my mother see reason. He has always felt the church she attended was more cult-like and their views didn't line up to his own beliefs. He assured me I was better off staying at Jenna's for a while just to keep the peace but I didn't mind.

My parents attempted marriage counseling to work through these issues but sadly, mom was too gone into her beliefs that dad filed for divorce last month. The day my mother received the divorce papers, she sent me a text, calling me the Devil's child and telling me how much my sins caused her failed marriage. I screenshot the texts to send to my father and then I blocked my mother's number. She's never going to love me or accept me for what I am and for who I love. And I don't need her toxicity affecting my mental well-being. I will always have love for her, and I occasionally say a prayer for her, hoping that one day she will have a change of heart. If that day ever comes, I may allow her back into my life but she is going to have to work for it.

I feel a kiss on the top of my head before he drops into the chair beside me. My dad beams at me with so much love and pride. I'm grateful I get to still have at least one of my parents. My siblings take the chairs next to him, happy smiles and everything. Mother moved out shortly after receiving the divorce papers. Dad offered to buy her a small home, but only if Hannah and Isaiah would stay with him. She agreed, stating how she'd rather not chance her other children becoming like me. They seem happier since she's been gone.

Payson's twin brothers sit next to Isaiah. The three of them have become the best of friends and I love seeing their friendship blossom. They hope Payson and I get married someday so they can officially be "brothers."

Thea and Colton take the chairs across from us along with their parents. Thea and Hannah chat away about typical teenage girl things but my eyes are focused on Colton. He hasn't been his quirky, happy-go-lucky self since Stacey decided to break things off. She's going off to Penn State in the fall and felt it wasn't fair for the both of them to do the long-distance thing since Colton has another year of high school left. My heart goes out to him because I know he's hurting. I just hope he heals from this and finds someone else who will make him happy.

A clinging fork against glass brings all of our attention to the head of the table where Payson's intimidating father, Hank, is standing.

"I'd like to make a toast before we say grace and dig in."

Everyone lifts their glasses of sweet tea or iced water above their heads.

"First and foremost, I'd like to make a toast to family, as well as the friends who have become like family. Blood doesn't make a family so when you find a group of people who you deeply care for, who have your back as you have theirs, treasure them. It's been a true pleasure and honor getting to know the Altwoods and Adams families."

Everyone takes a sip of their drink before Payson's mother, Leanna, stands. "I'd like to make a toast to our graduating seniors. You guys accomplished a huge milestone today. It took years of hard work and dedication, but you all did it. I think it's safe to say I speak for all of us parents that we are incredibly proud of you. Letting you go off into the real world is going to be so hard..." Leanna takes a moment to compose herself, taking a napkin and dabbing under her eyes. "Sorry, sorry. Ignore my motherly feelings...Here's to our 2023 seniors and to the exciting futures ahead of you."

We once again take a sip of our drinks before we bow our heads and say grace.

"Amen!" we say in unison.

"Finally, we can eat!" Payson says excitedly, rubbing her hands altogether.

We all make our plates, eating and laughing and just enjoying this moment in time. We have to take these moments while we can.

"So, Sadie, Jenna, what colleges have you ladies decided on?" Mrs. Reynolds asks us.

Jenna dabs her mouth like a lady before speaking. "Well, I'm off to California Institute of the Arts where I can major in animation and video graphics."

"Ohh, that sounds very interesting. How about you Sadie?"

I finish swallowing down a bite of my burger and take a quick drink of sweet tea. I glance around the table, noticing all eyes are on me.

"So, I have been waiting for a response from all the colleges I applied to, and I just received the email from the final school I applied for. I can't bring myself to read it though." It's a lie. I've already read it; I know what it says. I just need Payson to—

"Let me read it." And right into my trap she falls.

I open my Gmail to the email and pass my phone to Payson.

"Dear Miss Sadie Adams, we would like to congratulate you on your acceptance into the University of Southern California—holy shit!" Payson jumps up out of her chair, her eyes scanning the email.

"Language, Payson."

"Sorry, mom," she says quickly. Payson looks at me, "Sadie, is this for real?"

I give her my biggest smile. "Yes! I'm going to be a Trojan, too!"

Payson pulls me in and gives me a kiss before wrapping me in her arms. I can finally breathe now that I was able to tell her that we both will be USC students together. After Payson took our team to the South Carolina Championships and won it, USC scouts reached out to her, offering her a full ride scholarship. She was so thrilled to land her dream college but had been fighting her excitement out of fear of where I would be going. She didn't like the idea of a long-distance relationship but was willing to make us work. We both were. Thankfully, that is not something we have to worry about now. What's even better is knowing Jenna is only going to be less than an hour drive away so I can still see my best friend.

Looking back to the beginning of senior year, I never would have imagined my life ending up like it is today. I'm happier than I ever thought I could be. I have the love and support from the ones who matter most and best yet, I get to go to school with the woman I love, the one I plan to build a future with.

Acknowledgements

First and foremost, I must thank my wonderful husband. He has always been loving, supportive and my rock when I needed him to be. Ever since the idea of becoming an author touched my heart and this opportunity came about, he ensured I saw this through every step of the way. When at times I questioned if it was going to be worth it, he was there telling me it would be. I sure hope he's right. Thank you for supporting me and making me push past my fears and self doubt to achieve this dream of mine. I love you!

To my four, beautiful children — I hope I'm showing you that anything is possible when you put in the work and make it possible. I hope it motivates you to follow your passions and see them through. To give it all you have to achieve what it is your heart desires. I'll be behind you, cheering because I believe in you!

To my family and friends — Thank you for all the love and support you have shown me on this newfound journey of mine. Whether you are telling people about my books, reading them or just buying my work to support me, I am so appreciative that you are showing your love for me and it does not go unnoticed.

To Maria — Thank you for the All Write Well program and your always positive feedback as I stepped foot into the writing world. I would not be turning this dream into reality if it wasn't for you and the program you have created. I hope I make you proud! I will continue to use what I learned from AWW to help me build this author dream of mine.

To Aliciana, Alyssa S., Britney M, Kathryn and Tracey — You were the few people I openly shared this story and process with. Being fellow bookworms, I knew I could entrust your opinions and wanted to share with you the excitement of this journey with me. It is your love, support, and enthusiasm that helped motivate me to make this book what it is today. I love you ladies and I am so thankful to have you a part of my life.

To my book cover designer, Dee Garcia ~ You always have the magic touch when it comes to designing book covers. When I feel like I can't fully express my vision, you somehow manage to put together my visions and make them reality. The number of compliments I get in regards to the covers make me proud to showcase your talent for the world to see. Thank you for the amazing work you do!

Finally, to the readers who took the time to read this book. Thank you for taking a chance on a new indie author. It means the world to me that you chose to read my story. Whether you loved it or felt it could have been better, I appreciate you and thank you! If you could leave an honest review on Amazon and any other social platform, I would greatly appreciate it! Reviews help indie authors such as myself get our books out to more readers.

About the Author

Dev Hahn is a new indie author, learning as she goes and ready to bring her notebook of story ideas to life and share them with the world. Reading has always been an escape for Dev when her depression became too much or when she just needed to escape reality for a few chapters. She hopes she can do the same for anyone willing to take a chance on her books. Besides reading romance and falling for fictional characters, Dev enjoys watching American football, singing karaoke with her family, iced coffee all year round, and spending quality time with the people she loves most. She's a stay-at-home mother who writes around her children's busy schedules. She resides in Maryland with her husband, two fur babies and their four children who make life fun, chaotic and entertaining.

242

Also By Dev Hahn

<u>Standalones</u>
Beyond Broken Colors

<u>Bellwood Lady Baller Series</u>
Coming Out on the Sidelines
Catching Feelings in the End Zone
Tackling Temptations on the Line
Opposing Hearts on the Field, *Coming Fall 2025*

Connect With Me

Be sure to follow me on my socials for updates and new releases!

Bookbub: bookbub.com/profile/dev-hahn
Facebook: facebook.com/authordevhahn
Goodreads: goodreads.com/author/show/47750634.Dev_Hahn
Instagram: instagram.com/authordevhahn/
Pinterest: pinterest.com/authordevhahn
TikTok: tiktok.com/@author.dev.hahn
Threads: threads.com/@authordevhahn